Re:ZeRo
-Starting Life in Another World-

"—What a truly pitiful existence. In my great mercy, I shall grant you rest."
And having said that, Priscilla slowly drew a crimson sword from the sky.

"Gh, ahh?!"
"Let me see your hand!"
Ferris took his hand, examining it as he stared in shock. The light of healing magic enveloped the dark veins, but there was no trace of pain nor sign of the black affliction fading.

Re:ZERO -Starting Life in Another World-

The only ability Subaru Natsuki gets when he's summoned to another world is time travel via his own death. But to save her, he'll die as many times as it takes.

CONTENTS

Re:ZeRo

-Starting Life in Another World-

VOLUME 18

TAPPEI NAGATSUKI
ILLUSTRATION: SHINICHIROU OTSUKA

YEN ON
NEW YORK

Re:ZERO Vol. 18
TAPPEI NAGATSUKI

Translation by Dale DeLucia
Cover art by Shinichirou Otsuka

Yen On
150 West 30th Street, 19th Floor
New York, NY 10001

Visit us at yenpress.com
facebook.com/yenpress
twitter.com/yenpress
yenpress.tumblr.com
instagram.com/yenpress

First Yen On Edition: February 2022

Yen On is an imprint of Yen Press, LLC.
The Yen On name and logo are trademarks of Yen Press, LLC.

Library of Congress Cataloging-in-Publication Data
Names: Nagatsuki, Tappei, 1987– author. | Otsuka, Shinichirou, illustrator. | ZephyrRz, translator. | DeLucia, Dale, translator.
Title: Re:ZERO starting life in another world / Tappei Nagatsuki ; illustration by Shinichirou Otsuka ; translation by ZephyrRz ; translation by DeLucia, Dale
Other titles: Re:ZERO kara hajimeru isekai seikatsu. English
Description: First Yen On edition. | New York, NY : Yen On, 2016– |
Audience: Ages 13 & up.
Identifiers: LCCN 2016031562 | ISBN 9780316315302 (v. 1 : pbk.) | ISBN 9780316398374 (v. 2 : pbk.) | ISBN 9780316398404 (v. 3 : pbk.) | ISBN 9780316398428 (v. 4 : pbk.) | ISBN 9780316398459 (v. 5 : pbk.) | ISBN 9780316398473 (v. 6 : pbk.) | ISBN 9780316398497 (v. 7 : pbk.) | ISBN 9781975301934 (v. 8 : pbk.) | ISBN 9781975356293 (v. 9 : pbk.) | ISBN 9781975383169 (v. 10 : pbk.) | ISBN 9781975383183 (v. 11 : pbk.) | ISBN 9781975383206 (v. 12 : pbk.) | ISBN 9781975383220 (v. 13 : pbk.) | ISBN 9781975383244 (v. 14 : pbk.) | ISBN 9781975383268 (v. 15 : pbk.) | ISBN 9781975383282 (v. 16 : pbk.) | ISBN 9781975335250 (v. 17 : pbk.) | ISBN 9781975335274 (v. 18 : pbk.)
Subjects: CYAC: Science fiction. | Time travel—Fiction.
Classification: LCC PZ7.1.N34 Re 2016 | DDC [Fic]—dc23
LC record available at https://lccn.loc.gov/2016031562

ISBNs: 978-1-9753-3527-4 (paperback)
978-1-9753-3528-1 (ebook)

3 5 7 9 10 8 6 4 2

TPA

Printed in South Korea

PROLOGUE

A DARK TORRENT

His head was hot, and his mind was ablaze, but a chill coursed through his veins, and he felt like he was gradually freezing over.

"—Rghaaa!"

He gritted his teeth and slammed his fists together ferociously, willing his sluggish blood to start moving again. Skillfully using the silver steel covering his arms, he shield-bashed his enemy's thick arm, the impact shattering the stone pavement below them.

That attack contained every scrap of strength he could muster, and he could feel a powerful reverberation shooting through his shoulder, but there was no indication that it had been a decisive blow. If anything, victory seemed to be getting further and further away with every move he made.

The enormous, black-robed inhuman figure before Garfiel was unmoved. Its eight arms were moving wildly, absorbing his attacks, deflecting them, and delivering their own destructive counters with a practiced precision optimized for killing.

Garfiel's cheeks, chest, and legs were all battered, bleeding, or both. He desperately tried to hold his ground even as his thoughts threatened to scatter from the pain and impact of each blow. He knew his opponent's four swords were a complete offensive and defensive package—they were the famed set called the Devil Cleavers, the legendary blades wielded by the ultimate god of war. And Garfiel's opponent was using those famed weapons like an extension of its body. No, not *like* an extension. For a warrior who had true mastery and enough experience, a weapon really could become a part of the body.

—In which case, based on how this mysterious warrior was using the Devil Cleavers, then maybe—

"—Gah?!"

A solid punch connected with Garfiel's jaw, taking advantage of an opening right as his thoughts had started to wander.

"Bh, gh…aaaa!"

His bones groaned, and his vision started going red. The punch had rattled his brain, draining the strength from his knees for an instant. But that brief moment of vulnerability was more than enough to be lethal in mortal combat. And the war god who had once claimed to be the strongest in the land would not miss that moment.

Each following its own path, all four swords raced toward a different vital point. The head, the neck, the chest, the waist—if any of these swings connected, Garfiel would die or, at the very least, be unable to keep fighting. And at the moment, he could do nothing to drive back the specter of death fast approaching.

Gritting his teeth, he looked around his reddening world, searching for any way out. And as he desperately clung to life, a phantom came into view, as if amused by his impending doom.

A woman in a black robe with a crimson smile was peering down at him in his unsightly state.

"—Eyes up, numbskull!"

A roar rang out, followed closely by the sound of steel clashing and the dull thud of something biting into flesh. A broad, furry back appeared in front of Garfiel, shielding him after he failed to move in time. Ricardo had blocked the swords with his big hunting knife, using his torso to catch the one attack he'd failed to parry.

"Gh, gaaah! That hurt, ya son of a bitch!"

Coughing up blood, Ricardo pushed back with all his might, knocking away the swords. Taking advantage of the momentum, the war god leaped backward to gain some distance.

Now that he had some breathing room, Garfiel shook his head

and adjusted his stance as he stepped forward, lining up alongside the man who had protected him.

"My bad, tha—"

"This ain't the time for that! Are your eyes workin'?!" Ricardo cut off his apology. "It's do-or-die!"

"Y-yeah, don't have to tell me twice!" Hearing that, Garfiel tried to harden his resolve. "We gotta go all out just to have a shot at winning…"

But even now, he was having trouble. His spirit was flagging like he was a drenched alley cat. Irritation, impatience, and a growing sense of self-loathing churned in his chest, almost as if they were trying to put an end to his miserable self. And his head was filled with a vortex of pointless thoughts, so maybe he really was trying to get himself killed.

A powerful enemy was standing before him, one he couldn't afford to take his eyes off of, and yet a corner of his mind couldn't help but focus on the black-robed woman flitting in and out of view at the edge of his vision. Even though the city hall they needed to reclaim was right in front of him. Even though his comrades were up there waiting for them to come to the rescue. Even though every second longer he took meant another second of suffering for the girl he needed to help at all costs.

"Hoo-oooooooooohh!"

Recalling that bloody moment of regret sent his rage past the boiling point, and all the hair on his body stood on end. Goose bumps stood out for a moment before golden fur started appearing as he transformed into a beast.

His body creaked as his bone structure changed and his small body grew larger. He would stifle all his unnecessary thoughts, all his self-hatred—everything—and become a tiger to obliterate the foe standing in his way.

Transform, Garfiel Tinzel. Mow everything down. If you can do that—

"*—But will that really undo everything?*"

All of a sudden, a bewitching woman's voice tickled his ears, penetrating the consciousness that had been on the verge of dissipating.

It was a voice that shouldn't exist. And just when it stole away his focus—

"What?!"

There was a thunderous boom from above, and Ricardo was looking up, eyes wide. Seeing that, Garfiel looked up, too, his green eyes finding a scene that left him dumbfounded.

Flames erupted out of the top floor of the building. An enormous explosion blew out the windows, spewing fire hot enough to melt glass. The source was a black dragon sticking halfway out of the building, its wings covered in blood as they flapped.

—That black dragon had to be the loathsome Archbishop of Lust.

"General…!"

As Garfiel called out to the person who was supposed to be fighting the dragon, the strength he had put into his clenched fangs started slipping away. For a split second, the charred black corpse of his friend appeared in his mind, and his heart leaped into his throat.

And because of that, he was slow to react to the violent change that came immediately afterward.

"———"

Far in the distance, an ear-shattering roar erupted near the city's walls. The sound of something enormous groaning echoed throughout the city as a fearsome harbinger of what was to come.

Something colossal was approaching the city center, drawing closer to city hall, preceded by a growing tremor running through the ground. When he felt the vibrations beneath him becoming more intense, it set off alarms in Garfiel's head.

"C'mon now, this ain't even funny……"

Beside him, Ricardo's face stiffened. Even someone as brave and fearless in combat as he grew hoarse when faced with something so implacable.

It was only natural, though. Because the tremors they were feeling and the deafening boom they had heard were actually—

"—Sir Garfiel! Sir Ricardo! Get to high ground!"

A sharp voice broke through the mental freeze that had held Garfiel. The warning came from the Sword Devil, the old man who had been trading blows nearby with the longsword-wielding cultist for

the past two minutes. After crossing blades with his opponent one last time, Wilhelm quickly put some distance between them as he prepared to heed his own warning. But even leaping straight up, Wilhelm was unable to clear the gargantuan wave crashing toward them.

"Gh."

Wilhelm was swallowed up by a wall of water taller than most of the surrounding buildings. After witnessing that, Garfiel was only a moment away from suffering the exact same fate. He dug in his heels on the stone pavement, readying himself for the shock—

"—Bgh!"

—But his stance was easily broken by the intensity of the onrushing water. Hit by a force like the power of nature itself given form, Garfiel's body was completely engulfed and at the mercy of the pitch-black world he'd been thrust into. After what felt like an unbearably long time, his fingers caught on something, so he pulled with all his might, at last dragging his head out of the water.

"Ghah! Daaaamn it all! Where did…everybody go…?!"

Having grabbed the metal railing on a rooftop, Garfiel scanned his surroundings. The force of the churning water was ruthless, and everything around him had been consumed by the muddy torrent. Only a handful of particularly tall buildings were just peeking out of the water, and he was barely holding out against the powerful current.

"Boss man! Sword Devil…!"

He called out to the other two members of his party, who must have gotten caught up in the same disaster, and he was concerned about where their enemies might have gone off to—but that thought was erased just moments later.

As he clung there unable to move, he noticed something happening at the half-submerged city hall. The black dragon spread its wings and started flying away, leaving the upper floor still burning.

The dragon was covered in wounds, and its claws dexterously held two people—a green-haired woman and a black-haired boy.

"Gen—"

Garfiel's eyes widened, and he started to call out, but water rushed into his mouth, and he couldn't breathe. His fingers slipped, and he could do nothing but watch as the two of them were taken away by the enemy—

"—?"

Filled with shame, Garfiel desperately fought to keep his eyes on the damned black dragon. And as he did, he saw the dragon's flight suddenly get disrupted as it let out a shrill cry. The reason was the fangs of a great serpent that bit into the black dragon's wing. The serpent had suddenly appeared and lashed out at the dragon, calling the dragon a coward and viciously tearing into its wings.

An instant later, the boy was released from the dragon's claws as it shuddered violently.

"———"

His eyes wide open, Garfiel could only watch as it happened. He could only watch as the boy was swallowed up by the roiling waters that were in the process of consuming the entire city. He had fallen beneath the surface unconscious and was undoubtedly being carried away by the current, unable to resist, going far away, to a place where Garfiel could not reach him.

"Wait..."

Stretching his hand out toward the silhouette that instantly vanished somewhere below, Garfiel was dragged away by another surge. He desperately kept his head above water, shouting as he was pulled farther and farther away.

"Aaaaah!"

Eventually, he slipped beneath the surface, still seeking Subaru Natsuki and cursing his own uselessness. Screaming without making a sound.

CHAPTER 1

PICKING UP THE PIECES

1

"Emilia, are you a virgin? This is crucial."

For a split second, Emilia couldn't process what she was being asked.

"..."

She was surprised by the suddenness of the question, but the situation being what it was, she struggled with how she should respond to such an odd confrontation. With only a single blanket to cover herself, Emilia took a deep breath.

As she was forced to confront such an incomprehensible situation and try to understand what was going on, Emilia's instinct was to try to recall everything that had happened so far.

—Following an invitation from Anastasia, a fellow royal-selection candidate, she had traveled to the Water Gate City of Pristella, one of the five great cities in the Kingdom of Lugunica. During her time there, she met with Crusch and Felt, two other candidates who had also received invitations from Anastasia, and they all enjoyed the welcoming, peaceful atmosphere. The next day, after a rather tense breakfast, she set off into town with Subaru and Beatrice, running into the Songstress Liliana...and then finding out that Subaru and

Beatrice were facing off against one of the Witch Cult Archbishops by themselves. As soon as she learned this, Emilia quickly joined the fight. Their enigmatic foe may have been covered from head to toe in bandages, but she proved to be a powerful opponent, wielding flames and chains with equal skill. Emilia fought her hard, but they had been pushed to a point where defeat was looking inevitable when— What *did* happen after that?

When Emilia came to, she was lying on an unknown bed in a room she did not recognize inside an unfamiliar building. And when she stepped outside the room to see what was going on, she found herself in the hallway face-to-face with a white-haired man dressed in an all-white suit. Standing before him, she was unable to move, even forgetting to breathe.

—Who is he, where are we, and why am I here?

Now, as Emilia caught her breath and started to think—

"Ah, my apologies. It seems I've surprised you. I must admit that was an error on my part." The white-haired man—Regulus Corneas—smiled and raised his hand. "I am sorry for the sudden question. Truly, I apologize. You see, I'm the sort of man who can genuinely apologize when I believe I am in the wrong. There are utterly unbearable louts in this world who refuse to recognize their own faults and merely shift blame with an unending stream of excuses, but on a fundamental level, I stand apart from such lowly, inferior people. You agree, don't you?"

"Ummm… Yes, it's important to be able to apologize from your heart, sure…"

"Just so! That's it exactly. Being able to apologize is crucial. Thank goodness. People who can't even understand something as simple as that are far more common than you would think, but since we both share that understanding, I'm sure we will get along famously in our married life. That's a relief. There is no mistaking we were fated to be joined together."

Regulus's eyes sparkled excitedly as he nodded to himself over and over, completely ignoring Emilia's apparent shock. After looking her up and down, he continued.

"You see, I'm not inquiring as to your chastity out of a vulgar curiosity. As I said, we are husband and wife, and spouses must of course be joined together out of a powerful bond of mutual love and understanding. In order to maintain a relationship like that, it is only natural that it is a requirement that both parties must entrust all of themselves to their partner. Which is why I would like to be sure."

"Sure of what…?"

"Sure that you have not been touched by another man. But to be clear, I ask this with only love in my heart, so while it might cause you some small amount of discomfort, I really must insist. It's my duty both as your husband and as a man."

Regulus's thoughts flowed out with great expressiveness and verbosity. Emilia felt something was off about Regulus himself as she was tossed about by the flood of words.

"………"

She was overwhelmed by the vehemence of his insistence, but that was not all. His figure, his voice…something about him was stirring the depths of her memories. But she couldn't seem to figure out why, and it soon slipped away, before she could manage to figure it out. But she could say one thing for sure—this man was incredibly focused on one certain word.

"So please allow me to ask again: Emilia, are you a virgin?"

"Um, can you explain what that means? I'm sorry, that's not a word I'm very familiar with." Faced with the same question once again, Emilia averted her purple eyes apologetically.

It was clearly something that held great meaning to Regulus, but she simply didn't understand what he was getting at.

"…What?" Regulus's expression tensed when he heard that.

Right as Emilia was starting to feel uneasy, his eyes suddenly widened.

"—Marvelous. You truly are the manifestation of my ideal maiden!" Regulus exclaimed, grabbing her hands as an animated smile crossed his face.

Emilia's eyes widened in shock, but Regulus paid no heed to her response and celebrated like a child who had just gotten his hands on the toy he had been dreaming of for so long. He nodded to himself over and over, and his eyes gleamed with a feverish light as he stepped in closer.

"Yes, I knew it! I had always had some misgivings as to whether using virginity as a metric was really the best way to answer this question. But that's it exactly—true purity lies in the heart. Physical virtue is only natural and expected! But what truly matters is being immaculate in spirit as well… As fulfilled as I am, you have still managed to reveal a new truth to me!"

"Ah, um, that's nice, I think…?"

"Indeed it is. And let me say, you pass with flying colors. You are perfectly suited to be my wife. And in the future, I won't have to do something as silly as inquiring into the virginity of my brides. Anyone impure enough to understand the very concept would only diminish the value of the station. A woman who has committed adultery in her heart is not fit to be my wife."

Letting go of Emilia's hand, Regulus rapturously regaled her with the future he saw for them.

She still couldn't quite grasp the true meaning of what he was saying. In fact, all of his talk about being husband and wife had come out of nowhere. In her mind, *husband and wife* described the loving relationship her father and mother shared, which seemed at odds with Regulus's idea of marriage. Maybe he was thinking of something else that merely sounded similar?

"Ah, how careless of me. I've said too much. I shouldn't leave you standing there in such a state for so long. Let's get you a change of clothes." Noticing Emilia's bewildered silence, Regulus clapped his hands. "Come along, #184."

A door opened on his command, and a doll-like figure joined the two of them in the hall.

"———"

The beautiful woman in a white dress approached, elegantly trailing long blond hair. Her pure, unblemished white outfit must have been coordinated with Regulus, whose appearance radiated all white. Standing silently at Regulus's side, she politely curtsied as she looked at Emilia.

There was no emotion in the woman's expression. Emilia's breath caught as she noticed the lifeless, doll-like eyes.

"Prepare a change of clothes for her—for #79. Once she is ready, go help the others prepare for the ceremony. She will be joining all of you, so do try to get along and look after her."

"———"

"Mm-hmm. You've stopped smiling like I requested. Good girl. You are an excellent wife."

Regulus smiled, satisfied by the woman's silence and lack of expression as she did nothing more than nod. He then stepped toward Emilia, who still had not grasped what was going on, and, as if it were nothing, he reached his hand out and caressed her silver hair without a hint of hesitation. Her body stiffened in response to a gesture that felt entirely different when a certain black-haired boy did it.

"Well then, I shall see you later. She will make you even more beautiful."

"Right..."

Emilia was filled with doubt and resistance, but at the same time, her instincts were telling her not to openly defy this man, that Regulus Corneas possessed great power. A horrifyingly vast amount of power.

"Good girl."

Nodding at her short response, Regulus smiled and leisurely turned away. She watched him disappear down the hall, and when he was finally out of view, her shoulders gradually relaxed at last. Her body had instinctively tensed up, completely on guard against him without her ever realizing it.

His mere presence felt just as menacing as the horde of great rabbits—

"—This way."

The woman's voice was beautiful, like a perfectly tuned harp. But there was no emotion in her voice, either. And something about that pained Emilia.

"Your clothes."

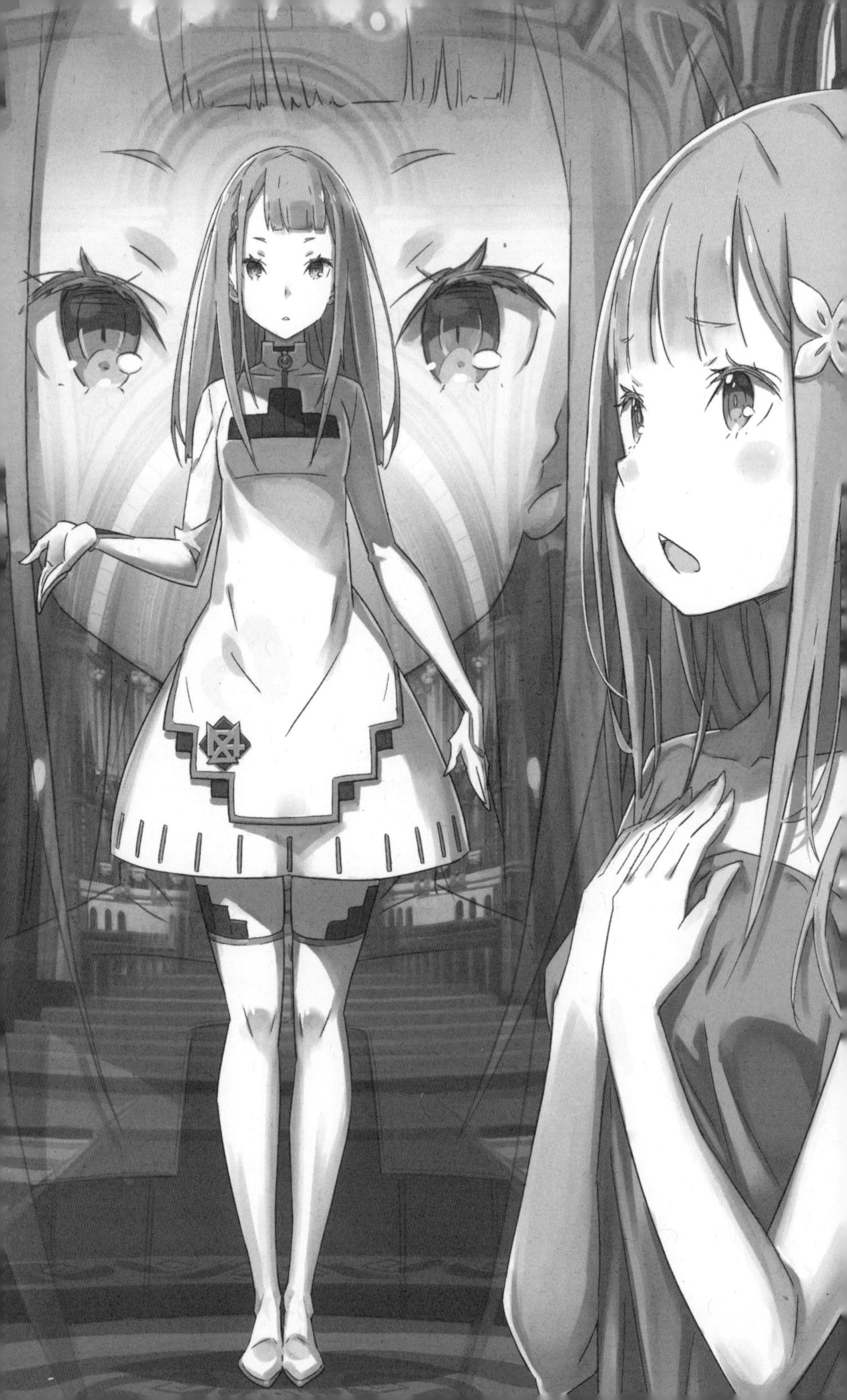

"Um, I *really* appreciate it, but I have a lot of questions. Like where is this, for starters? I was in the great plaza in Pristella, and then—Ah! Wait!"

Ignoring Emilia's questions, the woman had quickly started walking.

"Um, could you please listen? I really need to send a message to my friends. I'm sure they're all worried about me, and I'm worried about what happened to them, too..."

"———"

"Excuse me, are you listening? Can you hear me? ...Arghhhh."

The woman just kept walking forward, back straight, not lending an ear to Emilia. And as Emilia started to pout after all her questions were ignored, the woman finally led her to the room beside the one she had woken up in. It held all sorts of clothes and accessories, almost like the dressing room in a castle. But just like the place she had woken up in, something about this room made it feel different from the coldness that the rest of the building radiated.

"There are so many clothes, but...this wasn't originally what this room was for, was it?"

"These were all brought here by our husband. Please get dressed, #79."

"...Is that number supposed to mean me? He—Regulus called me that, too. Who are you?"

"I am #184, one of his wives—just like you."

Closing the door, her back to it, the woman who called herself #184 responded. Her voice was as cold and emotionless as before, but Emilia was still a bit relieved to just be able to talk with her.

"Thank goodness you finally responded. Um, what should I call you again...?"

"#184. Please be careful; he is picky about the numbers."

Hearing that warning, Emilia placed her hand on her own chest.

"...That number thing is bothering me, too, but I assume it's safe to say that when he was talking about marriage and spouses, he meant me? If so, I don't recall ever agreeing to marry Regulus..."

Thinking back, she could not remember ever arranging anything of the sort. #184 narrowed her eyes ever so slightly.

"You may not have such intentions, but he most certainly does. And your will has no bearing on his desires."

"That's strange, though. Marriage is something two people who love each other do together, right? I don't even know him."

This discussion about marriage didn't mesh at all with how Emilia understood the concept. And from what #184 was saying, Regulus sounded less like a good husband and more like…

"—It's like he's one of the wicked kings I've read about."

"———"

Emilia was still busy studying for the royal selection, and the names of many kings filled the pages of history, including some whose names were recorded for not particularly flattering reasons. Dictators, for example—rulers who refused to listen to others and insisted on obstinately following their own course above all else.

"That's a perfect description of him."

"Huh?"

"His bearing is undoubtedly that of a king… He is well deserving of the title 'the little king,'" #184 murmured softly.

Emilia could not catch what the woman had said, so she asked her to repeat it, but #184 tightly pursed her lips.

"……Your clothes."

"What? Wait…"

#184 was even more unyielding than before to cover up her momentary slip of the tongue. She stepped forward to remove the blanket Emilia was using to cover her body—

"—Gh?!"

Without warning, a loud noise and violent tremor rocked the town.

"Watch out!"

Emilia caught #184, who had stumbled from the sudden jolt and blast. Emilia swung her head around and then leaped to the window of the changing room. Searching for the source of the noise, she saw something unbelievable.

"That's…the floodgate?!"

Her lips quivered, and her purple eyes opened wide as she watched a huge floodgate—one of the massive devices that controlled the flow of water in all the city's waterways—open with an ominous groan.

With nothing to hold it back any longer, the water rushed into the city all at once. Pristella was laid out like a bowl, designed so that water would flow toward the lower levels—to the center of the town.

In the distance, the heart of the city was visible—city hall. And that tall structure was already being swallowed up by water.

"That's…"

The roads were flooded as a rolling wave swept away people and goods alike. Emilia clutched the windowsill in shock, hearing the imagined pandemonium in the back of her mind.

It was beyond anything she could imagine, and while she watched in shock, all the people were tossed about, desperately struggling to survive.

What had happened?

The city's residents and her fellow candidates who had also traveled here—were they safe?

And there was another who came to mind.

"Subaru…"

Her knight was somewhere out there, too. Was he safe?

She closed her eyes, imaging his smile as she prayed for his safety.

Praying, pleading, Emilia kept her eyes shut tight.

2

Voices were echoing far, far in the distance.

"______"

Voices that he could not identify. Male, female, young, old? Were they coming from above him or below him? He couldn't say. It sounded like a battle cry. Then it was more like a grieving wail. A scream, a sob, an enraged bellow, a jagged lamentation.

All these sounds rained down around him like a waterfall, crashed over him like a giant wave, swirled around him like an inescapable vortex. It was almost like someone he had finally met after a long, long time was opening up about everything they had held back for years.

And, swallowed up by the unending deluge of voices, he lost track of where he even was.

"______"

Hands, legs, head, bottom, chest, back—it all blurred together. In that enormous swell of voices, his sense of self was gradually melting away, losing shape. He was becoming indistinct, fading and scattering until the countless voices were all that remained.

The voices became dark and stagnant, intent on breaking down his identity, reducing and draining it. He was sinking into that darkness, unable to resist. But right when he was about to resign himself to merciful oblivion, he realized there was a thread bound inextricably around his core that rejected the stagnation around him.

"______"

There was something writhing deep inside him, a thread that refused to stop fighting the black stagnation—the two forces claimed ownership of his self, fighting, each trying to steal him away, to kill the other off.

And then finally…finally—

3

"—Imbecile. How long must you insist on imposing your clueless, carefree face on the world?"

"Gh, aaaaaaaah!!!"

Subaru Natsuki awoke with a scream as he experienced the feeling of his face being gripped by a crimson flame. He jolted up at the intense heat enveloping his face, and the pain of it scorched his eyes. He groaned and flailed on the ground while cradling his face. His heart was pounding, and it felt like all the blood in his body was boiling from the heat—

"Wh-what—what happened…?"

"Ohh, what a pitiful creature. Such an ill-kept head to begin with, and now that it has been bleached out by all the water, apparently nothing remains on the inside. At this rate, you won't even be fit for your role as a jester."

"That outrageous arrogance and lack of consideration for others…"

Subaru wiped away the tears welling up as he turned toward the source of the caustic voice verbally lashing him. His blurry vision gradually cleared, and what appeared was a beautiful girl who seemed like a walking personification of the color red—

"So it *is* you, Priscilla."

Priscilla sniffed haughtily, crossing her arms, almost like she was deliberately emphasizing her well-endowed chest.

"Who else would I be? As if another as beautiful as I could exist in this world. If your eyes fail to detect something that obvious, it would be best to spoon them out and at least save yourself the trouble of carrying around such useless appendages."

"There's no way that would be better! And I feel obligated to point out that when it comes to beautiful women, the other royal-selection candidates are all top-tier knockouts… Not that that matters anyway!"

Subaru had gotten sucked into Priscilla's pace and reflexively retorted before he got ahold of himself.

He had been unconscious and had woken up to discover Priscilla was with him. His first thought was that he had died and restarted another loop at the park, which would've placed him just before the Archbishop of Wrath, Sirius, was scheduled to start her atrocity in the plaza by the time tower.

Right as Subaru started to wonder why he had been returned to that point after dying…

"Where is this…?"

That guess went out the window as he realized he did not recognize his surroundings. There was none of the natural greenery that filled the park. He was in a narrow alley. And for some reason, it was muddy and filled with puddles.

"And it's not just the ground, either… I'm practically dripping here."

Grabbing the sleeve of his tracksuit, Subaru was baffled by his waterlogged condition. His whole body was wet. As if he had cannonballed into a bath with all his clothes on. Had there been some torrential rainstorm while he was out? If not, then—

"Did I fall into the canal? Or was there some terrible flood…?"

"—Yes, sirree! That's exactly what happened! Your humblest Liliana was trembling so much in awe at it all that it's almost like I've invented a new dance! See!"

Subaru's fearful guess was affirmed by the surprise entry of a voice that came with musical accompaniment. The source of both suddenly appeared from behind Priscilla. Dark skin and an oddly aggressive manner of speech marked her as the city of water's peerless Songstress.

"Liliana! I'm glad you're safe… Turns out you were with Priscilla!"

"I mean, you and Lady Emilia and the little lady all left me behind with Lady Priscilla in the park! And with the whole town gone topsy-turvy like this, I was so scared, I couldn't bear to move a single step away from the oh-so-reliable Lady Priscilla's side."

She didn't hesitate at all to whine before latching on to Priscilla's waist. It was the sort of brazen behavior that normally would've earned her a one-way trip to the executioner's chop from Priscilla, but for some reason she was extraordinarily tolerant of Liliana because of her rare talent.

Liliana was trembling like a fawn as Priscilla nodded and patted her head.

"As the diva said, soon after you left the park, a boorish rabble defiled the waters of the city. Exceedingly merciful as I might be, even I cannot forgive such an outrage. I was on my way to relieve them of their heads when I noticed a certain foolish commoner floating in the water."

"Ahh, I see. And this *foolish commoner floating in the water*… Did you perhaps mean me by that?" Subaru asked, pointing to himself.

Priscilla just sniffed as if to say, *Who else could it be?* Choosing to interpret that as an affirmative, Subaru felt his confusion grow.

"I was floating in the water…? Why? That doesn't make any sense…"

He thought back to the last thing he could remember: Subaru had been on the top floor of the city hall building. He had been defeated by a dreadful monster, the Archbishop of Lust.

Capella had used Lust's Authority to freely transform herself into a beastly form, and unable to withstand her fierce barrage of attacks,

Subaru's right leg had come free. After losing a lot of blood, he had been writhing in pain…

"But I've still got my leg. It's still connected. The bandage is coming undone, but… Ugh?!"

The wrap around his badly wounded leg had gotten filthy from being drenched in blood and fetid water. But as he removed it to check his leg, he shouted in disgust at what lay beneath.

"Wh-what happened?! Ugh?! Wh-wh-wh-what is that?!"

"——"

Drawn by Subaru's response, Liliana came closer out of curiosity and immediately turned pale. Beside her, Priscilla peered down, eyes filled with revulsion.

All three of them were looking at Subaru's right leg, which should have been torn off during the fighting with Capella. But despite his remembering differently, it was still attached—and covered by hideous black flesh.

"——"

He felt no pain in his foot.

Caught up in the shock of seeing the condition of his limb, he rolled up the leg of his pants, revealing the full extent of the black, wriggling, vein-like protrusions extending up from his foot. A cautious touch confirmed the leg had some give to it, similar to that of normal human flesh. Ignoring its appearance, he could even call it fully healed.

"To be clear, your limbs were all attached when we found you. That hideous leg has nothing to do with us. And judging from the look on your face, it's clear you weren't born this way."

"…Thanks for catching me up while I was dealing with the shock of finding this nasty stuff that someone embroidered on my leg without my permission… There's no way this is the result of healing magic, right?"

Nodding along to Priscilla's response, Subaru ruled out what seemed to be the most likely way it could have happened. As far as he knew, healing magic operated under the basic principle of increasing the natural recovery ability of a patient's body. It was not regeneration, so scars would be left after healing. In fact, there were plenty of those on Subaru's body already.

But the dark mass on his leg was nothing like those scars. He could confidently say it was not the result of healing magic. The healing magic he knew was a gentler, warmer, miraculous power that saved not only bodies but even souls. The sort of thing that Ferris was proud of, that Beatrice had mastered as if it came naturally to her, that Garfiel had studied for the sake of his wish, that Rem had so earnestly offered freely. This black mark on his leg was a blasphemous desecration of that sort of miracle.

"Just to be sure, commoner, am I correct in assuming that your leg was not originally some sort of oddity that could reattach itself even after being violently removed?"

"That sounds like you're asking just to ask, but yeah, my body doesn't work that way. I've had my leg torn off before, but I died...! Almost died that time."

"You've had a body part torn off before?! What a life!"

When Liliana heard such an absurd answer to an absurd question, her excitement bubbled up.

But when he thought back to what had happened before, at least during that first loop, there had been no sign of his body gluing itself back together. And there hadn't been any situation later in which he'd ever displayed any kind of hyper-regeneration, either.

Priscilla nodded and simply said "I see" at his response.

"Don't raise your voice," she ordered curtly as she swung the fan in her hand with the flick of a wrist. Unable to follow the red fan's path, Subaru and Liliana peeled their eyes in an attempt to figure out what was going on, but her target became all too clear before long.

"—Gh!"

There was a faint numbness, and then Subaru's leg was struck by a burning heat. The edge of her fan had grazed his leg, leaving a sharp gouge in his thigh.

Subaru was hit by two different shocks: The first came from the realization of how skilled she must be to do something like that with a fan, and the second came from the realization that she was the kind of person who could slice open someone else's leg with zero hesitation. But both thoughts were erased by the even greater shock of what happened next. The cut on his leg was deep enough to reveal bone—until the black flesh swallowed it up. Within seconds, it was as if it the wound had never been there at all.

"______"

Subaru gingerly touched the spot with his finger, at a loss for words at the revolting miracle that had just taken place. The site of the wound was completely fine. The pain had disappeared, too.

"Ummmmmm, I could be wrong, but there might be something wrong with your leg…," Liliana commented nervously.

"It's weird how normal it feels. What is even going on with my body…?" Subaru was shocked by the unnatural healing.

Something is *wrong with my leg. What the hell happened?*

"—Wait, is it because Capella dripped blood on my leg…?"

It had happened when his consciousness was fading from the pain and the loss of so much blood after he lost his right leg. It was not a clear enough memory for him to be absolutely sure, but he was fairly confident he remembered her cutting her own wrist and dripping the blood over his wound.

Capella had said something about it while he was suffering from the unbearable pain.

"Something about becoming a hideous lump of flesh and doing the same thing to Crusch…"

"Sharing her blood, you say? That sounds rather like some sort of curse. I've heard that many of the rituals that northern practitioners of such arts are fond of using involve such roundabout rites. Perhaps it's something along those lines?"

"Curses, curses… Right, a blood curse. That's it! A dragon! She said something about dragon blood!"

Priscilla's low voice triggered something in the foggy recesses of Subaru's memories.

Right before he had passed out, while he was writhing in pain from coming into contact with her blood, she had claimed that dragon blood flowed in her veins. Whether that was metaphorical or just a straight-up fabrication, it might be a good clue worth following up.

"Dragon blood… That's one of the three great treasures left to the royal family of Lugunica by the Holy Dragon."

"I dunno any details, just that something like that exists..." Subaru furrowed his brow.

"—It grants abundance to lands withered and barren, rejuvenates all destruction that has been wrought, heals the most incurable illnesses in an instant, and becomes a light to wash away indelible despair. Those are the properties of the blood of the great and Holy Dragon."

"——"

A lyrical response reached Subaru's eardrums. There was a mysterious look on Liliana's face as she plucked her lyulyre and softly sang. Acknowledging Subaru's gaze, she bowed solemnly.

"It's a verse from the fellowship of the Holy Dragon Volcanica as passed down in the Kingdom of Lugunica. The great treasures bequeathed to the kingdom were the dragon's blood, the Dragon Tablet, and the Covenant."

"...That dragon blood sure sounds like it could do just about everything."

Subaru was a bit taken aback by how different Liliana could be when it came to songs and folklore, but he was more concerned with what her verse had described. *Rejuvenated destruction* and *healed illness* came pretty close to describing his leg's strange condition, but the parts about treating barren lands and light that washed away despair felt more questionable when he looked at the hideous black pattern on his body.

And when he considered that this hunch was based on something Capella had said, it became even more dubious.

"I don't know what caused it, but considering the wounds I had before going into that fight were healed, too, I guess I should count it as a plus... Gh! Hey, that hurts! What do you think you're doing?!"

"You really do insist on being noisy. Don't make a fuss over something so minor," Priscilla responded in a bored tone after grazing the nape of Subaru's neck with her fan.

She looked at the edge of her fan and flicked it with her finger.

"Hmmm, wounds to other parts of your body don't appear to be affected. If we were to tentatively accept that leg of yours as the blessing of the dragon's blood, it would seem the sacred dragon is a far cry from the legends that have been passed down."

"What?! What are you saying, Lady Priscilla?! No matter how voluptuous and beautiful and buxom you are, there are certain things that cannot be said! No matter how voluptuous you are!"

"Oh, you would dare oppose me? Disdain for the Holy Dragon must sit quite poorly with you."

"Naturally! The Holy Dragon Volcanica is a living legend! To we who sing to preserve the legends of the past for the future, to us bards, the Holy Dragon is our greatest benefactor! If I let contempt for the Holy Dragon pass without comment, I and my honor would both cry!"

"That spirit is admirable. But now what? How will you make me retract my words?"

"Please remove Sir Natsuki's head from his neck! Right here and now! Then watch and behold as the Holy Dragon's blood and its miraculous power rejoin his severed head with his body where he stands! If you would please!"

"There's no way that would work!" Subaru howled at the absurd one-act play unfolding before him.

Unfortunately, the nape of his neck was still hurting. As Priscilla had said, it looked like the healing was limited to his right leg, and it would probably be safer to assume it was really just the parts around the black flesh.

"Anyway, this isn't the time for experiments. The authenticity of the dragon blood aside, if my leg is like this, I'm more worried about Crusch. If she suffered something along the lines of what happened to my leg…and also, before that…"

Setting aside the oddity of his leg, Subaru finally returned to his first question. The one that the weirdness with his leg had made him forget—why had he been floating in the water?

"What happened to everyone? Garfiel and Wilhelm and the others were fighting with me…"

"Ah, um, as to the reason, you see, the truth is…" Liliana raised her hand.

"Wait, you know what happened?!"

As Subaru leaned in, she pointed out into the distance. Following where she was pointing, Subaru was baffled by the sight. He could not see anything particularly special or out of the ordinary. It was just the wall surrounding the city and one of the four floodgates that held back the water around the city—

"Wha—?"

After getting that far, Subaru remembered that both he and the ground were soaking wet. Liliana had even said it at the start. The canals had overflowed.

"No matter how dull a fool you might be, even you should understand by now."

The crimson-eyed girl nodded when she saw Subaru's ashen face.

Priscilla opened her fan with an audible crack and covered her lips with it as she spoke.

"It is as you suspect. One of the great floodgates was opened, and a torrent of water surged into the city. You were floating because you had been caught in the flood."

4

One of the city's great sluice gates had been opened, allowing a deluge of water to consume Pristella.

The mass of water had left the confines of the city's channels, creating a flash flood that spilled out into every corner of the city. That much water was unheard of, and almost half the city had been submerged at one point. The still-flooded roads scattered here and there around the city were a remnant of that.

It was miraculous that Subaru had survived the flood and was simply plucked out of one of the canals.

"The one silver lining is that the gate that was opened was quickly closed again, which is way better than just leaving it open. And almost all the residents managed to escape to the shelters, too...," Liliana explained.

"But not all of them."

"...Most likely, yes. It's sad and unfortunate and heartrending to say, though," she said, nodding in response to Subaru's regretful murmur.

Thanks to her, he had a general grasp of what had happened to the city while he was unconscious. A massive flood from the gate being opened, which would have required access to the control towers that controlled the gates. The only ones who could have done it were the members of the Witch Cult, who were currently occupying the towers.

Meaning the flood had been their doing, and—

"It was revenge for attacking city hall, then. Makes sense." Priscilla had reached the same conclusion as Subaru.

"Ngh." Subaru grimaced.

"What, do you mean to tell me you didn't expect your actions to have consequences? If you act, so will your enemy. Making an example early on is just standard practice," Priscilla declared mercilessly.

"If anything, this feels almost half-hearted," she continued, fanning herself gently as she tried to deduce the Witch Cult's aims. "I would have expected something even more despicable if they are as disgraceful a rabble as the rumors say. I suppose I should assume they value the items they demanded on the broadcast as too important to allow themselves to get too carried away."

Hearing her cold, calculating deductions, Subaru was chagrined to realize that his actions were likely what had brought about the current situation. Ever since coming to the city of water, he had suffered a string of complete and absolute failures: He had been killed by Sirius three times; Emilia had been kidnapped by Regulus; Beatrice was in a coma after saving him; he had gone to city hall in order to face Capella with his friends, only to end up being toyed with by her; and to top it all off, the town had been almost totally flooded by the cultists in retribution. He was on the verge of exploding in anger at how pathetic he was.

Subaru covered his face with his hand and stared up at the sky.

"Um, um... Please don't brood, Sir Natsuki. The situation is definitely awful, though—almost 'What's next, tying my arms and legs and throwing me in a lake?!' levels of terrible!" Liliana was waving her hands and legs as she held her lyulyre against her scrawny body, and her twin tails flapped around on either side of her face.

That she still did not give in to despair, even in this dire situation, was splendid, truly worthy of praise.

And—

"Aaaargh! Damn it! You think I'll let it end like this after losing this much?!"

"Wah?!"

The hand covering Subaru's face clenched into a fist as he howled. Liliana, who had been intending to raise his spirits, leaped backward instead to cling to Priscilla in shock at the sudden shout. Naturally, Priscilla dodged the bard and casually knocked her aside. Ignoring Liliana's cute cry as she hit the ground, Priscilla looked at Subaru with something akin to interest for the first time.

"That's unexpected. So you refuse to break over something so trifling, I take it?"

"Setting aside the question of whether this is trifling or not, that's the general idea. This is nothing compared to that nasty Witch's trials. It's way too early to be giving up on anything."

Every battle had been a loss, his right leg was covered in some alien black substance, and the city was headed downhill fast—but he wasn't about to give in just because of all that.

Now that he had a firm grasp on the current situation, he steeled his will as he came to a conclusion about what he should do first.

"—I need to meet up with everyone who stayed back at the Muse Company. Once we regroup, we can kick those assholes out of the city for good."

"Can you really do that?"

"That isn't the real question. It's whether we do it or don't. And I'm not about to choose *don't*. Whatever we do, though, priority number one needs to be rejoining the crew. What are you going to do?"

"———"

There was a flame dancing in Priscilla's eyes. She stood there silently, waiting for Subaru to continue.

"You know, I still haven't forgotten what happened back at the Water Raiment Inn—if anything, I'm still holding a grudge about it—but this and that are two different things. But being with someone you know is good for peace of mind, and Al was with us, too, not long before this. It might be easier for you to find him if we stick together."

"Al was with you?"

"Yeah, though he left before the fight. He was wandering around the city looking for you."

Al had split off from the group before the assault on city hall, but Subaru was still a little worried about whether he had gotten caught up in the flood. He wanted to assume Al was safe, what with how aloof and perceptive he seemed to be, but…

Hearing that, Priscilla thought for a moment.

"I understand your line of thought, but I have something I must see to first. And I have no intention of accepting your invitation if it means putting that off."

"What could be so…?"

"But your show of resolve wasn't half bad. So I'll grant you a reward."

"A reward?"

Subaru cocked his head at the unexpected response.

Priscilla reached out and grabbed Subaru by the shirt and pulled him to the ground, where he fell down next to Liliana with a grunt. He looked up in order to give Priscilla an earful for suddenly throwing him down—

"What the hell was that for all of a…? Wha—?!"

—until he saw a misshapen silhouette leap out violently at Priscilla.

"—!!"

The grotesque being howled sinisterly as it launched itself high into the air. It had four short, hound-like legs and twisted fangs lining its mouth. Just that would mark it as little more than a particularly ugly beast, but everything else was abnormal. It had swords and spears protruding from its back and torso. Not hanging from its body. Not stuck into it. The weapons were growing out of its body.

It was literally a fusion of flesh and steel creating a truly hideous silhouette.

"That's...not a demon beast! What is that?!"

"Ahhhhhhh! That's a demi-beast!" Liliana screamed as she crawled across the ground.

While that was going on in the background, the grotesque monster that Liliana called a demi-beast took aim at Priscilla's pale neck. Its sickening, unclean fangs drew near, but Priscilla easily deflected it to the side with the fan in her hand, forcefully knocking it down. One of the swords fused with its body gouged the earth underneath, creating a groove in the ground between Subaru and Liliana. A shout froze in his throat as he saw how sharp and dangerous it was.

"Well? Unsightly, isn't it? These hideous, inferior brutes are rampant in the city right now. Not even beasts, and yet insufficient as tools. Incomplete from birth, a botched job from creation—thus demi-beasts."

Priscilla stood there calmly, having knocked aside the demi-beast with her fan as Subaru watched stiffly. He was shocked by how at ease she appeared as he pulled Liliana away from where the demi-beast had fallen.

Behind them, the demi-beast writhed in agony as it leaped up, its spit-flecked jowls twisting around as it searched for the one who had attacked it. Something about it felt off to Subaru, and he quickly realized why. Its eyes.

"It doesn't have any eyes... Did something blind it? Wait, did it just never have them to begin with? What?"

Its head looked similar to a dog's. It had a snout with a vaguely canine nose and jaws, but there were no eyes where there should have been. It was true that some creatures simply didn't develop vision, then, but this one had empty, hollowed-out pits where eyes would have been. It had eye sockets but no eyeballs. There were no scars or any other signs that they'd been removed, either. It was all incredibly cryptic. What were demi-beasts?

"Look closely, commoner. If you would wander this city, you

might encounter one of these monstrosities at any time. They are coarse and incomplete creatures, but they have enough strength to easily hunt down one or two helpless fools."

"Hey, who's supposed to be helpless?! I've…"

Subaru reached for his trusty whip to drive home his point, but he had lost it either in the fight with Capella or else when he fell into the water. Farewell, Guilty Whip.

And with him unable to deny the helpless-fool point anymore, Priscilla intentionally made a sound with her shoe, drawing the demi-beast's attention toward her. Gnashing its fangs, it obediently bounded toward her, drawn by the sound.

"Look how it clings to sound. It is comical how inexperienced they are in dealing with their world without sight. That shows this is not their natural state. But that is just the sort of being they are."

"What are you saying…? Hold on a second! You said they're all over town? There are more like this out there?!"

"They have spawned everywhere. Without eyes, without ears, without a mouth…like a mockery of a living creature, they are all flawed in some form or another. One can only assume their creator's sense of beauty is catastrophically broken."

Right after Priscilla said that, the demi-beast launched itself into the air again. Unable to see, it relied on its ears to leap toward her approximate location. Naturally, she swayed out of the way of such a clumsy attack with ease. When the demi-beast's fangs caught only air, it quickly turned after landing and prepared to attack again—

"—What a truly pitiful existence. In my great mercy, I shall grant you rest."

And, having said that, Priscilla slowly drew a crimson sword from the sky.

"———"

Subaru was shocked by the sudden appearance of the sword, but more than that, he was enchanted by the sword's beauty.

The bright-red blade that appeared was gilded with strange and beautiful ornamentation. It was radiant enough to be easily worthy of being called a treasure sword. From the hilt to the blade, it was entirely scarlet, and in Priscilla's hand it glimmered brilliantly, like she held a living flame.

"—Ah."

Cloaked in an inferno that enchanted all who beheld it, the sword flashed as Priscilla allowed the blind demi-beast to experience the blade firsthand in all its glory. The creature split down the middle and then burst into flames. There were no dying cries as the single crimson slash transformed the demi-beast into cinders.

"The gleam of this sword of sunlight and the knowledge that demi-beasts abound are my reward for your determination," Priscilla said as Subaru watched the demi-beast's death with eyes wide open.

Looking over at her, he saw that the crimson sword was already gone from her hand, replaced by her usual fan. It almost felt like it had been an illusion, but the demi-beast's ashes were proof enough that it had been real.

"That's quite the foolish look on your face. Don't tell me you missed your opportunity to see something you will never see again? If so, my whim shan't visit again, so you have only your own unworthiness to blame."

"...There's so much to comment on there that I'm not even sure where to start. What even is your actual power?"

"What an empty question. I can't even work up the will to answer."

Priscilla fanned herself leisurely as she openly ignored Subaru's question. Liliana, whom Subaru had forgotten he was still holding under his arm, started flapping her arms and legs.

"Come on, Sir Natsuki!"

"Huh? Ah, my bad. Did I touch somewhere inappropriate? Though where would that even be on you?"

"How rude! They may be small, but they are there! But this isn't the time for that!"

Twisting her body, she slipped free from Subaru's arm, hit the ground with a thud, and quickly leaped to her feet. She left Subaru and Priscilla behind and ran to the intersection up ahead. Peering around the corner, she waved at them to come over.

"I knew it! Look! There is someone hurt here! Help! Please help him!"

"There is?! Were they attacked by that demi-beast?!"

Subaru frantically rushed over to Liliana. There was a young man lying facedown in a pool of blood. He had wounds on his shoulder and back.

"Are you okay?! Hey! Crap, he's totally out of it. The wounds aren't too deep, but..."

There was no response when Subaru called out to the young man. After checking his wounds, Subaru quickly tore the man's shirt and performed simple first aid.

"You seem quite familiar with how to deal with this sort of thing..."

"It's the product of my mentor's spartan training. I'm amazed you noticed he was here, though."

"Yes, I was sure I heard something. Like a heartrending voice pleading for aid."

"What are you, some hero of justice...? All righty, that'll do for first aid."

Subaru sighed in relief after stopping the bleeding and tying off a splint. The wound did not look life-threatening, at least.

"But we can't just leave him lying here, either. What do we do...?"

"Then carry him, commoner. My goal is the shelter down this street. If you take him there, they should be able to stabilize him."

"There's a shelter nearby? Right, you mentioned having some errand or other when you turned me down..."

"Let's go. Do not slow me further."

Paying no heed to Subaru, Priscilla said whatever she pleased and then started walking away. Subaru silently shook his head and then lifted up the unconscious man. He felt a dark irony that he was practically relying on his blackened right leg to brace himself as he followed Priscilla. Liliana tottered along behind them, still full of concern about the young man's fate.

"Time and again you really do seem to be a man with good timing."

"What?"

Priscilla flashed a dark, crimson smile.

"You should etch into your eyes one more time just what the current state of this city is."

5

There was an odd air to the area. Even Subaru could notice almost immediately from the way his skin crawled.

"——"

When they stepped into the shelter carrying a wounded person, they were met by many different gazes. A moist, cloying, depressing emotion rested within those eyes. An oppressive, vague negative feeling that was uncomfortable to be around and made it hard to breathe.

This location was apparently a shelter that had been constructed in the basement of one of the buildings in the fourth district.

It had been designed to protect residents in the event of flooding, and its sturdy door had been sealed, keeping all the water out. But even so, the mere fact that they had escaped the flooding was not enough to soothe everyone's worries, given all the danger threatening their city. That much was clear enough from the way they buried their heads in their knees and from the potent fear that appeared in every face that wasn't just looking down at the ground.

"This is bad for the heart. What is this feeling…?"

Leaving the injured man in the care of the healer on duty in the simple medical room setup at the shelter, Subaru slowly looked around the underground area, gulping bitterly.

There were a lot of people. There were enough crowded here belowground to make the shelter feel cramped. But it was quiet. Very quiet.

They were holding their breaths, avoiding one another's gazes, looking down in silence. As if they were trying to avoid drawing attention to the fact that they were still alive.

"I see, he's not here, either."

Priscilla was cast from a different mold, though, able to carry herself without any hesitation even in this uniquely oppressive environment. On the one hand, it was certainly a regal quality to remain so unaffected by one's surroundings, but it also did nothing to ease the fear and uncertainty gripping people's hearts, which made her seem more like a tyrant than anything else in the moment.

Almost naturally, something akin to annoyance started welling up in Subaru's chest. Priscilla was always so full of arrogant self-confidence, and he felt a sudden urge to tear at her face, to peel away that haughty mask—

"At the end of the day, a mediocre man remains a mediocrity. You've been completely bewitched after such a short time."

"Wh-what are you talking about…?"

"There was a barbarous gleam in your pupils. It is only natural that the mere sight of me ignites lustful passion, but the desire to harm beauty is mere brute savagery. Can you truly say you know not of what I speak? Well?"

Interrogated by the woman whose face he had just considered clawing off, Subaru was suddenly dumbfounded.

"———"

Why had his emotions boiled over so suddenly? It was not that odd for him to feel antagonistic toward her, but there had been no reason for it to suddenly get so intense and violent.

—It was almost like he had lost control of his emotions.

"No way…"

As that thought occurred to him, a chill ran up his spine. The discomfort grew and grew until his arms and legs were trembling, and he couldn't keep his teeth from chattering.

The way his emotions were unnaturally shifting in a way he could not control reminded him of something.

"Sirius… Wrath's Authority…? Is that what's causing this?!"

Subaru pinched his cheek, clearing his head with a dose of pain as he gritted his teeth.

Naturally, Sirius was not in the shelter. Subaru could not hear her voice, either. But he could not escape that sense of gloom, that unpleasant sensation of being tossed into a pot of simmering emotions until they were all scorched black.

The moment after Subaru realized what was happening and how dangerous it was—

"—What's your problem? The hell do ya think you're staring at?!"

A middle-aged man near the back of the shelter shouted, teeth bared and face red. His rage seemed to be directed at a younger man near him. His anger still obvious on his face, the older man approached the younger man and gave him a hard shove in the chest.

"If you've got something to say, then say it! Well?! What's your problem?!"

"—Ngh! Fine, you really want to know?! Take a look around you! You aren't a boy anymore! Have some self-control! We don't all need to know how pissed you are! It's a pain in the ass for the rest of us, you washed-up piece of shit!"

"Stop it! Stop it! Please, just stop it!"

The younger man's rage exploded at the older man's provocation, and the woman beside him started crying as she cradled her head. Unable to hold back her emotions, she started sobbing uncontrollably, which only stoked the older man's anger and the younger man's righteous fury.

And the explosion of emotions did not stop there.

"This isn't good! The other people are getting affected…"

It was slow at first but quickly picked up speed—a wave of intense emotions spread throughout the shelter. The explosive increase in noise after the previous silence made it feel like pandemonium had broken out in the blink of an eye.

"This isn't good! Priscilla! If we don't do something, people are gonna die!"

"Fool. You've lost your calm as badly as they have. Just sit down and shut up."

"Is this really the time for that?! Even in a situation like this, you're still… Gh."

Impatience turned his vision red, and he tried to grab Priscilla, but she evaded his hands with a simple sway and grabbed his hair, pulling his face close to hers.

"Gah?!"

"Listen, commoner. Your fears will become reality. The unpleasant feeling that corrupted this city's water will warp people's hearts, steal their rationality, and rob them of their kindness. However—"

Priscilla coldly explained the tragedy that would befall the shelter as Subaru's face tensed and his lips quivered. But as she trailed off, she looked to the center of the room.

Subaru naturally followed her gaze. Standing there was…

"Hark. Lend me your ears—Pristella wavers, reflected in the water's surface."

The plucked strings of the lyulyre created clear, high-pitched chords that pierced the pandemonium. In an instant, that sound shattered the rage and grief that had gripped the shelter. Everything paused for a brief moment. And into that split-second gap, something slipped:

Music.

"______"

Right as feverish emotions were about to boil over, an ephemeral melody emerged from the lyulyre's strings. And everyone who heard it was shaken to the soul by the voice that accompanied it.

Liliana's tongue danced, giving form and shape to the song welling up inside her. That strain of music struck the people, Subaru, and even Priscilla alike, captivating the crowd from the moment the sounds hit their ears and making their bodies, their minds, and their very souls tremble.

Her song had stolen their hearts. There was no other way to put it. They were taken back and returned to their rightful owners.

Subaru could feel himself being set free from the confining emotions of Wrath's invisible web. This was the power of song. The brilliance of Liliana's music, the music the Songstress unleashed, was a power beyond reason capable of shaking people to their very core—

"—Thank you very much for your kind attention," Liliana said with a bow.

By the time she finished, the dark emotions that had dominated the shelter were long gone.

—There was only a thunderous round of applause that welled up naturally from all sides.

6

"Thank you! Thank you! My apologies for such an embarrassing sight."

"You..."

With her performance over, and after the ripples of her singing voice had faded, and she had finished introducing herself to her tearful audience, the Songstress faded away and Liliana took her place.

When Liliana winked awkwardly and gave Subaru a thumbs-up, his shoulders slumped—not because of some inexplicable emotion but because of his own exasperation.

"So you've returned to your senses. That is quite the accomplishment by the diva."

"I don't really have room to argue. You seemed fine even without the song, though...and for some reason that actually makes sense to me. Wrath's Authority was creating a resonance with everyone's emotions."

For Priscilla, whose ego was so strong and whose sympathetic impulses were so limited, it made sense that the effect of Wrath's Authority would be weaker. At least that was how Subaru interpreted it, given the calm demeanor she had projected both before and after the song.

The pandemonium in the shelter was unmistakably the effect of Sirius's ability. The worst possible outcome had been avoided thanks to Liliana's song, but it gave Subaru chills to think of what might have happened without her.

Most likely, the original impetus had been something trivial, but everyone in the shelter was under intense stress from the oppressive, closed-off atmosphere and the presence of a dangerous group in the city. And when they were unable to fully manage that pressure, darker thoughts started to slip into their hearts, which Sirius's Authority then amplified until even the most minor friction with someone else in the shelter could set it all off. And when it exploded, the resulting damage created a pandemic of intense emotions that could lead only to tragedy.

And that was—

"That is the unsightly, meaningless reality currently occurring everywhere around the city."

"______"

"You described this unpleasant atmosphere as an Authority, did you not? 'Wrath's Authority.'"

"...Yeah, that's right. This is the work of one of the Witch Cult Archbishops."

Priscilla's crimson eyes narrowed in distaste. Even without the effects of any Authority, Subaru could sympathize with the ire resting deep within her gaze.

Subaru had thought he had a sufficiently healthy respect for how dangerous Sirius's ability to amplify and propagate emotions was, but his understanding had been too simplistic. It seemed all too possible now that Wrath's Authority had extended its reach across every part of Pristella.

And the majority of people in the city had fled to the shelters. If they felt the effects of that ability with so much fear and unease in their hearts, the potential for disaster would be unimaginable.

"The careful training to always go to the shelters if anything happens has totally played into their hands here."

If Wrath's ability could share and amplify people's emotions, the strength of the effect should be proportional to the number of people inside the area of effect. The people around you became mirrors for emotions, and you in turn became a mirror for them, accelerating and amplifying the effect.

People being near others strengthened Wrath's ability and increased its potential to infect more people and spread. This observation spoke to the lie Sirius was hiding. Hers was not a power for allowing people to understand one another at all. It was a nightmarish power that forced people to isolate themselves and remain alone in a situation where fear and unease dominated the mood.

"That makes me a tiny smidge vexed, so I believe I shall have to hold out a bit longer."

"Liliana..."

Subaru absorbed Liliana's words with quiet surprise as she pointed to the deepening furrows in her brow.

It was clear now that her music had the ability to free people from Sirius's Authority. And she, fully aware that it had that effect, had been traveling from shelter to shelter, singing as she went.

—When she had been staying at Roswaal's manor and her music had invited trouble, she had gone so far as to say "I don't want my singing to be used as a tool," even when her life was hanging in the balance.

For that same Liliana to use her singing like this—

"What the situation calls for is captivating people with song, which is right up my alley!" Liliana said with another lousy wink.

There was no denying she was the city's Songstress.

"So then that goal you mentioned before is helping Liliana go around to all the shelters?" Subaru asked Priscilla.

If that was the case, that would mean Priscilla was also acting out of concern about the chaos that had struck the city. Right as Subaru was on the verge of reconsidering his view of her and realizing that perhaps he had badly misunderstood what lay in her heart, that train of thought was suddenly interrupted.

"Fool, as if I would bother with something so inconsequential as that."

Subaru pursed his lips at the textbook Priscilla response.

"Inconsequential? …Fine, then what *is* your goal? Why are you visiting all the shelters?"

"I'm looking for Schult. If I don't, he will almost certainly cry. And I cannot stand seeing a child's teary face."

"——"

Subaru's mind froze at the unexpected response. It was something only Priscilla would say. Not noticing his reaction, Priscilla shrugged as if to indicate she had little choice in the matter.

"Al can take care of himself. The fate of another fool is of no concern to me. But Schult's charm is irreplaceable, so I have to recover him personally. He's quite the troublesome retainer."

Considering there were no stronger emotions in her voice, it was a fair guess that was how she really felt. But the reason she gave for moving around a city embroiled in such trouble—to search for her lost young retainer—was not something Subaru had expected.

It was surprising, but he could accept it. It was indisputable that she was busily walking around looking for her servant, after all. And she just happened to be helping Liliana with her goal as well in the process.

"What's that look on your face?"

Priscilla looked over at him suspiciously, but Subaru waved it off with a vague "It's nothing" and a sigh. But he felt like he understood. And that was enough, given the situation.

Taking a deep breath and filling his lungs, Subaru looked out at the now-stable mood of the shelter.

"This shelter should be fine now. I'm going to go now like I said before. I need to meet back up with everyone."

"Aye-aye! Lady Priscilla and I are going to another shelter now. Music is still needed… I am grateful to be a bard, so now's the time to cash in and earn some more self-respect!"

"Phrasing!"

Despite the grave situation, Subaru could not help laughing and latching on to how she put it.

He turned to Priscilla again. It had only been a short while, but he was grateful for the many things she had given him. He never would have guessed the day would come when he could interact with her so genuinely.

"Thank you for all your help. Let's meet again after all this is over. And you should really look for Al, too."

"As if I would lend an ear to anyone's instructions. I will simply do as I please. You should run along now and worry about cleansing this city's befouled waters. If you manage to actually accomplish something, I shall personally reward you."

"Just so you know, unlike your retainers, I don't have any particular interest in licking your boots."

And with that, Subaru turned away from them as Liliana saluted, and Priscilla was not even bothering to look at him anymore. He departed from the shelter and started racing through the city.

Priscilla and Liliana would head to another shelter to stop another latent explosion of emotion that was just waiting to go off. He could trust them to take care of that, so Subaru would need to follow through on his own role.

"First is Muse… If everyone is still okay, then that's where they would go."

The Muse Company was far from the fourth district. But he had all the motivation he needed. All that was left was to steel his nerve.

This isn't even close to being over. Not by a long shot. And I'm going to prove it.

7

"______"

A blind, bloody-smelling demi-beast was sniffing at the ground in front of him.

Holding his breath to keep from being noticed, Subaru examined it, feeling a sense of righteous anger as he compared it to the other demi-beasts he had come close to encountering.

The demi-beasts Priscilla had labeled hideous, and Liliana had scorned earlier for their inability to sing, came in a multitude of forms, and Subaru had felt reluctant to lump them all together under the same repulsive description.

In exchange for lacking something—eyes, ears, mouth—their bodies were fused with swords or shields or other inorganic objects. They had been transformed into something that could not naturally occur in some horrible design.

The demi-beasts were the unnatural creation of an aberrant mind. So turning it around, if he could accept that they were unnatural life-forms, then it was entirely believable they had actually been designed. And there was at least one being currently in the city who was capable of manipulating the bodies of living creatures.

"Capella, you piece of shit…"

The demi-beasts' parent, or perhaps *creator* would be the better word, appeared in Subaru's head. The Archbishop of Lust, Capella, practically an embodiment of all the malice of the human world. Subaru could absolutely believe that she would create such incomplete creatures as demi-beasts and set them loose all around the city.

But that thought raised a question: *Then where is she getting the ingredients for the demi-beasts?*

"—!!"

"Ah."

When he gritted his teeth, he inadvertently twisted his foot slightly, grinding a pebble against the ground beneath his heel. The blind demi-beast immediately turned its head toward the sound and violently dashed over toward Subaru.

The ax growing out of its head was heavy, making it look absurd as it ran. The edge of the ax scraped the ground, sending sparks flying continuously as it closed in. Subaru leaped aside as it approached. Then he used a slight groove in the wall as a foothold to acrobatically launch himself over the demi-beast.

"And up we go!"

His right leg was in disgustingly good shape, and he could move better than ever because of it. He easily leaped over the demi-beast and left that stretch of road behind as it frantically spun around searching for him.

"—Girrrrrrrrrrah!"

All of a sudden, an awkward shout rang out. Subaru evaded the surprise attack by jumping straight up and spreading his legs. The demi-beast passed under him, but having lost his balance, Subaru rolled when he hit the ground. He was planning to use the momentum of the roll to start running away when—

"...Crap..."

Right in front of him was another demi-beast, quietly standing there, barring his path. It was one without a mouth, which was why it had grumbled instead of roared. The one whose charge he had just dodged had no ears, meaning all three types roaming the city were represented here.

"———"

They were surrounding him front, back, and to one side, cornering him.

Looking to the open side, he saw the wall of a dilapidated building that was deteriorating from age and lack of maintenance. With enough momentum and motivation, it wouldn't be impossible to get over. The goal would be something like what Felt had done when they first met.

The way she had run, leaving Subaru behind begging for help with Larry, Curly, and Moe surrounding him—thinking back on it now, he could not help feeling an odd sense of fate that those four had ended up in the same camp.

Soothing his nerves with some pointless thoughts, Subaru crouched. The demi-beasts surrounding him bent their knees, but Subaru was ready to go for the wall one step ahead of them—

"—Please don't move, Subaru. I don't want to miss."

But a voice that was far surer an option than trying to get out of the situation on his own made him abandon that desperate plan.

The three demi-beasts barreled down on Subaru as he stopped, all aiming to hit him with their blend of ax and fangs, swords and claws—but none of them reached him. Because each and every one of their attacks was deflected and knocked back by a single slender knight's blade.

"My apologies, but his continued survival is necessary for this city. I humbly request that you withdraw!"

The elegant knight Julius Juukulius attacked the three demi-beasts simultaneously with sword and spirits.

His sharp blade cut through the eyeless beast's torso in a single broad sweep while the earless and mouthless ones were swallowed up in a red glimmer and consumed by flames. Purged by a raging inferno, the warped creatures turned to ash and collapsed without a sound. But the blind beast continued to attack despite having sustained an obviously lethal wound.

"Julius!"

"You need not worry."

—The eyeless beast's head was sent rolling by an elegant, arcing slash.

This was not the time nor place for idle thoughts, but it was truly a beautiful slash, one that held Subaru's gaze. The flash of steel precisely struck at the weakest point of the demi-beast's neck, ending its life without prolonging its pain.

If there could be any mercy in the act of ending a life, then that attack had been the embodiment of it.

No matter how incomprehensible the creature's unnatural vitality might be, losing its head was still lethal. The same went for reducing its entire body to cinders. Subaru felt a strong sense of pity for the demi-beasts as they fell.

"Are you unhurt, Subaru?"

Flicking the blade that had cut down the demi-beast, Julius turned to Subaru.

"Yeah." Subaru nodded. "That was a dangerous spot to be in, though. Thanks for the help. And from the looks of it, you're doing okay, too."

"I cannot deny that. In the end, I was swept up in the flood from the gate opening, which left the battle at city hall unsettled. I was concerned when I saw you fall into the water and lost track of you."

Julius shook his head slightly as he placed his hand on Subaru's shoulder. Surprisingly, there was an unconcealable trace of relief in the gesture. As if he was still processing the fact that Subaru had returned alive.

"What happened at the tower? Honestly, I can't really remember much of the back end of the fight with Capella…with Lust."

"You don't remember? A black dragon attacked the upper floor and carried you and Duchess Crusch away. I immediately went after the black dragon to try and retrieve the two of you when the floodgate opened…"

"And in the chaos, I ended up falling into the water and getting washed away?"

"If I was to be honest, I had thought your chances of surviving were fifty-fifty at best. You did well to make it back safely."

Julius kept nodding to himself, his hand still on Subaru's shoulder, welcoming his return. Hearing that, Subaru realized his situation had been far more dire than he realized. But against all odds, he had returned safe and sound. And now he had been reunited with Julius.

"What about everyone else? Are they safe? I remember Crusch was in trouble. I was hurrying to get back to the Muse Company just now…"

"I understand the feeling, but for now calm yourself, please. Allow me to alleviate your first concern: Everyone who went to take back city hall returned alive… Knowing that you have survived and are safe, I can now say that confidently."

"Everyone made it back alive… I see…"

Overcome by relief after hearing that news, Subaru slumped down to the ground. He had been more anxious about that than he had realized, and for a moment he could not force his quivering knees to carry his weight.

"After facing so many powerful enemies, I'm glad everyone survived… And there weren't any losses to that flood, either?"

"It was a perilous situation. From what Sir Wilhelm said, they were close to being overwhelmed by the enemy when the water hit, and it was entirely possible we would have suffered losses if the battle continued. It's ironic to think that was the Witch Cult's doing."

Subaru furrowed his brow. There was more scorn directed at himself than regret in Julius's voice.

From what he was saying, it sounded like that flood that had exacted such a terrible price from the city as a whole had actually been a massive boon to Subaru and the others fighting at city hall. And it was probably at least partially because of it that Capella had failed to kill Subaru and Crusch when they were at death's door.

Which meant that the Witch Cult had shot itself in the foot by opening the floodgate when it had. Though it was also doubtful whether it put much stock in the outcome of a single battle.

"There are several other things that I have to tell you, but for now, it's good that we did not miss each other. Currently, the Muse Company is empty, and no one is there. You were about to waste a trip."

"No one? Why? Anastasia, Ferris, and my Beako should still be there…"

"Regarding that, try to remain calm while I explain."

Subaru gulped as things took a disquieting turn. Seeing that, Julius took a breath before continuing.

"…While we were attacking city hall, the Muse Company was also attacked. Their aim was the gentleman Kiritaka of the Council of Ten, but in the end, Lady Anastasia took command, and those who remained were forced to abandon that base."

"It was attacked?! But it was a shelter! There were lots of wounded people there, right?!"

Other than the Iron Fangs members there as guards, the vast majority of the people at the company had been noncombatants—including Beatrice, who was in a coma, and Mimi, who had sustained an incurable wound from the blessing of the grim reaper. Hetaro and TB shared the burden of their sister's wound and were in a dangerous condition, too.

There was no way they could have safely fled an attack with so many people in that sort of condition—

"Wait! What happened to Beatrice? To everyone?!"

"They succeeded in just barely getting all the wounded out safely at immense personal effort. Lady Beatrice and Mimi and her brothers were also safely carried away. However, the whereabouts of Mr. Kiritaka Muse and the members of the White Dragon's Scale who stayed behind with him at the Muse Company are currently unknown… We don't know whether they survived."

"Damn it! I'm sure Liliana would be sad if she heard that…"

Even hearing that Beatrice was safe, Subaru could not really be happy given the losses that might have been incurred. Considering the enemy's goal, it made sense that Kiritaka would be targeted. The Witch Cult's demand was for the Witch's bones to be turned over to them, and only members of the Council of Ten could tell them the location.

"Having lost the Muse Company, we have shifted to using city hall as a base. We should head there. Everyone is worried about you, and Garfiel in particular is running himself ragged."

"That's not good, but we're heading to city hall? We took it back?"

"When the gate was opened and our battle there was cut short by the massive surge of water, our enemies abandoned the building. However, they broadcast one final message before they did so. Did you hear it?"

"…That was right around when I was bobbing in the water." Subaru pursed his lips.

It did not sound like recovering city hall was really something that could be celebrated.

Hearing his response, Julius furrowed his brow and hesitated for a moment before responding.

"It was after they caused the canals to overrun and were wreaking havoc in every part of the city. I was struggling to grasp the chaotic situation myself when Lust's voice rang out from the sky."

"——"

Subaru quietly urged Julius to continue. Seeing that, Julius nodded and took a long, deep breath.

"Lust...or perhaps I should say the Witch Cult placed additional demands in order to free the city as punishment for attacking the tower. In addition to the Witch's bones, they had three new demands."

"...Which were?"

"—A book called the book of knowledge. An artificial spirit. And also..."

Just those two alone were more than enough to provoke Subaru, but the final demand actually made Julius pause even after he'd said that much. Seeing him hesitate, Subaru steeled himself as he wondered just how repulsive the final demand could possibly be.

However, Subaru quickly realized that that hesitation was out of consideration for him. Because the final demand was the most absurd, the most out of place, and the most impossible for Subaru to accept.

"...the wedding of the silver-haired maiden. Something you would surely never allow."

CHAPTER 2

WHAT IT TAKES TO BE A KNIGHT

1

Looking out at the flooding city, Emilia gripped the windowsill tightly enough to warp it.

There was another booming sound as the opened floodgate closed again. It was over in the blink of an eye. The city had escaped being completely flooded, but the damage was still massive. Buildings had been destroyed, and there was no question that people must have gotten hurt or worse. Thinking of the damage the water was causing, Emilia frantically started to go out the window—

"Whatever you might be thinking, it would be wiser to stop."

A cool voice stopped Emilia, who had already stepped onto the windowsill and was getting ready to leap down. It was the cold beauty #184, who seemed entirely unshaken by everything that was going on.

Faced with her piercing gaze, Emilia narrowed her purple eyes sharply.

"Wiser how? You saw what just happened, didn't you? I have to go help!"

"Your feelings are understandable, but were you to leave now, it would only cause even more suffering, since he…our husband does not wish for you to leave."

"That again?!"

Emilia bit her lip in irritation that Regulus could overtly restrict her freedom. It was clear from their interactions up to that point that #184 was entirely subservient to Regulus, but that was not how Emilia felt. She was resolute that she was not his wife.

"Even if you disagree, can you truly not imagine what he might do if something he found undesirable was to come to pass?"

"That's..."

"First he would punish the wife who acted against his wishes. Then he would punish whatever or whoever motivated his wife to act against his wishes. I am absolutely confident that is how he would respond."

Hearing that, Emilia thought back to her brief encounter with Regulus.

He liked to talk, but that by itself was not necessarily bad. The boy Emilia knew so well also often had a lot to say. But unlike him, Regulus showed absolutely no regard for the person he spoke with. His speech and actions and focus were all one-sided—because of his sense of omnipotence. Regulus Corneas was stronger than almost anyone else Emilia had ever encountered before. He might even be a match for Reinhard. And now #184 was earnestly warning Emilia not to upset him.

And yet—

"—That isn't enough of a reason for me to stop."

"...Even if your life is in danger?"

"There are people out there who are in danger right now. If I just secretly slip out and then slip back in, wouldn't that still be fine?"

Emilia's magic should be useful in dealing with flooding. She could freely shape ice, manipulating it in such a way that it would not cause any problems when it melted. If it would be a problem for Regulus to find out, then she could just do it stealthily, even if that was not really her forte.

#184 paused for a few seconds and then let out a long sigh.

"...Are you actually serious?"

"Huh? I was *really* serious... Did I not sound serious?" Emilia asked in shock.

She had been trying to plead as earnestly as she could, so if it had come across as a joke, that would be a problem.

Seeing Emilia's reaction, #184 looked outside.

"If you are concerned about harm befalling the residents due to the flooding, you needn't worry. The vast majority of people should have already fled to the shelters and should have escaped the worst of the flooding."

"Shelters…? Right, the morning broadcast mentioned that! Then everyone is hiding out there?"

"Since several hours ago."

"Oh, I see… That's a relief, then." Emilia placed her hand on her chest.

Of course that would not make the physical damage of the flooding disappear, but it was fortunate. At least that meant there would be no tragedy of countless people getting swallowed up in the floodwaters.

"…You trust what I just said?"

"Eh? Should I not?"

"I am his wife… Do you really think I wouldn't lie for my husband's sake?"

#184 was clawing away at Emilia's heart, as if testing her. And accepting that provocation, Emilia considered her words for a brief moment.

"—But you seemed sincere, so I'm sure you weren't lying." Emilia shook her head, choosing to believe in #184's sincerity rather than assume malice.

And if she was going to lie, there would have been easier, more convincing lies, but she had responded without any doubt at all in what she was saying. Because her conscience did not trouble her about it.

"—Ah."

#184 opened her eyes slightly in surprise. Seeing that reaction, Emilia felt like it was the first time she had gotten a glimpse of her natural range of expression.

"So you can actually look surprised. Maybe we can finally have a proper conversation."

"…That was unbecoming of me. Anything more will incur his ire."

"Getting upset that his wife showed a little emotion when she would be so much more beautiful if she could smile just seems *really* weird."

"Weird doesn't begin to describe it... Ngh— I should warn you."

Her emotional control fraying in the face of Emilia's smile, #184 quickly caught her breath before continuing.

"What he likes is your normal face, that exact expression. I suggest you not change it in front of him—do not get visibly happy or sad, things like that. It would probably be best if you don't open your mouth as well."

"I shouldn't talk? Why not?"

"Because no one knows what might draw his ire."

#184's behavior around Regulus was dictated by her fear of crossing one of his lines. Fear was limiting her emotions. Emilia wanted to do something to help her. She could tell from talking with her that she was wise and the sort of beauty who could light up a room with a smile.

"You mustn't furrow your brow, either. It upsets him."

"I'm thinking as hard as I can about what I can do to keep Regulus from getting between us having a proper conversation," Emilia responded earnestly.

Hearing that, #184 caught her breath slightly. There was the slightest hesitation in her cool eyes.

"Ummm..."

Something about what #184 was starting to say was different.

But—

"Hello, all you meatbags! I hope this finds you in good health as you tremble in the fetal position! In my deep and praiseworthy benevolence, I'm broadcasting my beautiful voice for you little shits to cling to for comfort! Are you happy now? Are you having fun? Are you dancing and singing and writhing in agony? Ah-ha-ha-ha-ha-ha-ha-ha!"

A shrill voice rang through the air, cutting #184 off.

"—Wah! Wh-what's that?!"

Emilia looked around in shock as a callous voice suddenly filled the sky above the city. Instinctively looking up, Emilia realized that it was a broadcast using a metia. The same one that had been filled with concern for the people of the city in the morning, and the same one that had carried Liliana's singing across the whole city. The impression the broadcast imparted could change dramatically depending on how the speaker used it.

At the very least, Emilia certainly did not believe that the person speaking now had much claim to deep and praiseworthy benevolence.

"Well then, I have an important announcement for all you twisted sacks of shit! Somehow, even after all the warnings you were given, a swarm of incompetent meatbags came after me in a good old-fashioned raid! Well, not that I expected any less, so I had already made arrangements to greet them. But it's still annoying, you know!"

The voice was light, and the broadcaster almost seemed to be indulging in the moment, but there was also a clear irritation mixed in as the sinister proclamation continued.

"Anyway, I was honestly thinking, *Ah, whatever, screw it. Just open the floodgates and sink the whole place to the bottom of the lake, and them's the breaks*, you know? I mean, it's hurtful when people just straight up ignore everything I make the effort to say! In fact, I've still got some wounds aching from it all. It's an affront and an assault on my goodwill and on me personally!"

"—Ngh."

Emilia shuddered at the threat of opening the floodgates. The massive flood that had just happened was from just one gate being open for just a few seconds. If they were all flung open it would cause far, far more damage. The shelters were currently still safe, but if the entire town was completely flooded, they would surely not escape the destruction.

For such a sadistic broadcaster to have that sort of power was immeasurably dangerous.

"But…"

Emilia noticed that the broadcaster did not seem to have any intention of actually following through on that threat at the moment. If they were really serious, they could have just left the gates open to begin with. But they had not done that. There had to be something they wanted more than they wanted to submerge the city.

"But I'm not some witch, after all. I'm magnanimous. Like the loving mother you never had. So in light of my generosity, I decided why not give you shitheels one last chance."

And just as Emilia was thinking there must be more they wanted, the voice on the broadcast offered an alternative, confirming her hunch. However, it was not going to be an alternative that demonstrated the speaker's magnanimity and loving, motherly generosity.

"Hooooowever! Out of consideration for how you've hurt me, damages have to be considered, too. Just accepting the previous ask won't be enough! So in addition to my first request, there are three new ones…ah-ha-ha-ha-ha! Three more things we want!"

The voice continued huskily.

"—The first is the charitable donation of the book of knowledge, which I'm sure someone has brought into this city."

The voice continued mockingly.

"—The second is the charitable donation of the artificial spirit that's wandering around this city."

The voice continued sneeringly.

"—And the third is… Huh? Ah, the wedding of the silver-haired maiden… In other words, just don't get in the way of it happening. As if I know what that's about, though."

The voice continued detestably.

"And finally, the Witch's body that I requested before makes four! Fulfilling these four requests is the one and only thing you mooks can do to survive! Everything else is pointless! Impossible! Mad! As proven by how that little attack on city hall failed!"

The broadcaster's voice one-sidedly and abusively assaulted all corners of the city.

And just like Emilia had thought, the enemy had made demands in exchange for not flooding the city entirely. But her gut was also telling her that there was no way they would honor their end of the deal. They would surely open all four of the floodgates around the city the moment they got everything they wanted.

"Aaanyway! That's all the happy news from me! I suggest you start your unsightly scramble to find the things we want so you can beg for your lives! Every one of them is definitely somewhere here in this city! Figure out which of your neighbors or which of the bigwigs or whoever is hiding them so you can steal them and present them to me! Ah-ha-ha-ha!"

High-pitched laughter was the final sound anyone heard before the broadcast abruptly ended. As the echoes of that sharp laugh faded, all that remained was oppressive silence. When Emilia felt like a restraint had suddenly been removed, she finally realized that she had been holding her breath.

It had been a terrifying voice with the power to ensnare the hearts of those who lent it an ear. It was not just a natural devilishness, either. The person behind it was extraordinarily skilled at using her voice to manipulate others. It was a skill born from natural talent carefully honed and fully brought to bear.

"That voice just now…" Emilia touched her hand to her throat.

"—That was the Archbishop of Lust, Capella Emerada Lugunica," #184 responded coldly.

Looking over at her, just an arm's length away, Emilia saw that all emotion had disappeared from her expression and eyes. Emilia felt both frustration and shame when she saw her emotionless gaze. Just before the broadcast, she had been about to tell Emilia something, but—

"As you heard, currently the town is at the mercy of the Witch Cult. They will not hesitate to punish careless actions. I'm sure you understand that, yes?"

"Wait… I understand about the Witch Cult, but before I came here, I ran into someone else who called themself an Archbishop. Not Lust though, Wrath…"

"Yes. There are multiple Archbishops here in this town currently. Our husband is one as well," #184 said, averting her eyes.

"—Regulus is…an Archbishop." When she heard that, it all clicked for Emilia.

The pressure she had felt from him was similar to what Sirius had radiated when Emilia had encountered the Archbishop of Wrath in front of the time tower.

If that was true, then there were at least three Archbishops in Pristella, and they had the ability to control the floodgates. And the broadcast just then as well as the current situation were demonstrations—

"So do you finally understand now what a precarious position you are currently in?"

"—? My position?"

"...Please recall the four demands that Archbishop Capella mentioned."

Emilia thought back to the broadcast. Setting aside the Witch's bones and the book of knowledge, which did not ring a bell, she could think of a connection for the artificial spirit. And the other one, which did not make any sense...

"'The wedding of the silver-haired maiden'... That one seemed weirder than the others."

"———" #184 stared at her silently.

"—Wait, you don't mean... Is that last one about me?" Emilia finally realized what that demand might mean and went wide-eyed.

She had never been called something like a silver-haired maiden before, and she had no interest in getting married, so she had been slow in realizing *she* was part of the Witch Cult's objectives. But if the broadcast's demands were for the things the Archbishops wanted, then the only person who would be planning a wedding had to be Regulus. And Emilia was the only person to whom he was proposing marriage.

So if Emilia ran away without a plan—

"—Pristella will be turned into the bottom of a lake."

"It seems you now understand the situation. Let us take care of your clothes. Fortunately, I took your measurements while you were sleeping. A bridal outfit matching his tastes has already been prepared."

#184 reached out to the blanket Emilia was covering herself with. For a second, she froze, but thinking back to the broadcast, she stopped resisting. Besides, her running around with nothing but a sheet for clothing would have deeply bothered Puck and Annerose.

"So then, you were the one who undressed me?"

"Did you think he did that? He would not touch a woman's skin in that way. He just wants to assert his ownership... That's the reason why he inquires about his wives' virginity, too."

"There's that virginity thing again. What does that mean?"

"...I could hardly believe it before, but do you really not know?"

Apparently, it was entirely standard knowledge, but Emilia in her ignorance was hit by a cool response from #184. She made a note to herself to make sure to look it up later. Once everything was over.

"I wonder if Subaru and the others are okay..."

If the entire city was under the control of the Witch Cult, then she was certain Subaru and Beatrice were doing their best to take back the town. And there were other candidates for the crown besides Emilia in the city. It would be nice if they were all safe...

"—You mentioned that name before as well. Is it the name of a male?"

"Yes. He's my knight. I'm sure he's *really* worried about me. But I'm at least as worried about him... I hope he isn't doing anything too reckless."

Or so she said, but she still knew he almost certainly was pushing himself terribly hard. And she had definitely made him really worried by disappearing like that.

—The worry that Subaru might have died did not even cross her mind. He had Beatrice with him, and she could not really imagine him ending up in a life-threatening situation in the first place. He could probably manage to find a way out no matter what happened around him. But that did not keep her from being worried about him or feeling guilty for making him worry. Emilia was badly disappointed in herself for troubling him.

"......" #184's eyes opened slightly as she watched Emilia thinking about Subaru. "Please be careful never to mention that man's name in front of our husband."

"...Just to be sure, why?"

"To put it in his terms, because he will start to doubt whether you truly are a virgin at heart."

"There's that word again..."

Having that used as a reason without any explanation of what it meant was bothering Emilia. But #184 just picked up the white dress she had prepared for Emilia and held it up to her body before nodding in satisfaction.

It looked resplendent while feeling refined to the touch. It was a truly beautiful dress that was very obviously of high quality.

"It looks a little hard to move in."

"It would be wise not to say complaints aloud. Now, let's get you dressed."

Emilia did as she was told as #184 helped her with practiced ease, slipping Emilia's arms into the sleeves. For now, she decided to do as #184 and Regulus said.

A thoughtless attempt to escape would only expose the city to further danger. She would need to carefully plot her actions.

2

"—You *useless*—!"

When he entered city hall, the first thing Subaru heard was grief-stricken rage. His ears were assaulted by a cracking, agitated voice. It was a familiar voice, but that was the first time he had ever heard such raw emotion in it. The shout was filled with unbearable resentment and accompanied by a sharp, dry slap that filled the room.

"Quit it! What's the point of tryin' to pin the blame like this! It's not any one person's fault, and you know that as well as any of us!"

A heated argument was taking place in the lobby, fracturing the mood. Seeing that, Subaru bit his lip, feeling pathetic as a twinge of regret hit his chest.

The lobby was big, with a reception counter and a waiting room. There were still signs of the struggle, broken chairs and tables pushed up against the walls, but it had at least been cleaned up some.

And in the very center of the lobby were three people: a teary-eyed Ferris, Ricardo, who had grabbed his arm and whose fangs were showing, and Wilhelm, whose cheek was red after he'd stood there and taken Ferris's slap to the face.

The old swordsman looked down weakly, his blue eyes remorseful as the other two argued.

"...I have no excuse."

"Make one up! Tell me there was some reason, any reason why

there was no other way! Give me something so I can accept what happened! Apologizing won't change anything!"

"I get how you feel. We're all feeling rotten about what happened. But..."

"'Feeling rotten'...? How is that supposed to help anyone? You're useless! Spineless cowards! Every last one of you! Why...why didn't anyone help Lady Crusch...?" Ferris was breathing raggedly as he glared at Wilhelm and Ricardo before falling to his knees.

Neither of them had any response to his tearful reproach. Ferris clawed at the hard floor as they—Subaru and Julius included—could only watch. His beautifully kept nails and fingers warped painfully, almost like he was punishing himself.

"...What's the point of fame and title if I'm useless in a moment like this...?! Worthless! ...Worthless, worthless, worthless!"

Tears poured from his eyes as he cursed himself. It would almost have been easier if he had pointed his rage at any of the people around him, but knowing that his rage was directed at his own powerlessness, no one could do anything to ease his grief. Everyone in the room was already regretting their own weakness, their own failures.

"...You made it back, Bro. And you too, Julius."

Unable to say anything to Ferris, who was collapsed on the ground, Ricardo called out when he noticed Subaru and Julius standing at the entrance. Subaru nodded slightly and walked over to the three of them.

"Sir Subaru...it's good to see you safe."

"You too, Wilhelm. Ricardo. Though it's not all sunshine..."

"Apologies for such an unseemly scene... Ferris..."

"—I know, I know."

Nodding to Subaru, Wilhelm called to Ferris. He violently wiped his face with his sleeves and stood up, acting like nothing had happened. He reached his hand out to Subaru's body, examining him as he stood there, still shocked by the scene he had walked in on. Finally, Ferris peered into Subaru's eyes.

"...Yeah, you seem fine. Nothing strange or out of order. What's your name and where are you from?"

"Huh? Oh. The name's Subaru Natsuki, and I'm from Japan."

"It must be deep in the countryside, because I've never heard of it… Anyway, I'll be with Lady Crusch."

Ferris listlessly brushed off Subaru's answer as a bad joke before turning away and departing from the lobby. Subaru could not think of the words to say as his slender frame moved away.

"Sir Subaru, apologies, but I'll be taking my leave. I'll also be with my master," Wilhelm said before following Ferris.

When the two of them left, the tense air of the lobby softened ever so slightly.

"I got word from Julius that he went out to get you. The lass there and Wilhelm happened to get into an argument, and, well…"

"It's understandable. Ever since we joined back up, Ferris has been concentrating on healing the wounded and caring for Lady Crusch above all else… Though, it has been a particularly harsh time for Sir Wilhelm," Julius said as he tapped his conversation mirror in his pocket.

He had used that metia to give Ricardo a heads-up that he was coming back with Subaru while they were on their way. Ferris had come down to check out Subaru, which led to starting that scene.

"*Haaah*, what a shit show…"

Subaru couldn't get Ferris's voice, or the grief and rage he directed at himself and everyone else, out of his head. But he also felt uneasy, wondering what about Crusch's condition could be that bad.

"By the way, you dropped this, Bro."

"Hmm? Wait, what?! This is…"

Ricardo tossed something over to Subaru, whose expression had started to cloud. He caught it only to realize it was a shiny black whip—Guilty Whip, his trusted weapon that he thought he'd lost forever.

"You found it for me? Thanks. That gives me a couple more cards I can play if needed, at least."

"You don't have to thank me. You were the one who used it to tie the duchess girl and that black dragon together. All I did was just untie it and hold on to it."

"If I tied the black dragon and Crusch together, then...? What happened...?"

Ricardo's response just left Subaru with more questions as he hooked the whip back on his hip.

"Exactly what it sounds like. The black dragon that sped out of the top floor flew you and Lady Crusch away from Lust. The duchess was unconscious, so you tied her to the dragon using your whip to keep her from falling."

"And then, after managing that final act, I ended up falling myself? If she ended up okay in the end, I'd call it a pretty clutch play if I do say so myself, but..."

"——" Julius paused slightly before affirming Subaru's suspicion. "Ferris has been trying everything he can, but the duchess's condition remains poor."

Crusch had been bathed in Capella's blood, just like Subaru—remembering the fleshy black pattern on his right leg, Subaru felt his mouth dry out.

"Can you be a bit more specific?"

"...I'm sure it has to do with something Lust did. A foreign substance has taken to Lady Crusch's body and is afflicting her. Ferris's lack of composure is the result of her current state. It is unbearable to see." Julius's tone dropped.

Judging from that, Crusch's condition was very serious. Subaru had experienced the terror of something foreign eating away at him right after he was splashed with Capella's blood. It was not just pain or distress—it was repulsive on an entirely different level. If Crusch was suffering the same torment that Subaru had felt in that moment, then...

"—Right! Dragon blood! Capella said something about dragon blood!"

"Dragon blood? You mean the Holy Dragon's blood passed down in the kingdom?" Julius asked, furrowing his brow.

"I don't know if it's anything as showy as some sacred dragon or whatever. Did Crusch say anything herself?"

"No, the duchess has yet to regain consciousness, so I'm sure Ferris has not heard anything about it."

"So she hasn't woken up… Do you think the blood thing might at least give us a clue?"

"I could not begin to say, but Ferris might be able to figure something out, so we should let him know as soon as possible."

"Ah, yeah, that's right. I'll hurry…"

"—Hold up, Bro. I'll go for you."

"———"

It was something that might be able to change the situation. Subaru leaped at the mere possibility, but Ricardo stopped him short. The massive dog-faced man who was like the dictionary definition of a kindhearted person had folded his arms with a rather gentle look on his face, shaking his head with a depth of consideration fitting for a man of his age.

"You haven't seen her yet. Better off stayin' that way."

"…What do you mean by that?"

"Exactly what I said… She's a beautiful lass, which makes seein' her like that all the harder."

It was an answer that not only fanned Subaru's unease but actively made him imagine an even worse situation—but Ricardo was not trying to hide anything, either. He was simply telling Subaru to accept and understand the situation.

He was a nice guy, but he was not trying to protect some youngster's heart from everything bad in the world. In that sense, his was a fittingly wild way of living that respected strength. He did not treat Subaru like a child. He had an adult's thoughtfulness, but he made it clear he was not going to always watch over him like that, either.

"I'll take care of this. You take him to see my boss." Ricardo scratched his head before grabbing Julius's shoulder with his big hand. "—And this ain't like you. Straighten up, ya blockhead."

"—My apologies. I'll leave Ferris to you." Julius furrowed his brow in self-reflection.

"See ya later, Bro. I'm glad you made it out okay," Ricardo said before heading deeper into the building.

"We are using a large room upstairs as an infirmary. Lady Beatrice and Mimi, Hetaro, and TB are there, too, naturally. But Duchess Crusch is…"

"In a different room, right…? Do you agree it'd be better for me not to see her?"

"…Unless the duchess herself desires it."

In other words, he agreed with Ricardo. Honestly, Subaru wanted to confirm with his own two eyes that Crusch was really okay. Even if his comrades were all advising against it. But that was Subaru's ego talking—no one wanted him to go see her in her current state.

"Over here. You should speak with Lady Anastasia."

In the end, Julius brought him to the center of the building without his being able to say anything.

As they left the battered lobby, the walls and floor of the hallway they walked down still showed traces of meaningless destruction. It was clear just what sort of acts the Witch Cult had committed while in control of the building.

Naturally, this was not the only building hit, either. Similar destruction had been visited on several other important structures, but Lust and Gluttony had gone wild on city hall in particular.

—Lust and Gluttony. Thinking of them again caused feelings of shame to well up in Subaru's breast.

"Julius, about Gluttony…"

"…Both sides suffered casualties, but there was no decisive blow. Like the battle on the ground, the chaos of the black dragon's appearance and the flood made escape possible."

"I see…," Subaru murmured faintly.

From the fact that it had not come up yet at all, it had seemed the hope of actually defeating Gluttony was pretty slim, but hearing confirmation that Gluttony had gotten away was unexpectedly depressing.

In just a single day, he had crossed paths with four Archbishops, but Gluttony—the one who had sent Rem into a slumber from which she could not wake, the very person who had removed all memory of her from the world—was special.

Honestly, if nothing else, Subaru wanted to tear Gluttony limb from limb with his own two hands.

"…My apologies, I failed to accomplish the task you entrusted to me."

"Stop it. If you keep apologizing for everything, it'll turn into a habit. Ricardo already mentioned that you're not yourself lately. Don't make me call you a blockhead, too."

"______"

"We all screwed up here, so all of us are going to have to work together to fix it—or is the Finest Knight going to call it quits after one little blemish on his record?"

Julius's eyes opened wide as Subaru shrugged provocatively. Julius's lips quivered.

"...You really don't hold back. Talking so big even in a situation like this... You really don't know the meaning of fear, do you?"

"I know the meaning of fear. I know the scariest thing there is in this world. I've experienced it, too. Which is why I'm always struggling so hard to avoid going through it again."

Subaru was painfully aware of what had gone wrong. He blamed himself, too. He was reflecting on his own failures. Which was exactly why he could not stop moving forward. The scariest thing in the world was losing the connections he shared with someone precious. No longer being able to wish for the shared blessings that should have been. To have that possibility cut off for all eternity.

And that most terrifying of possibilities was currently threatening every person in the city. So—

"There are still things we can do."

Putting his renewed determination into words, Subaru nodded to Julius.

If you mess up, then make up for it by taking action. You aren't the only one who's frustrated.

Before the threat was broadcast, Julius's brother Joshua had left the inn in order to gather information about Gluttony. From the fact that his name had not come up since, it was safe to assume his whereabouts were unknown. In a way, that gave Julius and the rest of them a strong connection with Gluttony, too—

"—Well, you look better than I expected. That's a relief."

As Subaru was thinking about that, a voice called out from the other end of the hallway. Looking up suddenly, he breathed a sigh of relief on seeing the woman at the other end. The beautiful woman with a soft, gentle face—the woman Julius had sworn to serve, Anastasia.

"What, were you listening? That's not very nice."

"I was walking around a bit to clear my head when I happened to hear your voice. I thought it'd be rude to interrupt y'all in the middle of such an important conversation." Anastasia elegantly touched her hand to her cheek before turning her pale-aqua eyes to Julius and thanking him for his service.

"It's good you managed to bring Natsuki back. Now Garfiel will finally be able to calm down and talk some when he gets back."

"From the sound of that, I guess Garfiel isn't here."

"He's running all over the place out there, hardly taking a break at all. Checking the situation at nearby shelters, hunting down those odd brutes who appeared in the center of the town…and more than anything, searching for his precious general."

"He was looking for me…?"

It was obvious once he thought about it. Subaru had gotten swallowed up by the flood and gone missing in the middle of the fight. There was no way Garfiel would be able to sit still in that kind of situation. He would definitely try to use his nose to go looking for Subaru, so it was not strange at all that he would be rushing all around the city.

"But with the situation being what is, even Ricardo said the scent was gone or too muddled together with everything else. It's funny that Julius was the one to find you when he was originally just going to the Muse Company."

"So then Garfiel's still running around town without knowing anything?"

"I told him to come back and check in here once every hour to be sure, so the next time he comes back, you should be able to see him. But more importantly…"

Anastasia slipped into a deep silence as she looked Subaru over. Subaru instinctively straightened his posture, feeling like his body was being appraised by her intellectual gaze. Anastasia's expression suddenly softened a bit when she saw his reaction.

"Yeah, it doesn't look like you're forcing yourself. There's no hiding from my eyes."

"I'm not trying to hide anything. So now that you've decided I'm healthy, what of it?"

Anastasia stepped closer to Subaru.

"—I was kinda hopin' to have an important conversation with ya, Natsuki," she said quietly.

Subaru lightly deflected both the close range and the pressure behind her voice with a simple "What kind of important conversation?"

"You heard it, too, right? Before she left the tower, the Archbishop of Lust changed the deal and added a bunch more demands— You aren't planning to just give in to them, right?"

"Damn straight. I'm pretty pissed. About ready to snap, even."

When he realized she was referring to the unacceptable marriage demand, a vein practically popped out on Subaru's forehead. Hearing that, Anastasia nodded, satisfied.

"Julius, I'm going to have an important conversation with Natsuki now. Can you manage things while I'm doing that?"

"If those are your orders. However, what might be the nature of this important conversation?"

"You don't have to worry; I won't do anything bad to him—honest."

A not-very-cute, impenetrable smile crossed Anastasia's face as she puffed out her chest.

Acknowledging his master's clear-cut orders, Julius did not question her any further. Looking away from her knight, Anastasia turned back to Subaru. She smiled as he caught his breath, lost in her pale-aqua eyes.

"So then, let's have a little chat. This is a big one, since it'll affect the fate of this city." Anastasia casually stated this as she put a hand to her white fox scarf.

3

An important discussion that would affect the fate of the city.

Most likely that was what she really thought and not an idle exaggeration.

And quickly realizing that made Subaru far more tense. It was like his disorganized resolve and determination had been given direction.

"—After I split off from Priscilla and Liliana, I headed for the Muse Company by myself. And along the way I met up with Julius, which is how I ended up back here."

Subaru took a little breath after briefly explaining what had happened to him.

The two of them were talking in a conference room on the second floor of the building. A map of Pristella was spread out on the table in the center of the room with various characters and signs written on it. The floodgate control towers at the four edges of the city, the floodgates, and even more precise details—

"All the shelters, too? No surprise a city this big has a ton of shelters… That really minimized the damage from the flooding, but they're causing their own problems, too."

The chaos he had encountered at the shelter flashed through the back of his mind as he looked at the map.

Sirius's Authority amplifying the feelings of unease and trapping the city's residents into a negative feedback loop. That same sort of scene was surely happening all around the city. And the ones dealing with that problem in an unexpected way were—

"—Mm-hmm, mm-hmm… Yeah, thank you. That explains a lot. I wouldn't have guessed the missing princess gallivanted off to do that, but if anything, I guess that's very much her kind of thing."

"Ah, yeah, I get you there. She's reliably unpredictable."

Anastasia's mouth curled into a vague smile when they briefly mentioned how Priscilla's insane drive for action was often directed in an entirely unpredictable way, but her expression tensed again just as quickly. She looked straight at Subaru.

"So about that leg of yours that got torn off and then stuck back on… Is it really okay?"

"Fortunately, there haven't been any issues even when I'm running or jumping around. It looks terrible, but I can show you if you want."

"Yeah, let me see it." Anastasia immediately nodded.

Subaru was a little surprised, but he rolled up the right leg of his pants. Seeing the blackened flesh consuming his leg, Anastasia winced slightly.

"It really doesn't hurt? It looks like it should be aching."

"I won't ask if you want to touch it, but yeah, it really doesn't hurt. It feels the same when I touch it, too. But anytime I get injured here, it seems to heal faster."

"…I assume that isn't the greatest feeling, either. But if it doesn't cause you any issues while running or jumping, then I guess that's good, since we're going to be needing you to do a lot more before this is over."

While she still had some hang-ups, Anastasia had accepted the situation as it was and come to the same conclusion Subaru had. There was no way to get rid of the blackened flesh, but it was not affecting his ability to act. Given that, it could drop to the back of the priority queue, and they could focus on more immediately pressing problems. For example—

"—The victims of Lust's Authority, the people working here who were turned into flies… For now, they've all been gathered in one place here on the third floor."

"How did you find out about them without me or Crusch…?"

"The black dragon that was carrying the duchess. We managed to figure out how to communicate. And the people who were turned into flies were still conscious and willing to follow our directions… I can't really say whether it was the right thing to do, though."

Subaru did not have an answer for her doubts, either. If their brains were changed along with their appearance, then there would not be any worries about their anguish at getting transformed, but that would be the same as them losing their sense of self, which would be its own unbearable problem.

But was it even possible to say that they maintained their sense of self after being transformed into entirely different entities? That was not a question that could begin to be answered by someone who had not experienced it firsthand.

"They can't even control their bodies freely, which has at least prevented any suicides. But I'm sure some of them still haven't accepted what has happened to them… It was at least good that we could protect them before it came to that."

"Suicide? That's just…"

"Do you really think that's something we don't need to worry about?"

"Ugh…"

Subaru did not have an easy answer for that question, either. But it was clear that even with how far off the rails the situation had gotten, Anastasia was dealing with things in a much more coolheaded way than Subaru. And it was also clear that she was genuinely relieved at having managed to get things there without letting anyone get hurt or getting hurt themselves.

"As long as you're still alive, there's still hope. But if your body or spirit dies, then hope dies with it. Don't stop, no matter how grim things seem. Just stay alive," Anastasia murmured, more to herself than to Subaru.

And if that strained, desperate clinging was her view on life and death, then Subaru was in full agreement. Stay alive no matter what, even if it meant guzzling down mud to survive. As long as life remained, a chance to fight back would come someday.

And in order to get that chance—

"There's a mountain of other problems to deal with. Wrath's Authority running rampant, Lust's victims going through hell, Gluttony wherever they are and whatever it is they want, and Greed, who doesn't make any sense at all…"

"All we can do is take it one step at a time and crush them one by one." Subaru clenched his fist.

Anastasia looked up at him from her seat in front of the map on the table. Subaru met her gaze before taking a deep breath.

When he stopped to think about it, it was an odd situation. He never would have imagined that, by themselves, he and Anastasia would try to figure out how to deal with the problems afflicting a city that had been plunged into chaos.

"—We haven't spoken face-to-face like this since the night before the White Whale hunt, have we?"

"What a coincidence. I was just thinking the same thing. We were talking about facing off against a dangerous enemy that time, too, huh…? I guess this'll be our second time as witnesses to history in the making," Subaru replied.

"Witnessing history, huh? That's a pretty haughty way to put it. But yeah, I suppose it's true."

Subaru looked dubious as Anastasia nodded to herself, mulling something over. It felt out of character for her. She was usually so direct about everything, but she seemed to be hesitating for some reason.

"Let's not beat around the bush, Anastasia. I guess we don't really know each other well enough to say we don't need to hold anything back, but you went out of your way to have Julius leave us alone, so you must have something you wanted to talk about, right?"

She had instructed Julius to leave the two of them alone because she had a reason. And hearing that, Anastasia said "Yeah" with a nod and exhaled. And then she looked Subaru in the eye as she began to speak.

"Let me ask you directly, then: Beatrice is an artificial spirit, isn't she?"

"———"

Subaru caught his breath. Something about Anastasia's question made it sound like she was already certain of the answer.

Beatrice was an artificial spirit who had been created by the Witch of Greed, Echidna. But there was no way anyone outside Emilia's camp would know that. Which meant that regardless of Anastasia's apparent confidence, Subaru could just play dumb. But—

"—Yeah, that's right. Beatrice is an artificial spirit, and most likely the cultists had her in mind when they mentioned it in their demands."

Subaru quietly acknowledged Anastasia's suspicion without trying to dodge the subject.

Of the three demands added in the broadcast after the flood, the one about turning over the artificial spirit meant, in other words, giving the cultists Beatrice. Which was one of the two main reasons Subaru's response to them was to flip them the bird and tell them to buzz off.

"Her origin is a little unique, but other than being incomparably cute, there isn't anything particularly special about her. I can't even guess what they might want with her."

Not that there was no cause for concern, though. Her mother was that nasty Witch, after all. It wouldn't be that shocking if the same Witch of Greed who had tried to make Subaru a puppet in order to indulge her curiosity had also left some kind of bomb lying dormant in Beatrice, and it was possible the cultists were after her because of something like that.

"I doubt anyone else in the city is carrying around an artificial spirit, so it's safe to assume that they are after Beatrice… Anastasia…?"

Having said that much, Subaru cocked his head. Anastasia was listening to his answer with wide eyes and a look of shock on her face.

"Huh? Uh, yeah…" She nodded, still surprised. "You're awfully… open about it. Even though it might put her in danger."

"We're trying to figure out who the enemy are after, right? They're the only ones who would benefit if I held back now. And given the situation, I'm the one who needs everyone's help the most, so it's natural I lay my cards on the table first," Subaru responded with a shrug.

"…Yeah, they really are the only ones who benefit from us holding back…"

Anastasia's soft response had a heaviness to it, but before Subaru could probe further, Anastasia touched her scarf, which was seeming more and more like a nervous habit of hers, before shaking her head.

"I had thought it would be difficult to say in front of everyone else, but I guess I was worried over nothing."

"Everyone in our camp knows about Beako, so it would've gotten out sooner or later. Besides, I have no intention of negotiating with terrorists, and I assume we're on the same page there, right?"

"Agreed. I don't know what a terro-whatever is, but I refuse to let the cultists get even one of their demands met. If we gave them what they wanted, there's no mistaking they would just sink the city anyway—and I refuse to let that happen."

Anastasia's suddenly overwhelming resolve gave Subaru goose bumps. Feeling it that powerfully from up close finally made him realize what the source of her intense emotions was.

She was burning up from a rage that she could not fully tamp down. It had been hard to notice with her beautiful figure and gentle demeanor and the calm way she behaved, but even so, her wrath had lit a fire inside of her. And the source of that anger was surely something that had happened before she fled to city hall—

"Anastasia, what happened at the Muse Company?"

He had heard from Julius that the Muse Company had been attacked and that at the end of a deadly fight, Anastasia and the others had barely managed to escape with their lives, but at the cost of Kiritaka Muse and the White Dragon's Scale, one of the city's council members and his personal guards, going missing—meaning the already grave situation had only gotten worse.

And on top of that, the normally calm and collected Anastasia could not fully control her own emotions. Subaru was careful broaching the topic, aware that something particularly bad had likely happened.

"...It was after Julius and Ricardo went with y'all to take back city hall." Anastasia did her best to contain the emotion creeping into her voice.

At the same time that they had been fighting over there, Anastasia and the Muse Company had been viciously attacked—

"—An Archbishop with bandages covering her whole body attacked us."

4

"Lady Anastasia, we've ascertained something troubling." Kiritaka looked pale as he broached the subject.

Anastasia furrowed her brow. She had just received a report from her conversation mirror on the table that the squad dispatched to retake city hall was engaging the cultists. Once the battle started, all she could do was sit and wait for good news. It was frustrating, but given that she could not take part in battle, her only choice was to ride out times like this with prayers and faith in her people. That was why she had silently prepared herself in front of the conversation mirror like always, but—

"That doesn't sound like good news. What happened?"

"I imagine you are aware that I've ordered my subordinates to protect the members of the Council of Ten."

"You mentioned that, yes. If they are captured by the other side, then it would only be a matter of time before the location of the Witch's bones you are hiding gets out. You don't mean to say..." Anastasia's expression clouded. "Has someone been caught—and the location already been revealed...?"

"...No, it is far graver than that. The Council of Ten has been wiped out. According to the reports, every last member other than me has been slain."

"What?"

Anastasia had prepared herself for the worst, but that was even darker news than she could have imagined. Seeing her reaction, Kiritaka shook his head, visibly agitated.

"Every last one. My subordinates confirmed they were all found dead either at their homes or in their workplaces. Judging from the conditions of their bodies, they were likely dead before the first broadcast occurred."

"Wait a minute; that doesn't make any sense. Aren't they after the remains...?" Getting that far, Anastasia suddenly came to a perfectly reasonable explanation. She had just naturally said "they," but the Witch Cult was not the sort of group that logically worked together toward a single goal. Currently, there were at least three different Archbishops whose presence in Pristella had been confirmed, but the plan to take back city hall had been predicated in part on the assumption that they were ill-suited to working together. When she considered that as well as the fact that the members of the council had been killed, a hypothesis started to present itself. Though it was hard to believe...

"Only members of the Council of Ten know the location of the Witch's bones. And the recovery of the remains is their goal. And yet someone is murdering the people who know that location one after the other... It doesn't make sense unless there are two competing goals at work here."

"One faction that wants the Witch's bones, and another faction that wants to stop them?" Kiritaka had apparently reached the same conclusion.

"...If Natsuki is to be believed, it might not even be *only* two different sides." Anastasia responded with an even more unappealing thought.

Honestly, it would almost be funny was it not so deadly serious: The cultists were maliciously illogical. Their inability to work together was both an opening to exploit and one of the sources of their utter unpredictability. And as galling as it was to say about the lost members of the council, their deaths could not even really be called the worst outcome, since they meant the remains were still safe from being stolen, and the city wouldn't be immediately plunged beneath the waves. But they also made clear—

"I'm sure you realize it, too, Mr. Kiritaka, but..."

"Their next target is surely this company and me. Lady Anastasia, you should prepare to evacuate the premises."

"—What are you planning?"

Dispensing with the details, Anastasia questioned Kiritaka directly about what he intended to do. She recognized his resolve as a representative of the city and his strong sense of duty as a member of the Council of Ten. She could understand his position, but—

"Don't go throwing your life away, y'hear? No matter what happens, just keep breathing."

Kiritaka raised his eyebrows in surprise as Anastasia forcefully stared him down.

"...I'm surprised. I would have expected you to be more inclined to cut losses."

"Did you think I was obsessed with money above all else? My company trades under the motto 'Your friendly neighborhood shop.'"

"Pardon me. Were time permitting, I would have loved to get to know you better over a meal, but..."

"You've got your Songstress you've set your heart on, right? Don't go cheating on her behind her back."

"Yes, you're right—and unfortunately time won't permit it, either."

Anastasia's jaw clenched. He was right. There was no time. If the enemy who was after the council members was coming for Kiritaka next, then the Muse Company would be an ideal hunting ground—and there were far too many people there who could not fight.

"I'm aware it is not my place to do so, but I've already ordered my subordinates to begin escorting all those who fled here as well as anyone who is injured to the nearest shelter. You should take the members of the Iron Fangs and Ferris and escape as well. My subordinates and I will act separately. It is too dangerous for me to go with you."

"You have some place in mind to go, right?"

"Of course. I have no intention of sitting around waiting to die..." Kiritaka straightened the sleeves of his white outfit and flashed a smile.

—And then, all of a sudden, a shock wave shot through the building, breaking all the windows at once.

"—gh!"

The crashing sound of a storm of broken glass pummeled Anastasia's ears. She immediately dove to the floor.

Always be on guard— Was it not for the habit she had formed as a young girl, it would not have been a pretty sight. She would have been showered by a wave of jagged glass shards. Slipping the conversation mirror she had reflexively grabbed into her pocket, Anastasia looked up.

Kiritaka had also dropped to the floor, but he immediately leaped up and shouted out the door.

"What happened?! Someone report..."

"—Sorry? And thank you."

The voice sent a shudder down Anastasia's spine, and she immediately grabbed Kiritaka's sleeve and pulled him down with all her might. She was light, but when she used her full body weight, the slender Kiritaka could not resist and fell down backward. A golden chain tore through the stone wall, passing right through where he had been standing. A cloud of dust jumped into the air, accompanied by the grating cacophony of destruction as the golden chain spun and wreaked havoc across the entire floor.

"———"

Kiritaka just barely avoided the attack thanks to Anastasia pulling at his sleeve. Just a second slower, and he would have been split in two at the stomach. After just barely avoiding disaster thanks to that split-second reaction, the two merchants had barely any time to recover before an unwelcome guest greeted them.

"Ahh, aaaaah, magnificent. Caring for one another, helping one another, entrusting oneself to another—those bonds are what allowed you to survive! You've shown me something so…so wonderfully beautiful. It deserves a round of applause."

A high, cracking voice rang out as someone approached, glass crunching underfoot with each step. Anastasia and Kiritaka caught their breath as the footsteps finally reached them. The half-broken door was kicked in.

Breaking through the door by force, a grotesque figure emerged from the dust cloud—a hideous presence covered from head to toe in white bandages, with silver hair and purple eyes that seemed to be glaring at everything in the world.

It was someone who matched a description Anastasia had heard just recently—

"…The Archbishop of Wrath…"

"Oh, to think you would know little old me without even needing an introduction! How embarrassing. My reputation precedes me, apparently. It would be nice if it wasn't due to nasty rumors."

When she put her hand in front of her mouth, the chain rattled intrusively. And there did not seem to be any deceit in the way she showed embarrassment. It seemed to be her genuine reaction, which only made her seem all the more abnormal.

Her figure, her presence, her speech—it was almost like she was a foreign entity in the world.

"I am Sirius Romanée-Conti, serving as Archbishop of Wrath. I hope you'll treat me kindly."

The monster, Sirius, bowed politely, greeting them with unreserved affection. In the face of such a twisted being, Anastasia could not help but gasp for air, as if her soul were desperately trying to free itself.

The monster smiling endearingly at them had just seconds earlier wrought destruction on the building. It was weird that she did not seem to feel any shame at that. That she did not seem to think anything at all of it.

"Can you stand, Lady Anastasia?"

The monster was just a stone's throw away. Kiritaka cursed his quivering knees as he forced himself to his feet. Anastasia had started to respond when she felt a swell of animosity rising in her heart.

"Huh? Wh—? Do you even need to ask…?"

A swell of fear rose, threatening to break her spirit as she tried to stand. She could not maintain the strength in her slender legs, and her gasping for breath grew more and more pained. Forget standing; she was on the verge of collapsing on the spot. But right as that concern flared—

"Ugh!" "Hah!"

"—gh?!"

An intense shock wave turned the shards of glass scattered around the room into a deadly whirlwind. The bandaged creature absorbed the full brunt of it with a groan and fell back.

The ceiling cracked between the monster and Anastasia, and two shadows fell to the ground—two small figures, orange ears and tails standing on end, the cat siblings howling on all fours.

Anastasia had been overwhelmed by dread, but when she saw them, her eyes shot open.

"Hetaro! TB!"

"Are you safe, miss?!" "That's the Archbishop… Gh!"

They only glanced back, still focused on Sirius. Their high shouts stirred Anastasia's heart. She stomped her foot with everything she had.

"I'm…fine. This is nothing! But are y'all okay?!"

The kitten siblings were supposed to be sleeping and recovering from the heavy wounds they had endured in order to keep their elder sister Mimi alive despite the incurable wound she had received. They should not have been able to move, and yet here they were. Anastasia was worried that something terrible had happened to Mimi, but…

"That's not it, Lady Anastasia!"

"—F-Ferris?"

Overhead, Anastasia spotted a cat-eared girl—who turned out to actually be the knight who specialized in wind, Ferris—peering down from the hole the two had made in the ceiling. Ferris shook his head as he pointed to Hetaro and TB.

"Ferri used a forbidden technique! The same thing I did with Subawu's leg!"

"Natsuki's..."

Hearing that, Anastasia remembered what condition Subaru had been in when the attack squad departed. After encountering cultists earlier, Subaru had been badly wounded, to the point where he had trouble even walking. But he was still determined to fight, so Ferris had performed a special intervention, using a technique that let him not feel the pain. But if that was the only reason TB and Hetaro were standing, then—

"______"

Blood was pooling at their feet. Crimson already stained the bandages wrapped around their bodies beneath their white robes. In exchange for not feeling pain, the two of them—no, all three of them were having their lives shaved away.

Unease swelled, tearing at Anastasia's heart, burning away inside her—

"—Miss! Eyes forward!!"

"Hetaro..."

"Sis would have told us to help you no matter how much it might hurt! We're just following through! What about you? What will you do, miss?"

"I..."

Anastasia gulped at Hetaro's question. He was normally so well behaved and reserved, usually having to be the responsible one who held back the uninhibited Mimi or the boisterous Ricardo. But this time, he was howling and coughing up blood.

Faced with that, what would Anastasia—what would Anastasia Hoshin do?

"—Hetaro, TB, stall for time. Can you two hold out for two minutes?"

The strain visible on her face, she asked them to carry a heavy load on their small backs. The two of them did not even turn, their long tails swaying left and right.

"Sis would say, 'Leave it to me!'"

"We'd be pretty cool if we could pull it off!"

Hetaro and TB were still smiling, even in the face of everything. They kicked off the floor—and then the wall, closing with the enemy. Sirius blocked their staffs with her arms. Faced with the two brothers' teamwork, the monster's purple eyes flared.

"Such adorable sibling love. Are you twins? Ah, how truly endearing…"

"Sorry, but—!" "We're the younger two of triplets!"

The metallic chain spun, crashing into a blue magic barrier. Leaving the battlefield being viciously carved away to the brothers, Anastasia looked up.

"Ferris! Use my people to get Mimi and Beatrice out of here! We'll meet back up outside!"

"—Ngh. Y-yes, ma'am! Understood!"

Seeing Ferris slip away from the hole, Anastasia grabbed Kiritaka's sleeve and ran to the window. The door out of the room had become a battlefield that the two of them could not pass, so they would simply have to use an emergency exit, and it wasn't like there were any other choices.

"Ugh, kh…"

Stepping out of the window frame, she set one foot on the ledge outside. At the lip was an emergency ladder that was set up to allow travel downstairs along the outside of the building. Anastasia clenched her fingers tightly, using the pain to stop trembling before climbing down. They had been on the third floor of the building, so they went back inside at the second-floor window.

"It's a little…too soon…to breathe easy…"

Hetaro and TB were still fighting strong on the floor above. The longer it took, though, the more dangerous it became for them, and the more dangerous it became for Mimi, too. It would not be difficult for Ferris to get everyone out of the fourth floor if he directed the Iron Fangs well. The problem was where to go after escaping the Muse Company building—

"—Meeting up with everyone who went to city hall would be best," Anastasia concluded after getting her head in gear.

"Agreed. It would be best to preserve the greatest chance possible of you joining up with them," Kiritaka said, panting.

She understood what he was getting at. It was the same sort of logic he had expressed before Sirius appeared. The enemy was after the Council of Ten, so they needed to limit the damage while preserving a way out as well as they could. Knowing just how hard it would be to get away with that Archbishop harrying them while they tried to escape.

"Try to hurry to the center of the city as quickly as you can. My subordinates and I will draw that thing's attention."

Anastasia could not say anything in the face of his determination. The more calmly she tried to think it through, the clearer it became that that was the most reasonable conclusion. They could not save everyone, so at the very least they needed to make deliberate decisions that would save the most people instead.

"Young master, we've made our preparations. Let's do this in style."

As the two of them went out into the hall, Kiritaka's subordinates, the White Dragon's Scale, were gathering. Seeing them already prepared for battle, Kiritaka calmly shrugged.

"In style, huh? You know, I was always more partial to reserved and calm performances..."

"I don't want a lecture about reserve from the man who fell head over heels for Liliana! What a crock!"

The men waiting for the order to rush past the line between life and death burst into laughter.

It was too close a relationship to be described by a word like *subordinate*, but Anastasia could see herself in Kiritaka. He loved the White Dragon's Scale just as she loved the Iron Fangs, and he was putting his life on the line to protect his beautiful city alongside his beloved comrades.

No one who saw it could fail to be struck by the tragic heroism of it. The faces of men going off to fight for something they loved, for something they took pride in.

"...That's not fair at all..." Anastasia murmured to herself.

"—Lady Anastasia, I leave Pristella in your hands."

Kiritaka entrusted Anastasia with his beloved city as he prepared to set foot on the battlefield.

Anastasia bit her lip at his earnest plea as he continued—his voice filled with love, expectation, and devotion.

"Please protect this beautiful city...and my beloved Songstress from these villains."

5

"Mr. Kiritaka and the folks from the White Dragon's Scale stayed behind while we retreated with Hetaro and TB—that's what happened at the company building."

"And you joined back up with everyone else here at city hall?"

"Mm-hmm. It was rough with the floodgate opening while we were in the middle of moving everybody. If we'd been any slower to notice, we'd be up the creek by now...but we avoided the worst of it."

Anastasia paused, having finished telling her lurid story. Subaru heaved a big sigh. They had done well to hold off Sirius's assault on the Muse Company and then escape with such minimal losses considering how little fighting power had stayed behind after they committed almost everything to the city hall assault.

"The city's representatives, the Council of Ten, have been destroyed. Mr. Kiritaka's gone missing...and that same Mr. Kiritaka left this town to me to protect—and there's no way I'm not living up to that promise."

Anastasia shook her head at what Subaru was thinking, her clenched hands white as her nails dug into her palms, almost like she was engraving the duty with which she had been entrusted into her skin like a curse.

Subaru finally realized what the real source of the rage she was feeling was.

"Getting saved is a debt, and debts have to be settled. That's my pride as a Kararagi merchant and my obligation if I'm gonna call myself Hoshin."

Anastasia's powerful, pointed determination, her firm stance, made it clear to Subaru just how fierce the struggle at the Muse Company must have been. There was no telling how bad the damage would have been was it not for Kiritaka and his party's heroic rearguard action—and that did not even begin to describe the true impact of the events that had transpired there. If it had not been for him, not only Anastasia but also Beatrice would have been in danger. Every one of Subaru's comrades there, everyone he knew at the Muse Company, had been saved by Kiritaka's decision.

"Debts have to be settled, huh…? Then I don't have much choice but to pay my dues as well."

Subaru apologized from the bottom of his heart to the man who had gone missing for all the rude things he had thought about him before.

After everyone did every last thing in their power to hold the line, they had managed to just barely hang on to a chance to stage a comeback—but there were still many dead who could not be saved anymore, a fact that tortured Subaru's heart. And it only made it worse, given how much he now owed the man, to think that Kiritaka was likely one of them.

"Sorry for going out of order on you. But the gist of it is: I've got my reasons to not back down. And I'd bet you're in the same spot, right?"

"Yeah, you got that right. I dunno what they want with an artificial spirit, but I'll be damned if I let them lay a finger on my Beako."

Subaru clenched his fists, his hatred for the cultists clear to see.

"Mm, that'll do, then."

Anastasia looked down at the map on the table again and pointed to the control towers at the four edges of the city.

"In that case, let's press on. The other things the cultists demanded…"

"About that, I've got something I should tell you."

Of the four demands the cultists had listed in the broadcast, they had covered the artificial spirit, but there was another one that Subaru happened to know about. Naturally, since what they were asking for was—

"The book of knowledge—it no longer exists in this world anymore. Burned to ashes."

"…Care to explain? I couldn't figure anything out about that book, and it has been bothering me."

If he was being honest, it was nothing more than an abominable cursed tome as far as he was concerned. It had been the impetus for Roswaal's actions behind the scenes while they were in the Sanctuary and had driven Beatrice to four hundred years of solitude in the archive of forbidden books. It would be hard for him to view it in a positive light even if he tried his hardest.

And that was also because it was unique in what it contained.

"How do I put it...? The book of knowledge is sort of like a prototype of the Gospels that the cultists have...it's what the Gospels were originally based on and is also a more complete version. It's set up to predict the future the same way the Dragon Tablet works, apparently."

"That sounds pretty hard to believe, but you said it was burned?"

"Yeah. There were two books, and they were both burned. So it shouldn't exist anymore."

"You keep saying 'exist.' Where'd you hear that?"

"...From the Witch who made them..."

Subaru's face screwed into a scowl. Anastasia's eyes widened at his response. She chewed over the word *Witch* for a moment, as if making sure she'd heard him right.

"And this isn't your usual joking around, right? You're serious?"

"Yeah, deadly serious. You said it before yourself, right? There were other witches besides the Witch of Jealousy. One even died in this city, and her remains are still here somewhere, right?"

"That's a dead one, though. That's still believable. But from what you said, it sure sounds like you actually met a witch and talked to her. And from the look on your face, it wasn't exactly pleasant, either."

"Yeah, I met one and talked to her, all right. And got tricked and set up by her, too. And, well, a lot happened. You get the picture."

It would be a long story if he talked about everything that had happened in the Sanctuary and in the tomb. It was a bit rude, but there was not much Subaru could say about the Witch Echidna. Or more bluntly, he really did not want to talk about her.

For better or worse, Echidna had lodged some sharp thorns deep in Subaru's heart that were not going to just go away.

"Anyway, the only two copies of it that existed in this world were both burned, so the cultists missed their mark there. It should be safe to just ignore that demand of theirs."

"—But can you really trust what that witch you met said?" Anastasia fired back adroitly.

"_____"

Subaru was at a loss for a moment, his eyes snapping open in shock at how the gears in his head had just stopped turning.

"You've got your thoughts about her and clearly don't trust her at all. But you still believe what she said. Sounds like she is a bit of a troublesome sort of person for you."

"...I couldn't agree more. You pretty much summed it all up perfectly. I have no intention of trusting her, so it's weird that I don't doubt that at all."

The things Echidna had said, the understanding she had shown: They had all been a performance in order to turn Subaru into her puppet. But did that mean he should assume everything she'd said was a lie? And was that vague uncertainty just him wanting to believe there was more to her, or was he still just getting led around by the nose by that know-it-all Witch?

The same Witch who had sympathized with how painful Subaru's Return by Death was.

"I can't comment on your connection with that Witch, and I'm grateful to at least get a little more information. But..."

"But?"

Subaru furrowed his brow, his uncertainty about what he really thought leaving a bad taste in his mouth.

"The cultists went out of their way to demand it on the broadcast. Maybe they just didn't know the book had been burned, but...I think we should consider other possibilities."

Subaru looked down as Anastasia gently talked around the point.

It did not exist; that was what Subaru wanted to believe: The book of knowledge did not currently exist. If that was a lie, it would mean Echidna had lied to Subaru again. And while he could not explain why, that would make him feel disappointed for some reason.

"—Natsuki."

But as he slipped into a sea of thoughts, Anastasia's voice pulled him back.

"Ah, my bad. Um, so what's left is..."

"There's still the Witch's bones, but we can just leave that for now.

The city hasn't been sunk, which is proof enough they don't have the bones yet…though it doesn't tell us anything about Mr. Kiritaka's current status."

"Yeah…and the last demand was…"

"—'The silver-haired maiden's wedding.'" Anastasia supplied the words Subaru struggled to say.

Her gaze bore only a simple question. There was no particularly deep meaning to it, just a doubt born of not being able to grasp what his aim was.

There was no one who could fail to guess who 'the silver-haired maiden' meant. As for why the cultists insisted on that demand—

"That bastard doesn't have any ulterior motive or anything. He absolutely meant it exactly how it sounds. He's serious about putting on a wedding."

"…With everything going on here?"

"He's an Archbishop of the Witch Cult. He'd do what he wanted in the middle of Armageddon. They all would. And what pisses me off even more is he has the strength to make it happen."

The image of the white-haired man carrying Emilia under his arm flashed through his head. When he was taking her away, he had insisted that all that mattered was appearance. A villain with nothing less than a loathsome level of transcendent strength—the Archbishop of Greed, Regulus Corneas.

Subaru could not say exactly who was responsible for the other demands, but he could confidently say that the marriage demand was 100 percent Greed's.

"That freaking nutjob… No, I guess that fits all of them. Beatrice, the book of knowledge that may or may not even exist anymore, the fate of this whole city, and Emilia! You think I'd let them have anything?! Over my dead body!"

It was hard to believe they could concoct a more insane setup. The only explanation he could come up with was that they were all, every last one of them, living under some different idea of rationality or common sense, some extradimensional way of thinking.

—A monster, a blasphemer, a mystery, and a villain. Throw in the not-so-dearly-departed, crazed evil spirit for good measure. They were a gathering of all the mortal realm's sins, incarnations of the world's dark side: the Archbishops of the Deadly Sins.

"...I was hoping for just that sort of reaction, but that was even better than I expected."

Seeing Subaru breathing hard after getting so worked up, Anastasia relaxed her expression in a moment of approval. But there was no mistaking it for a cheerful smile. It was a manifestation of the rage that had created an unstoppable impulse in her heart.

"You looked an awful lot like Ricardo there."

"I'll pretend I didn't hear that. Can't go messing things up between us until after we take back the city," Anastasia joked before her expression turned serious again. "Like we discussed, we won't give them anything. I've got a duty to see through here. To Mr. Kiritaka, for sure, but also to Emilia and Crusch."

"——"

"Emilia and Crusch and the rest of you came to Pristella on my invitation. All of you are my guests. Letting you get hurt like this... I ain't gonna take this humiliation lying down."

Her pale-aquamarine eyes were filled with deep resolve, and she stared into Subaru's eyes, asking if he was ready to fight.

"We'll need to be prepared to make the necessary sacrifices. Looks like you've made up your mind, too."

"Necessary sacrifices..."

"Everyone's shrinking back 'cause we lost, but can y'all accept where things are standing right now? I sure won't. I'm gonna fight with everything I can lay hands on. I'll worry about excuses for why I lost when I'm dead."

Her usually gentle, peaceful expression was consumed by a savage drive.

"There is always another chance, as long as you're still alive. I won't let people throw away their lives. It's too heartbreaking."

The determination welling from her small, slender body was powerful enough to make Subaru forget she was not someone who spent her time out on the battlefield— No, that wasn't quite right. They were already standing on her battlefield. And when it came to talks like these, Anastasia Hoshin was a grizzled veteran.

"It's entirely possible Lust has the ability to change Crusch and the people she transformed back. And we still don't know where Mr. Kiritaka is, but that's all. And you aren't planning on just leaving your precious princess in some stranger's hands, either, right?"

"—Hell no! If they're going to give us four demands, then we should hit back with a little something of our own."

Subaru was tired of getting pummeled so one-sidedly. Fed up with just doing what he was told.

"We'll save Emilia from that freak, kick Gluttony's ass and get him to spit out Rem's memories, bash Sirius for screwing with the entire city's emotions, and make Capella beg for mercy while changing everyone back! Then we save the city, and boom, everybody lives happily ever after!"

"Yeah, that sounds good to me."

Subaru thrust out his fist, and Anastasia gently wrapped her hand around it. It was not the reaction he'd expected, but it was at least proof they were on the same wavelength.

Anastasia still wanted to put up a fierce fight, and Subaru could stand behind that sentiment wholeheartedly. So—

"Let's save this city, Ms. Anastasia. We'll do it with our own hands."

Nodding to Anastasia, Subaru looked down at the map on the table again. It marked every location in the city, but it could not show the faces of the people living there. So he closed his eyes and imagined something else instead.

He etched Emilia, Rem, and all the people he wanted to save onto the insides of his eyelids.

—In order to keep fighting to save the city and all the people who were precious to him.

6

"Milady. And Subaru, too. So you were here."

Julius was standing in the doorway, a trace of relief appearing in his eyes. Stepping over the crack running through the floor with his long legs, he entered the room and approached the two of them.

In what was surely an unconscious habit, he touched his bangs as his golden eyes looked out across the trampled, scorched-black room on the top floor of the tower.

"Why are you here?"

"Natsuki said he wanted to check something. We only just came up here," Anastasia said, gesturing with her chin to where Subaru was kneeling on the sooty floor. Subaru was looking farther back in the room, to where a distinctive-looking metia was located.

It was the broadcast metia used to communicate with the entire city. It should have been swept up in the battle with Capella and the black dragon's attack, but it had almost miraculously avoided any damage. Subaru breathed easily as he made sure it was still working.

"I see… How did your discussion with Subaru go?"

"It went a little long, but I'd say it was a constructive talk. It looks like he's had it up to here with everything, same as me. How are things on your end?"

"As you instructed, I set the members of the Iron Fangs to patrol in shifts. For better or worse, there have not been any noteworthy developments…"

"That sure sounds like bad news. Without an obvious turn for the better, things are just gonna get worse as time passes… That's just how unease works," Anastasia responded as she gently caressed her scarf.

Subaru looked up at Julius.

"I visited one shelter before coming here. Any word how things are at the other ones?"

"It pains me to be unable to share good tidings, but unfortunately the situation is poor everywhere. In most shelters, the people are currently in no condition to act, and most are just staring at their feet in fear and anxiety. The cultists' proclamation has had a profound effect on morale."

Subaru stood up and murmured, "Proclamation…"

"Lust's final threat before abandoning city hall. In addition to announcing the four demands, she also announced that those of us who attacked the tower had been turned back."

"…So she told everyone we lost. Framing it as a defeat is definitely exacerbating things."

Which was precisely what Capella had been aiming for. Sirius's

Authority combined perfectly with the psychological effect of the broadcast. Between that and Sirius's attack on the Muse Company while they were going after Capella at the tower, despite their not making any effort to work together, they'd still managed to create the worst possible duet. And because of that, the townspeople's will had been broken, and they were getting pulled into a downward spiral, which was inexorably dragging them further into the depths of despair.

"It pains me to say, but it would be good fortune if they merely lost the will to remain standing. There are many who are responding in other ways. Several places are on the verge of crossing a dangerous threshold."

"What's happening with those shelters?"

"We are rushing over as fast as we can to limit injuries to the best of our ability, but..."

Julius hesitated, but that was more than enough to make the dark implication obvious.

Still—

"—There's no stopping the flood once the dam bursts. Some shelters are beyond saving. And there have been more than a few deaths, too. It's cowardly to avert our eyes from reality."

"...Milady..."

Anastasia's words forced him to face head-on the fact that there had already been losses. A more satisfactory look finally appeared on Julius's face, and seeing that, Anastasia focused her increasingly scrutinizing gaze on her knight.

"Pretending you don't see it won't make it disappear. The truth is all around us... What's gotten into you, Julius?"

"I would never..."

"This isn't like you at all."

At first her voice was harsh and stern, but it gradually grew softer and more fragile, her eyes wavering. For just a second, the concern she was feeling for him was visible. But she hid it again in the blink of an eye, reopening her pursed lips.

"...There have been victims. And there will be more. Given that we are trying to save as many people as possible, there is no avoiding the fact that we'll have to give up on a few. We don't have enough hands to do everything. So at the very least we can't turn a blind eye to what that entails."

"______"

"At least Natsuki is properly standing on his own two feet. Accepting that there have been losses and demonstrating the resolve for what's to come. But what about you, Julius?"

Doubt filled Julius's golden eyes—no, it had been there the whole time, swaying faintly, unsteady.

And seeing that doubt in Julius's eyes, Subaru finally realized something.

—Wrath's Authority was affecting city hall, too.

Ferris wallowing in his grief, Wilhelm bound by self-doubt and self-reproach, Ricardo baring his fangs in righteous indignation and annoyance, Garfiel running all over town in a fit of anxiety, Anastasia almost desperately doing her best to meet the expectations of the duty she had been entrusted with, and Julius struggling to break free from his indecision.

They were all expressing their emotions, baring their hearts more because of the influence of Sirius's ability. And Subaru was surely doing the same, too.

"______"

As Subaru came to that realization, Julius and Anastasia stared at each other. Julius was unable to escape his doubts, and a look of anguish crossed his handsome face as he closed his eyes.

Anastasia's logic was sound. She was telling him not to look away from the reality in front of him and demanding he show the resolve to face a fight in which sacrifices would be inevitable. And hearing that, Julius knew that he needed to set aside the troubles eating away at him. He tried again to steel his resolve. To join his master on the path to a victory that would only open up after he made many sacrifices and suffered many losses.

If you tried to carry a giant armful of abbles, it would be impossible to avoid letting one or two slip away. And eventually the whole thing would come falling down. In order to avoid that, you had to pick which abbles to carry and which to leave behind. Even a child could understand that concept.

However—

"—I think you're misunderstanding something, Anastasia," Subaru cut in for the first time.

The other two looked over at him. While the feelings in their eyes were different, Subaru could tell they were not just emotional. Both were still thinking.

"I swore to rescue this city together with you, but I have no intention of trying to sacrifice the few for the sake of the many."

"...We decided on our main goal. I was pretty sure of that from what we discussed." Anastasia's eyes narrowed. "Don't tell me you're gonna start with that unreasonable stuff now, too? If so, then you haven't changed at all from that first time I laid eyes on you back at the castle. Even if it wasn't the usual path, you've become a proper knight now, haven't you?"

"That's right. I'm a full-fledged knight. And because I'm a knight, there are some things I just can't give up on. That I refuse to give up on. If I gave up on them now, my reputation as a knight would be ruined," Subaru said as he changed positions, moving next to Julius.

He shrugged as Julius stood there frozen in place looking at him, and then Subaru puffed out his chest.

If you were holding an armful of abbles, it was only natural that you eventually could not hold on to all of them. But because he was a knight, the things that Subaru was holding in his hands—what Julius was holding in his hands—they were not just a bunch of abbles. They were something far more precious. Something irreplaceable. They were not abbles that would not say anything if you gave up and let them fall. They were the lives of people. People who could cry and who got angry, too. People with families, with friends and people they loved.

"I have no intention of letting a single one of them fall. Talking about resolve and determination sounds cool, but that's just giving up with extra steps. And there's nothing cool about that."

"—Ngh. Again with your foolishness... There were sacrifices during the battle with the White Whale and in the fight with the cultists afterward, too, but you weren't spouting this same stupidly stubborn stuff then."

"—Don't take me for a fool, Anastasia."

Subaru's gaze sharpened when Anastasia brought up the White Whale and Petelgeuse. He was not going to back down on that point or let it go unchallenged. She was barking up the wrong tree if she thought that was how things would go.

"The people who fought and fell in those fights were ready to give their lives. It's sad that they died, and they definitely didn't want to die, but they knew what they were getting into. And that makes all the difference—we can't assume the residents of this city are the same."

It was a convenient argument, and maybe it did not really follow, and it was certainly easy to point to the double standard of criticizing one form of resolve while holding up a different kind. But it was a fact that there was a discernable difference. There was a certain resolve required in situations where lives were being put on the line.

"The cultists made this city a battlefield, and that's on them. But it's wrong to let yourself get dragged into that same thinking and start talking about resolve when it comes to the normal, everyday people who got caught up in all this."

"Whether we like it or not, the decision the cultists made is going to cause a lot of people who aren't resolved to get hurt anyway, at which point they're just going to have to steel themselves."

"There. That's wrong. The cultists have made their own decision, and people who actually have the resolve should be the ones to go after them. If you ask me, having that resolve while always keeping that distinction in mind is what it means to be a knight. That's how I would hope a knight would act, and that's what I teach the kids in the village, too."

After he had been knighted and gotten fawned over here and there, when Subaru finally became a proper knight like he had always imagined, that was the path he had naturally chosen. And when he swore to always live that way, the children had looked at him with sparkling eyes, so ever since he had tried to never bring shame to that vow.

—And because when Emilia, who had been beside him, heard it, her eyes had shone, too.

"I'm Emilia's knight. I want to fight for her. But that doesn't mean I'm only fighting to protect her. Julius is your knight, Anastasia. He wants to fight for you more than anyone else. If you order him, he'll listen to you—but that isn't enough to be satisfied. Because knights are by nature greedy people who want to look cool."

"______"

"I always try to look cool even if it kills me. And so does Julius. Because he's the Finest of Knights. That means he tries harder than anyone else to look the part."

Subaru pointed to Julius with his thumb as Anastasia fell silent. Partway through, Julius, who had been listening silently, suddenly caught his breath, and his eyes widened.

An out-of-place, satisfied grin appeared on Subaru's face when he saw how badly that had caught the both of them off guard.

"You talked about necessary sacrifices before. But what I said was 'Let's save this city.' Cities and countries aren't just a bunch of buildings or swaths of land. They're made up of people. At least according to a bunch of mangas and games."

Choosing at the outset to give up on someone and trying to save someone but failing were two different things. It was easy enough to convince yourself to discard a person in order to create a world you could be satisfied with, but—

"—Infecting other people with that self-satisfaction is what makes you no good. That there's a heroic delusion that'll swallow a crowd whole."

"______"

Another person suddenly butted in right as Subaru was in the process of trying to turn his naive belief into an idealistic theory.

Subaru caught his breath and turned around. It was a slightly muffled voice that sounded familiar. There was almost a hint of irony in the voice, a cynical, pessimistic, philosophical tint to those words as the man wearing a black helmet met Subaru's gaze.

"Stare as hard as you like, it's not going to change the fact that I didn't bring you any presents. You'll just have to make do with my smile. Not that you can see it like this, though."

"—Al."

The man in the iron helm shrugged as he joked with Subaru from the doorway.

He had chosen to act independently before Subaru and the others left for the assault on city hall, and his whereabouts had been unknown ever since. He slowly stepped into the room and headed over to them. Still under the influence of her intense emotions just before, Anastasia responded gruffly.

"You're back awfully early."

"Strictly speaking, I'm not back, since this is a different place from before, but I feel bad about appearing again right after leaving, too. Sorry for being a nuisance, but I didn't come here because I particularly wanted to, either."

Al remained aloof in the face of Anastasia's sharp response, but he wasn't making light of the situation. As the mood in the room tensed, Subaru spoke up again.

"Hey, I've got a lot I'd like to say, but at least you made it out safe. I was worried you got washed away."

"...I was lucky I happened to be on high ground when the water level started rising. And by chance, I happened to get a message for you, Bro. So don't go shooting the messenger."

Subaru furrowed his brow as Al responded with a casual tone and a shrug. Given the situation, Subaru was hard-pressed to imagine whom the message could be from.

"Messenger? Who would send a message in a situation like this...?"

"—It's from your precious, precious princess."

"—?! From Emilia?!"

Subaru was thunderstruck by Al's startling revelation, and he stared wide-eyed as if questioning whether the man was serious. Because of Al's obscuring helmet, there was no way to glean any information from his eyes, but he nodded.

"Even I wouldn't joke about something like that. It's exactly what I said, a message from your young master—she's seriously doin' crazy stuff behind enemy lines. Scaaaary," Al said with a causal shrug.

In contrast to his usual flippancy or his stinging irony, he gave an actual sigh. He looked Subaru in the eye and continued.

"The blushing bride is waiting for her Prince Charming to come take her away before the wedding—I'm jealous, Bro."

CHAPTER 3

THE NEWEST HERO AND THE OLDEST HERO

1

"—Yes, that's it exactly. As I thought, white really suits you."

"...Thank you..."

Regulus responded cheerfully to seeing Emilia in her new white dress. After getting dressed by #184, she had been led from the changing room to Regulus's room, where he was waiting.

"——"

This room was adorned with a twisted splendor far removed from the building's overall cold feeling. Emilia furrowed her brow slightly, chalking it up to Regulus's tastes.

Also, he was wearing a different outfit from when she had seen him in the hallway. It was still all white, but this time it seemed more formal.

Noticing Emilia's gaze, he lightly plucked at his collar.

"Our wedding is a special occasion, after all. I considered wearing my standard, unadorned outfit, but I would never think to embarrass you with a pointless fixation. Consideration for each other, a mutual give-and-take—that's the ideal relationship between a husband and wife. And of course, you needn't worry yourself about troubling me over something as minor as this. I just want you to understand the depths of my generosity and willingness to change myself to a reasonable degree for your sake."

As usual, he talked a dizzying amount. As far as Emilia could follow, the basic content of what he was saying was entirely reasonable, but for some reason, she could not help but hesitate a bit before nodding along.

But one thing she could say for sure was that he was unmistakably one of the Witch Cult Archbishops. It was clear enough from the broadcast and what #184 had said, and understanding that and then actually standing across from him again in person, it was impossible to ignore the bizarre presence he had.

Her instincts were screaming out in her head. They were telling her that an immense threat to her life was standing there before her. And that reality caused her soul—as it would cause any person's—to cower and want to plead for mercy. That was why he felt so abnormal.

"You look down. A sunken look does not suit your face at all… No, this complex expression is cute in its own way, but it isn't your best look. Is there something troubling you?"

"——"

Emilia froze as Regulus casually touched her cheek. She had not thought that she had looked away, but he had closed the wide gap between them in the blink of an eye. Regulus closed one eye as he examined Emilia's still-tense expression.

"#184, did something happen while she was getting dressed?" Regulus pressed the woman standing next to Emilia when Emilia did not immediately respond.

"…Apologies, but perhaps it might be the effect of Lady Capella's most recent broadcast," #184 responded smoothly, as if she had already thought of the response.

"Broadcast? Ah, that. I just ignored it, since that animalistic reprobate's voice is as grating as ever, but I see—hearing that for the first time could certainly upset a girl. That was an oversight on my part."

Loathing and scorn crept into Regulus's expression as he scoffed, accepting that explanation.

“You need not worry yourself about the vile slurs of that blighted, shallow-minded mass of inferiority complexes masquerading as a woman. Unlike her, utterly unworthy of any being’s love, your face is worthy of my affections. From the day you were born, you stood above that thing. Have confidence in yourself.”

“Ummm…”

“Still troubled? That reprobate really went overboard. I cannot stand seeing that hideous face, but I’ll have to lodge my complaints with her directly after this is over. Setting that aside for now, though…what should we do in order to rescue the bride’s mood with our joyous ceremony right before us?” Regulus asked, cocking his head.

Emilia thought carefully about how to respond.

She could imagine two main choices if she wanted to escape. The first was to break free from her position as essentially a hostage. Honestly, she could most likely slip away from #184 and get out of the building without too much difficulty. But if she did that, the floodgates would be opened, drowning the city. And from what she had seen of Regulus so far, if she was asked whether he would really go that far, she would be forced to say he almost certainly would. There was just too much risk involved with that gamble, so she had no choice but to scrap that plan.

There was the bank shot where she fought and beat him then and there in a surprise attack—but that was most likely impossible. Her instincts were telling her that she could not defeat him by herself.

The fundamental problem was a lack of options, so Emilia chose the other path: the bitter, painful choice of avoiding a rash decision and devoting herself to using this as a unique opportunity to gather information.

“Such a troubled expression. I was merely asking what to do in order to improve your mood, but do you not have an answer? It is true that we are not officially husband and wife until the ceremony is carried out, but in effect, we should for all intents and purposes already treat each other as such. Given that, what should a proper wife do for her husband? For the sake of our future harmonious matrimony, should you not also strive to fulfill your duty, nay, responsibility?" Regulus's speech accelerated as he quickly grew impatient with Emilia's silence.

"Ah, I'm sorry. Right… I may be a tad tired still. Would it perhaps be okay for me to rest a bit?"

"Tired?"

Regulus arched his brow, putting his hand to his chin, repeating the word *tired* several times.

"—I see. I was not attentive enough. My apologies. I shall strive to do better. It's only natural that you would be tired with all the sudden happenings occurring all at once. In that case, there is no issue with you returning to your room and resting for a while. There is another outfit planned for you for the ceremony, so you need not worry about lying down in the dress you're currently wearing. My wives and I will take care of the venue's preparations."

"The venue…"

"Yes, there's a chapel attached to this building. It is modest, but well suited for our purposes. We are preparing for the wedding ceremony there. All my wives are here to welcome the newest member of our family. I'm sure that's reassuring news for you. My pride and joy, my admirable, beautiful wives."

He nodded to himself smugly as he threw open the window of the room and waved Emilia over. Standing next to him like he gestured for her to do, she could see the neighboring building by looking out the window.

It was a chapel—or more precisely, a building where weddings and other ceremonies were held. She could see the bustling activity happening inside through the open doors and the big windows lining the walls that allowed in voluminous sunlight. There were several figures moving around the building, bringing in decorations and ornaments and generally preparing for the ceremony. Every person she saw working down there was a beautiful woman, and every last one was wearing a stunning outfit.

"I have had a total of two hundred and ninety-one wives…though sadly, death has forced me to part with many of them. Currently, I have fifty-three wives with me, and that will rise to fifty-four once our ceremony is complete. It goes without saying, of course, that I love all of them equally. *Twisted* does not begin to describe the idea of a husband who plays favorites. I would never do something so dishonorable. I share the appropriate love in the appropriate way at the appropriate time for all—I will love you and all of them equally."

"Th-thank you… I'll be…sure to keep that in mind…"

Emilia was taken aback as she carefully, nervously tried to find her way to an answer that was maybe correct. She was behaving almost exactly the same way #184 reacted in her fear of Regulus.

Being constantly exposed to his violently oppressive presence was enough to wear down even the strongest hearts. That was likely the main reason his wives all had their will to resist sapped away.

"Good girl. Now head on back and rest. I'll have someone send for you once the preparations are complete."

Fortunately, her limp response did not seem to have hit a nerve, and he merely indicated she should return to her room out of a seemingly genuine concern for her condition. Not resisting, Emilia stepped away from him and headed for the door with #184. She could go back to her bedroom and start planning how to get out of the situation—

"I was thinking, though, it was careless of me not to notice my bride's fatigue, but does it not strike you that the person who was by her side the most should have noticed it, too?"

"—!"

—when Regulus's voice called out right as she was about to open the door. A chill ran down her spine, and she immediately grabbed something else with her outstretched hand.

"—Watch out!"

"Eh?"

#184 widened her eyes at suddenly being grabbed. Emilia pulled her close and leaped to the side. And immediately afterward, a breeze blew through the spot where #184 had been standing, and the wall and door exploded like they had been hit by a giant's hand. The floor peeled away, and the destruction continued in a straight line out into the stone hallway.

"______"

The wave of devastation splintered the room and crushed the entrance. Seeing that overwhelming show of force, Emilia was speechless as she clung to #184. Realizing the target of that destruction, #184 tensed and curled up, making herself smaller.

Regulus, who had only casually swung his right arm, tilted his head at the two of them.

"Ah, apologies, apologies. That was careless of me—thank goodness nothing happened to the two of you."

"______"

"Anyway, I have something to attend to, so I'll be in the other room. Oh, and perhaps we should have your hair done up before the ceremony? I think that would really amplify your natural allure. You are lovely as is, of course, but no effort should be spared at becoming even more beautiful. Naturally, I am content with my happy and satisfied state, but I would never protest your efforts to improve yourself. Doing one's best for someone who loves you is the most fundamental level of etiquette a person can express, after all."

Regulus smiled at Emilia as if that earlier act of destruction was of little note, then he left behind his wife and soon-to-be wife, holding each other on the ground.

Once his white back was no longer visible down the hallway, Emilia let out a long breath.

"...What was that?"

It made no sense at all. Both the reason for the action and the way that he acted, neither of them made any sense.

"...Thank you for saving me," #184 said before slipping free from Emilia's dumbfounded embrace.

The agitation she had just felt disappeared from her face, and she stood up and adjusted her hair. And then she began to clean up the destruction wrought by a wave of Regulus's hand.

"Wait! This doesn't make sense at all! You were almost killed just now!"

Emilia took issue with how #184 accepted the violence of just a moment before and moved on to another task. Regulus's presence was menacing, and maybe there was some logic guiding his actions and words that others could not follow, but even if that was the case—

"If I hadn't pulled you away, that would have hit you. You were even trembling."

"And what of it? I thanked you for saving me. Please don't expect any more than that from me. Anything more would be overstepping bounds."

"This isn't about bounds or obligations! It's more important, more precious than that!"

#184 stubbornly refused to face Emilia. And Emilia could tell that it was simple self-preservation that was keeping her heart locked away. She could understand it, but that did not mean she could accept it.

"Regulus said that everyone was equal. So does that mean that all the wives in the chapel are like this, too? Everyone is just cowering in fear of him, always watching him, trying to get by without drawing his attention? Just accepting that he tried to kill you… It doesn't make sense at all!"

"That's just one dynamic between husbands and wives. Once you've experienced it more, you will grow used to it…or if you don't, then that will be the end of you."

#184 did not even turn to answer Emilia's desperate pleading. It was enough to make Emilia feel like she and #184 were living in two different worlds.

"That doesn't make any sense at all… Isn't getting married what people who are happy together and love each other do? But I'm not happy, you don't look happy, and none of them look happy, either. Am I wrong?"

"…Yes, you are wrong. Being happy together is not a requirement for getting married. There is no requirement that a husband and wife love each other, either. The only requirement is being around each other all the time—you get used to being married."

#184 did not deny that she did not want to be in her current position, and yet she still affirmed her current status. It was a twisted, misguided point of view. Marriage was something that was supposed to be desired, not just something that couples got used to.

"Please do as he said. Go back to your room and try to rest. Take the dress off if you would like. I will come by before the ceremony to do your hair."

"———"

With that, #184 focused on cleaning up the rubble and tidying the wrecked room. Emilia tried to say something to her, but her words faltered and failed to come out. No matter what words she chose, they would not have any weight to them as long as she was unable to do anything about Regulus.

She pulled back her outstretched hand, clenching her fist regretfully at her inability to reach out.

2

"—All right, that should be good!"

Wiping her forehead with her forearm, Emilia nodded in satisfaction at her handiwork.

Rejected by #184, she had returned to her bedroom, but she had not sulked at her own powerlessness in a fit of depression or anything cute like that. She had of course been depressed at her powerlessness, but it also spurred her on.

She could not abandon #184 and the other women forced to be Regulus's wives and constantly endure his whims. Her spirit was roiling with determination. But no matter how much she screamed or pouted, there was probably no way she could change Regulus's mind. And if she tried to fight fire with fire, she would just lose against his overwhelming strength. So she had searched for another path forward, following Subaru's example.

"Subaru wouldn't just rush into things without thinking it through first. It all starts with preparation."

She pulled the sheets over the ice sculpture shaped like her that was lying on the bed, making it look like she was obediently sleeping. No one looking in from the door would be able to notice it was not really Emilia. And having done that, she would spend the time until the ceremony—

"Here we go."

She smoothly slipped out the window and headed out to gather more information. Raising her hands, she crafted a ledge of ice on the outside of the building and easily escaped her room. She could have simply escaped at this point, but that was out of the question, given the situation, so she started looking for useful information instead.

"This really was one of the floodgate control towers."

Emilia had headed for the top of the building first in order to get a grasp of her surroundings and where she was being kept, and it perfectly matched the control towers she had seen earlier.

—With the cultists occupying the towers, they had control of the city's floodgates. There was a sinister red flag hoisted from the top of the tower, emphasizing that it was being occupied. And the three other towers all sported the same red flag.

"They took all four of the towers, so the city is helpless..."

Straining her purple eyes to see the other towers in the distance, Emilia slipped into thought.

Just a single gate opening had caused that much damage, so even if she entirely froze the tower she was in to prevent it from activating, there were still three more.

"If only there were four of me..."

If there were, she could freeze all four towers at once. And also, if there were four of her, two of them could teach each other her studies while one learned how to cook and the other chatted with Subaru. It would solve a lot of different problems all at once, but unfortunately, things were not that simple.

"There's still just one of me, no matter how much I might wish otherwise...which means I'm going to have to get someone's help."

Her reliable friends and the other candidates would surely be planning something to take back the city. And they were all either clearer thinkers or stronger or able to do more than Emilia.

But Emilia was probably the only one who had been caught by the enemy, which meant she was the only one who could probe the enemy position from the inside.

—I'm alone. I was separated from everyone else and now I'm in the middle of enemy territory.

Turning that hopeless situation around in her head was something she had learned from Subaru Natsuki.

"There is a chapel right next to the tower, so that means this should be the tower in the third district. With so many Archbishops here, it should be useful to know which one is in which tower."

As best as Emilia could tell, the upper hand in the fighting would be more an issue of compatibility than one of true strength. Regulus and Sirius were powerful, too, but beating them would come down to which people were arrayed against them. And unfortunately, Emilia could not imagine how to defeat someone as powerful as Regulus.

"If they can just tell who is where, though, then they should be able to think of a way to pull it off."

Putting a massive amount of trust in that assessment, Emilia leaped down from the roof in order to carry out her role.

The hem of her white dress fluttered in the wind as she used a scaffold of ice to clamber down. If anyone looking up happened to see her, they would almost undoubtedly think her a witch beyond human ken, but there were not many in the town with the courage to raise their heads and look to the towers where the Witch Cult's flag flew.

Emilia flew down the control tower, enjoying that one small blessing.

3

"—Tell me, do you think I want to be having this pointless conversation right now?"

The moment she heard that annoyed voice, Emilia landed on a larger ice foothold, leaned her back against the wall, and held her breath—Regulus's voice was coming from a room in the chapel right behind her.

—Emilia had learned a lot in just a short time running all around the tower. First of all, there were no signs of any cultists other than Regulus at that tower—she could not see any trace of anyone other than his wives. She had struggled to believe it, but she had even carefully approached the control room for the floodgate, so it was safe to say the tower's defense was full of holes.

It was hard for her to determine if it was from carelessness, confidence, or was just natural given Regulus's impossible strength, but she took it as good news that they did not have to worry about anyone other than Regulus here.

But that was still not enough. She needed to get something more decisively useful. And just as she was thinking that, she heard his voice. Emilia created a foothold from ice just beneath the window to his room and hid there, listening to what was happening inside. Her nerves tensed when she realized he was talking to someone. She was afraid it was one of his wives, in case he was about to attack her like he just had #184. If that happened, she would have to stop him, even if it meant revealing her rebellious intentions.

"———"

Emilia pursed her lips as she made a mirror of ice in her hand and carefully peered into the room. The cool mirror reflected a waiting room on the second floor of the chapel. Unlike the control tower, it had a majestic appearance appropriate for a building where ceremonies were held. The waiting room was not gaudy; instead, it gave off a tranquil and sublime feeling.

—Or at least, it would have if not for the ominous and dreadful white-suited figure standing in the middle of the room.

"...No one's there?"

Tilting her ice mirror to look around the room, Emilia furrowed her brow. There were no other people visible in the room. Had it only been a loud complaint to himself? That would not have been that shocking, but straining her eyes, Emilia realized it was not that, either. He was definitely talking to someone—more specifically, he was addressing a mirror in his hand.

"How many times must I repeat myself? I only came here to find my fated bride. And having found her, I am holding a wedding. A wedding is something to be celebrated—and certainly should not be disrupted. A brute who would do such a thing betrays themself to be a petty, small-minded villain who begrudges others their happiness. Though I am well aware you all have always been filth."

Regulus was talking to someone on the other end of the mirror. It was a conversation mirror—a metia that allowed its user to speak with whoever had the other mirror, wherever they were. Regulus was using it to talk to someone somewhere else.

"It is not as if I have any particular interest in your actions. But opening the floodgate, that is unacceptable. It is not a part of the plan. And I can only interpret your willingness to do something unplanned that upsets my bride as a desire to ruin the wedding I'm painstakingly preparing. And clouding my bride's face, sullying the joyful occasion of my blessed marriage—what should be the most sunny and happy of stages in my life—that is an injurious infringement of my rights."

Regulus's annoyance was growing as he spoke. Emilia could feel a burning sensation on the back of her neck as she realized that he must be talking to another cultist, seemingly one connected to the flooding that had just hit the city—

"—!"

"You are aware, are you not, that I can see your tower quite clearly just across the city from here?" Regulus said, suddenly throwing the window open.

Just beneath the window, Emilia stifled a shout at the sudden movement. She held her breath, praying that he would not notice her below as she focused on what he was saying. Fortunately, he seemed oblivious to her presence and continued speaking from his vantage point like nothing was out of the ordinary.

"It isn't even so far away that I can't see it. It would be a simple matter for me to blow your tower away from here if I so desired it. A word of caution: Do not assume that you and I are equals. You'd best treat this with the imperative of an order... What?"

Judging from how Regulus was looking off into the distance, Emilia gathered that the person he was talking to was in the tower directly across the city. And that person was—

"You weren't the one who opened the floodgate? What sort of excuse do you think that is supposed to be? You were the one who made that grandstanding threat on the broadcast, were you not? Claiming now that you were not the one who opened the floodgate is utterly unconvincing... You shouldn't tell such pointless lies, you repulsive reprobate."

"———"

"Well, either way, I've conveyed my demand. And after your tactless display, at least the people in the city won't interrupt the proceedings between my bride and me… Once the stage is properly set, I shall hold my marriage, and then I will leave the city with my wives. It is on you to achieve whatever it is you want before then."

Spitting that out, Regulus closed the cover on the mirror in his hand. Standing at the window, he narrowed his eyes as he brushed back his hair.

"What an asinine excuse. 'Some rat sniffing around.' Do you take me for a fool? Trying to hide your own incompetence while treating it as a word of caution. You only confess your own pettiness by clinging to such trivial pride. And assuming just because you were had that others would be, too, is the mark of a rotten character, though that is not the only thing rotten about you, I suppose."

Regulus expressed a heartfelt loathing for someone who belonged to the same organization that he did. Sitting outside the window, Emilia was the only one who heard his muttering, and recognizing Regulus's remoteness from others, the way he was in conflict with everyone and made no effort to change that, she felt a gloomy despair.

Just then, there was a knock on the door.

"—May I enter, sir?"

"…Come in."

A woman stepped into the waiting room. Another woman besides #184, though she was also beautiful and similarly dressed up. It was clear at a glance from her frozen eyes and expression that she was another one of Regulus's wives.

"The preparations for the ceremony are continuing apace. We have begun the interior decoration, however…as you requested to direct the interior design personally, I came to let you know we are ready," the woman responded with a polite curtsy.

"Ah, it's already time? Yes, right. Let's get to it, then." Regulus nodded.

He walked away from the window and left the room together with the woman. The door closed, and Regulus's presence faded into the distance. Silence fell over the waiting room.

"*Haaaah*… That was close. I almost made a sound."

Emilia patted her chest as she hopped through the window and into the room once she was sure it was safe. She still had plenty of mana in reserve, but that bit of covert movement had drained her mental reserves. Taking a deep breath at clearing the first hurdle, Emilia parsed what she had heard.

"The control tower visible straight across from here… If I'm right, this is the third district's tower, so the one across the city is in the first district—and based on the conversation, the one there should be the Archbishop of Lust."

Parking herself where Regulus had been standing, she looked out in the same direction he had, confirming her guess for the location. He had not mentioned a name, but he had identified the person he was talking to as the one behind the broadcast and called them a reprobate, which all but confirmed he had been talking to Lust. That meant that Lust was based in the first district, and Regulus was in the third. Even just that much should be at least a little bit useful for the others.

The only remaining problem was—

"How do I tell them?"

Emilia cocked her head in thought as she crossed her arms. Sharing the information she had gathered was the most challenging part. Even though she had managed to get something worthwhile, it would be meaningless if she could not find a way to share it.

The only thing she could think of was perhaps making a big sheet of ice on top of the tower and writing it out on that, but that would be visible to anyone and would likely fail.

She could maybe rush over to them directly to tell them and then slip back into the control tower as if nothing had happened…

"If I was out that long, it would definitely get noticed…"

The defenses seemed full of holes, but counting on that to save her was as good as acting without a plan at all. She could not endanger so many people's lives on such a risky gamble.

"If only there was some reliable way… Huh?"

As she looked around the room, desperately trying to think of something, she arched her brows. It looked the same as when she had peeked in using the ice mirror, but there was something on the desk that caught her attention. The conversation mirror that Regulus had just been using. He had tossed it down in a fit of frustration after he was done. Picking it up, Emilia stared at it.

"If would be nice if it could just connect to any mirror..."

But unfortunately, conversation mirrors were not that convenient. They could only communicate with mirrors imbued with matching magic. There were some capable of communicating with more than just a single paired mirror, but for the most part, they only worked in fixed pairs. Even if Emilia activated it, the person on the other end would be none other than the Archbishop of Lust.

"It would be nice to try to talk with that Lust person once."

But Emilia didn't have it in her to hold a composed conversation at the moment, and it would only reveal that she was moving around behind Regulus's back. Thinking about it realistically, she had no choice but to give up on using the mirror to communicate with everyone.

She could also just break it there to keep Regulus out of contact with the other cultists, but—

"It doesn't really seem like they are working together anyway. What do I do...?"

She could not afford to take a pointless risk that would reveal the presence of a mole.

But while Emilia grappled with what to do, something happened.

—The mirror she had set on the desk activated, and a white light shone out from behind the cover.

"Ah."

Emilia took a step back from the desk in surprise. But the light from the mirror did not stop. It meant that the person on the other end was trying to connect. All Emilia had to do was open the cover, and it would connect. But she was not sure what to do.

It went without saying that the person on the other end was almost certainly someone connected to the cultists, if not Lust herself. There was no benefit to answering, but it was also possible for things to be leaked via the mirror, as they had been when she overheard Regulus. In one sense, it was possible to justify turning a blind eye to the downsides.

After worrying and thinking about it, Emilia decided to—

"______"

She flipped the mirror so it was pointing away from her before opening the cover. The two mirrors connected, but the person on the other end would not be able to see Emilia. They would surely notice something was off, but if she was lucky, they might let something slip first. That was her working theory, at least, and she ended up getting rewarded from an entirely unexpected angle.

"—Oh, there's a response. Wait, there's no one there. What's going on? That ain't how it's supposed to work. Did I mess something up?"

"Eh?"

Unexpectedly, the voice she heard through the mirror was a man's voice. She was caught off balance after having assumed she would be connected to Lust. But that was not the only reason for her shock. The voice was familiar. She had heard it just that morning at the Water Raiment Inn—

"—Al? Is that you, Al?"

"...Whoa, whoa, hold up, it went this route?"

Emilia flipped the mirror, blinking as she saw who was on the other end. It was Priscilla's black-helmed retainer, Al. Naturally, he could see her, too, and even though she could not see his face through the helm, she could tell he was shocked as well.

"Um, this is unexpected. How did you happen across this conversation mirror?"

"The truth is: I'm in the middle of sneaking around investigating things. And just as I was looking around the room where this mirror happened to be, it started flashing... Oh, right!"

"Wh-what?"

"Hey, Al, can you get in contact with Subaru and the others? There was something I wanted to let them know."

Eyes sparkling at the miracle of someone she knew having been on the other end of the mirror, Emilia decided to make the best of the situation. Caught up in her momentum, Al responded without thinking too deeply on it.

"Y-yeah...I guess so? I'll let him know you're safe and want him to come save you..."

"Tell him Regulus, the white-haired Archbishop, is in the control tower in the third district. And also the Archbishop of Lust is apparently in the first district's tower. There aren't any other cultists in the third district, but Regulus is really strong, so don't let your guard down."

"______"

"It would be better if I could investigate the other towers, too, but I don't know where Sirius is. But there was that broadcast, too, so tell him to make sure to protect Beatrice, too. And, um..."

"—Wait a second."

Emilia was going through the list of things to tell Subaru when Al stopped her. Hearing that, she looked surprised as she asked, "What is it?"

"I knew you were tough and hyper-positive, but there's gotta be some other things on your mind, too, right? Considering the situation you're in and all."

"This was all I could manage after thinking hard about what to do and following through... Was there a better way I missed?"

"Nah! That's not what I mean... I mean you don't have to be trying so hard, forcing yourself to do this and that. You're a captured princess, after all."

"Hmm..."

Emilia's eyes wavered as she caught her breath, taken aback by his strong tone.

"No need to be reckless or try the impossible. It's okay to want Bro...Subaru Natsuki to save you..."

"I'm sorry for worrying you, Al. No, I should say thank you—but it's okay."

"It is...?"

"I'm not forcing myself to keep going. And it might sound a little strange, but—"

Emilia naturally broke into a smile. Despite being all alone behind enemy lines, despite being so close to such a powerful being, and despite being in the most danger she had ever been in in her life.

"—I never doubted that Subaru will come save me. That's why I want to do everything I can to make it less dangerous when he eventually does."

"______"

That was unmistakably how she truly felt. She was absolutely sure that Subaru would come save her. But she was also determined to not just sit back and leave everything to him.

"Please, Al. I'll be sure to apologize to Priscilla later for asking for your help with such a selfish favor..."

"...You really don't doubt that there will be a later, do you? Damn, that's sure something."

Touching the seam of his helm with his finger, Al heaved a deep, heavy sigh.

"Fine, I got it. I'll let them all know what you told me. You can rest easy and just play the captured princess now. All that's left is for you to wait for Prince Charming to save you."

"Subaru's the one who will save me, though, not some prince..."

"Ah, right! Bro, right! My bad! I messed that up! But seriously, just sit still and don't do anything crazy. This isn't a game."

"Mm-hmm, I understand. You be careful, too, please."

Emilia nodded at the serious warning that followed Al's joking response.

Hearing that, Al snorted a little and then shut off the mirror. The light disappeared from Emilia's end, and it went back to being a simple mirror.

"...Phew. Now it will at least get back to Subaru and the others."

Blessed with an unexpected opportunity to share what she had learned, for once Emilia was grateful for her fortune.

Putting the mirror back on the desk, she left out the window again, careful not to leave any traces of her having been in the room, and then returned to the control tower and back to her room.

She judged that she had reached her time limit for wandering around gathering information. The mirror's connecting to Al had been a coincidence, not something that would ever happen again. Considering that, she really had been blessed. It was unbelievably lucky that it had just happened to connect with someone outside the Witch Cult so she could send a message—and that that someone had been Al, of all people.

—If it was Al, he would definitely be able to get her message back.

"...Huh? Why am I so sure of that?"

Emilia was confused as to why she was so confident that her preparations were perfect after having left the rest to Al. But an answer soon started to form in her head.

Something about Al reminded her almost of Subaru. That was probably why she was so sure.

Emilia did not think about it more deeply than that as she scrambled back up the ice scaffolding.

4

—The blushing bride is waiting for her Prince Charming to come take her away.

After claiming to be a messenger sent by Emilia, that was what Al said.

Subaru caught his breath and then slowly chewed it over.

"Don't gimme that 'I wouldn't lie to you' bullshit. There's no way Emilia would say something that on point. Don't make me kick your ass."

"Sheesh, the two of you together couldn't find a funny bone if it smacked you in the face. Got me worrying I'm losing my edge."

"Like I give a damn about your edge! Quit screwing around, man..."

Al could not hide his disappointment, his shoulders slumping as Subaru shouted. Subaru started to approach him to seriously demand what he really meant, when—

"—General!"

"Whoa?!"

He was stopped by a bolt out of the blue that came tumbling into the room and ran straight into him. Subaru took a big step back to keep from being bowled over by the unintentional tackle. Somehow managing to stay on his feet, when he looked down at his waist, he saw a blond mop of hair clinging to him. Between the shout and the hair, he quickly realized it was the little-brother figure he had not seen for a few hours.

"Garfiel! You were all right! Where'd you come from all of a sudden...?"

"That's my line! You were...and I...I was...!"

"Wh-whoa, are you crying...?"

From the way his voice was catching and how he was hiding his face, Subaru was worried he might be crying, but Garfiel looked up with his face all disheveled.

"I'm not crying! I was a little on edge is all...! You and Bro and Lady Emilia and Beatrice and everyone were all..."

His eyes were just barely still dry, but he was red all the way to the ears, almost failing to hold back the tears that were threatening to come bubbling up. But this was not the time or place to be teasing him. It was plain to see exactly how distraught Garfiel had been.

Everyone he had come to Pristella with had been either unconscious or missing. And on top of that, he had come as a guard, and yet he was the only one who had made it out safe. Just imagining the despair he must have been feeling was plenty uncomfortable. And in the end, he had spent the past several hours not listening to Anastasia or anyone else and constantly searching all over the city for Subaru.

"I'm sorry for worrying you. But as you can see, I'm okay. Though I came back a little darker in some places..."

"Huh? Darker? What do you...?"

"We can discuss that later. So is it just a coincidence that you showed up at almost the same time as Garfiel?" Subaru asked Al as he patted Garfiel's head.

"I can wait if you want," Al said, cocking his head. "This is your moving reunion with your little bro, right? Take your time."

"A part of me is screaming that this probably can't wait. So what is it?"

"Well, in that case... Yeah, you ain't wrong. I agreed to deliver your princess's message, but it's not like I can just be casually wandering about, you know?" Al nodded in confirmation before alluding to the dangerous state of the city.

He most likely was referring to the demi-beasts prowling the streets in search of prey, and perhaps he even meant people who had lost control and were acting under the impulses of Sirius's Authority, too.

"So you just happened to encounter Garfiel while headed here?" Julius asked.

"...I was searching for the general since he got swept up in the water, but because of the floodgate opening, the whole city got sloshed, and I couldn't track his scent. I was still desperately lookin' for any new scent, but just when I thought I found somethin' similar..."

"It was me. I wish I could show you how fast he just deflated. It's not like I did anything wrong, either, but I still felt kinda bad," Al explained lightheartedly.

But it was no laughing matter for Garfiel, and as expected, he glared at Al angrily.

"Who asked you, coward? And I sure as hell wouldn't be bringin' ya here if ya didn't claim to have a message from Lady Emilia."

"That makes two of us. It's not like I wanted to go out of my way and come here if she hadn't asked me to deliver a message. I haven't even found my own princess yet."

Between Al's going his own way before the city hall fight and this most recent spat, he and Garfiel did not get along well. Subaru slipped between the two of them, holding Garfiel back as he started to snap at Al.

"Quit making fun of someone not even half your age. And if you're still looking for Priscilla, I ran into her in the fourth district. She was there with Liliana, the Songstress, going around to all the shelters looking for that Schult kid."

"Really? Weird how we ran into each other's masters like that. Was she all right?"

"It looked like she was doing fine. She's a weird one."

Subaru had originally chalked Priscilla up as unaffected by Sirius's Authority due to some inherent inability to empathize with others, but he'd eventually realized that wasn't really the case. Which meant either there were differences in how much it affected individuals, or else—

"We've gotten a little off track, but…do you really have a message from Emilia? Or was that just another one of your bad jokes?"

Growing increasingly exasperated by the aimless conversation, Anastasia finally asked Al for the message directly.

"The former," Al said as he scratched the visor of his helmet. "I wasn't lying about her waiting to be saved, either, but that's not the main point. Since she was up close and personal with the enemy, she seized the chance to gather some information about their positioning and managed to get word back to us."

"She did what? …Emilia-tan? She did something that smart?"

"You're Lady Emilia's knight, are you not? You should take more care when speaking of your master," Julius scolded.

Still, Al's message from Emilia was unexpected in any number of ways. Most importantly, the information she had passed along would be unfathomably useful.

"Lust is in the control tower in the first district, and there is a white-haired Archbishop in the third district. She also said the white-haired guy didn't have any cultists with him. And that you have to take care of Beatrice."

"Those are all pretty important, even that last bit…and that's a huge help, actually."

Emilia had somehow managed to figure out where two of the Archbishops were stationed and had successfully passed her findings to Al. Knowing how impossible Regulus was to deal with, it wasn't hard for Subaru to imagine the dangers she must've braved in order to secure that information.

But—

"How did you manage to get in contact with her? There's no way you could have just stumbled into each other out on the street."

"Like I said before, it was just by chance. The stars were all aligned or something. I was out walking around in the city when I picked up a conversation mirror that the cultists were using. And it happened to connect to her."

"How lucky can you be…?"

Al's explanation was lacking, and it was clear he had no intention of being more forthcoming. But it was not an out-and-out lie, and it clearly wasn't a joke or just him shooting the breeze, either. Subaru could sense a certain seriousness to Al's response that made him trust it.

"I know it's weird to say when I'm the one who brought this guy here, but are you seriously gonna take him at his word, General?"

"I believe him. The last bit about being worried for Beatrice sounds exactly like something she'd say."

"——"

"That's not enough to be sure, but...I'd like to think Emilia would do her best and not give up, even in this crappy situation."

If she could be that single-mindedly positive and believe in Subaru despite everything that had happened, then he would give his all and try to save her in the same way.

"Though, it would be nice if she didn't overdo it and try anything too reckless, either..."

"I'm with you there, man. She's way too energetic for someone stuck behind enemy lines."

Judging from Al's reaction after he'd actually spoken with Emilia, she was not at all acting the part of the damsel in distress, even if she seemed like she was born to play one in some theater show or movie. If anything, that unusual bravery was just like her, which made Subaru proud.

"Anyway, that was her message, so my job's done here... So what are all you doin' here, and what's that huge metia for?"

"Naturally, this is the headquarters for the take-back-the-city-from-the-cultists squad. And the metia back there is a broadcast device that can carry a voice to the entire city... It's our trump card for turning this thing around."

"You don't say." Al chuckled at Subaru's self-assured response.

On the other hand, Garfiel was shocked enough for the both of them. His sharp fangs were trembling as he looked at Subaru.

"Did you think of something that can turn everything around, General?"

"Yeah, something that might have a decent shot— Do you know how to use this metia, Anastasia? Or if not you, does anyone else?" Subaru asked as he looked over at it.

"...Something like this wouldn't be too hard for me to get going," Anastasia responded.

Subaru nodded to himself as he continued looking around the room. Garfiel and Al, plus Julius and Anastasia—four people who were well suited for sounding out his idea.

"As you all know, Wrath's Authority is currently putting everyone inside the shelters around the city on edge, and these places are ready to blow. It's okay as long as they're still just smoldering, but there's no telling when they might go off."

"Yeah, you've got that right. I checked in on a bunch of them while lookin' for you, but..."

Garfiel's expression clouded. He must have seen something unsettling in the short time that he'd been running around. It looked like he was struggling to stay calm, as if there was something bothering him besides his general concern for their friends.

Subaru noticed it but decided to keep the focus on the current topic first. If things went the way Subaru was imagining, then whatever was bothering Garfiel might be resolved in the process, too.

"Between the cultists' broadcast and the current state of the city... it's only expected that everyone's worries would balloon while they're stuck far from home and forced to hide out without any sign of things getting better. And that only gets worse when people are crammed into a small space together. The shelter system is actually stoking the fire...though, even without them, people would end up congregating anyway, I guess."

"That is the most insidious aspect of Wrath's ability. It makes you feel more alone, eats away at your heart, and even threatens your life. It's absolutely unforgivable," Julius commented with quiet anger.

Anastasia glanced over at him as she touched a hand to her fox scarf, then looked at Subaru.

"—I have a good idea what exactly it is you are thinking of doing."

"Well, yeah. I mean, I did come all the way up here to make sure the metia was still functioning, after all," Subaru said, grinning awkwardly as he scratched his head.

Al and Julius also caught on from their exchange and turned

toward the metia in the back of the room. Garfiel alone hadn't figured it out yet, cocking his head in confusion.

"What…? What are you planning to do, General?"

"Basically, Bro is thinking of turnin' Wrath's Authority on its head."

"Huh? What does that mean…?"

"—Sirius's ability is amplifying the unease that all the residents of the city are feeling. And Lust's nasty broadcast was what lit the fuse. In which case…"

"We just need to inspire people's hopes the same way that the cultists preyed on their fear." Julius said, finishing the thought, and Subaru nodded in hearty agreement.

Sirius's Authority shared and amplified people's emotions—but that was all it did. While it could heighten existing emotions, it couldn't do anything to emotions that weren't already there.

And if that was true, then if they could just paint over the unease and fear running rampant through the city and replace it with hope…

"That hope would spread and fill the city instead."

"—! Ohhhhh! That's right! If you do that, no one'll start killing one another! And all the people who've given up will feel better…!" Garfiel's eyes shone as he punched his fists together in front of his chest. There was a resounding *crack* as they hit. "Time to make it happen!" Garfiel grinned. "We've got the metia right here. No point wasting time. Let's do it now…"

"Wait. It ain't that simple. It's not like I didn't consider that option, too." Anastasia cut in, putting the brakes on the idea.

"Huh? Why are you stopping us? You know what's happening out there right now."

"Yes, I do, and I've thought about it at least as much as you have. But that's exactly why I can't just say *do as you please*… How do you think the cultists will react when they hear the broadcast?"

Garfiel gulped.

"The floodgate opened after we attacked city hall, almost like it was meant as retaliation or like they wanted to show what happens when people go against them. If that happens again, they might not close the gates next time."

"I'm worried about that, too...but there's something about that theory that doesn't quite fit."

While agreeing with her concern, Subaru glanced at Julius.

"Yes?" Julius's eyes narrowed. "Allow me to ask, what is it that seems off to you?"

"...I was unconscious, so I can't really say for sure, but the person who got transformed into a black dragon carried Crusch and me away from Capella, and right after that the floodgate opened, and the water interrupted the fighting. That's when I fell into the water. Does that sound about right?"

"Yes. That matches what I remember of the events. What of it?"

"Doesn't the order of events seem kinda off? And which floodgate was it that opened?"

"Which floodgate? If I recall, it was the one in the first quart... Ah."

As she thought back to answer Subaru's question, Anastasia's eyes widened. A moment later, Julius also murmured, "Oh-ho."

"The first district's gate was the one that opened. But if Lady Emilia's information is correct, then that would be..."

"But Lust wasn't in the tower then, right? And the timing of the gate opening doesn't make sense at all. Because the flooding was what helped us escape, and then it closed again immediately after, right? It's true that the cultists don't act super consistently, but there should still be *some* logic to what they do."

It would be foolish to write off everything the cultists did as irrational just because they were cultists. The Archbishops all acted on thought patterns that were incomprehensible to normal people, but each still followed their own twisted logic or set of rules.

And in that context, opening the floodgate at that point just did not make any kind of sense at all. It was almost like someone else with a different goal had been behind it.

Of course, it was possible that that whole line of thought was off base, but—

"They left the metia here without breaking it. And after we were gone, they even sent out another broadcast before leaving. They had plenty of time to break this if they wanted to."

"So are you saying that us using the metia is part of their calculations? What could they possibly get out of that…?" Anastasia's voice trembled as she tried to understand.

"—They don't have a reason for anything," Al cut in with a husky voice. Then, as if regretting his unintentional remark, he clicked his tongue in annoyance. When he caught Subaru looking at him, he shook his head slowly. "They don't care one bit about anything we do. They've never lost, and they've never even considered the possibility. A dragon doesn't give a damn what some ants crawling around its feet are planning," Al spat.

He sounded awfully confident in his analysis.

"——"

Al looked away as if he had said something he shouldn't have. His behavior was very unusual lately. Was it because of Wrath's Authority? If so, what was being amplified? Anger? Sadness?

The only thing Subaru could say for sure was that Al had given them advice about the Archbishop of Sloth before they had gone to the tower before. It was clear he knew something about the Witch Cult that he wasn't sharing. But even if he pressed Al on it, it was clear as day he wouldn't answer.

Right as that thought crossed Subaru's mind—

"—Let's go for the broadcast plan, then."

"Anastasia…"

Perhaps having reached the same conclusion as Subaru, Anastasia changed her vote.

The main strike against the plan was that they didn't know how the cultists would react. But if she was satisfied on that point, then there was just one hurdle left.

"So who do we get to do the broadcast, and what do they say to inspire the townsfolk?"

"Who…?" Subaru furrowed his brow and looked over at the metia.

The broadcast would have to inspire hope in the people around the city and blow away the unease eating at their hearts. The person best suited for that—

"Aren't you perfect for the job, Anastasia? You're a royal-selection candidate and famous around these parts to boot. If you tell them we're still fighting the good fight, then…"

"It really pains me to say this, since it's practically admitting I'm not good enough, but I don't think you should really expect me saying somethin' here to have that big of an effect."

"———"

Anastasia outright rejected Subaru's suggestion. He couldn't understand why, though. She was one of the candidates for the throne. It had been announced all throughout the country, so the people in Pristella would all recognize her. And she was famous enough that few could claim to be as well-known as she was in the whole kingdom, let alone in Pristella.

"If all we were talking about was fame, then sure, I'd be a solid choice. If that was all it took, then I'd gladly say whatever I had to. But that just ain't how these things go. My name doesn't have the sway to rid people of their fear of the cultists. I'm better than someone they've never heard of, but only just."

"B-but—!"

"That's not enough, and you know it. They need hope. The kind of hope that can blow away all their fears and convince them to stand up again."

Subaru was speechless. Honestly, he wanted to tell her she wasn't being strong-willed enough and that she should reconsider. But it was painfully obvious that she was the one most disappointed in herself for her lack of power.

"———"

Seeing her small fists white and trembling as she clenched them tight, Subaru tamped down his irritation. She hadn't spoken up without thinking. It was the opposite. After thinking it through from every angle, she had correctly judged that she was not the right person for the job.

"If it was enough to just trick them, then it wouldn't be impossible. I could probably convince half the people listening. But that's not what you want to do, right? You're the one who didn't want to cut our losses before we even tried anything."

"That's... In that case, what about Crusch? She had a gravitas to her words during the ceremony at the castle and during the White Whale fight, too. If it's her, then..."

"...Yeah, if it were her, then that might be enough. But we're talking about the Crusch from back then. She doesn't have that same gravitas now, and in her current state, we can't drag her up here and stand her in front of the metia anyway."

"———"

Subaru was the only one who hadn't been able to confirm her condition with his own eyes, so he didn't know what was causing Anastasia's pained expression or the pity drawn on Julius and Garfiel's faces.

Ferris and Wilhelm's grief from earlier flickered at the back of his mind.

"Then what about you, Julius? You could..."

"Apologies, but I cannot meet your expectations."

"Mm-hmm... I'm proud of my knight, and he's certainly an elite member of the Royal Guard. But how well do his personal accomplishments stack up when it comes to dealing with the Witch Cult? If we're just talking fame, then I'm more famous, and if you wanted skill at speaking, then I'd still be more likely to succeed."

Crusch could not fill the role, and both Julius and Anastasia shot down the possibility of putting Julius forward. In that case, the only choices left were Wilhelm and Ricardo, or maybe if they could pull Priscilla or Liliana away from their tour of all the shelters in the city—

"...Ummm..."

As Subaru struggled with all the options being shot down after they'd finally come up with a way to deal with Wrath, Garfiel raised his hand. His clear green eyes widened as he looked straight at Subaru.

"—Is there any reason you can't do it, General?"

"...Huh?"

Subaru was completely caught off guard. He opened his mouth, not totally sure what he had just heard. He could not believe that Garfiel would joke around in a situation like this—

"______"

But that thought shattered when he was faced with the gleam in the boy's straightforward gaze. A blank formed as his thoughts crumbled. And Garfiel stepped firmly into that opening.

"There's no one but you. Not a royal-selection candidate, not a knight from the Royal Guard, and not the famed Sword Devil. You. I mean…it's obvious."

"Garfiel…"

"You're the one who has already defeated a Witch Cult Archbishop—you defeated Sloth. No one else's got that to their name. And right now, that means more…it means more than anythin'."

There was passion in Garfiel's voice, and his gaze grew gradually more intense. Gritting his teeth, he looked up at Subaru pleadingly.

"Here's a man who's already beat one Archbishop in this town occupied by cultists. There can't be anyone better for the job. Maybe the Sword Saint Reinhard if he were here, but there's only Subaru Natsuki! You're the only one, General!" Garfiel spread his arms, almost howling.

"Ngh!"

Overwhelmed by the force of his words, Subaru unconsciously took a step back, bumping into someone standing right behind him. Glancing back, he saw a tall, slender figure supporting him.

It was Julius. He looked at Subaru with the same straightforward eyes as Garfiel and nodded.

"I agree. If we're going to do this, then you're the only choice that makes sense, Natsuki."

"Not you too…"

Behind Julius, Anastasia was burying her face in her scarf. There was a swirl of indignation and annoyance at herself for her own inability to play the part, but it was also colored by a silent understanding—because she wanted to protect the city whatever the cost.

Having understood that point at last, Subaru finally realized the huge burden of hope that had just landed on his shoulders.

"You too, Julius? Are you serious?"

"...Do you remember back at the castle, your outburst at the knights and when I defeated you on the training grounds?" Julius asked.

Subaru caught his breath and then slowly exhaled.

"That moment is a finalist in my top three for regret and humiliation. I'll never forget it for as long as I live."

"I remember it well, too. Your baseless proclamation, the disgraceful way you besmirched the knightly order...but I also remember you joining in the Battle of the White Whale after that, and when you managed to defeat Sloth as well."

"———"

"If there is anyone in this city whose voice could ease the fear and unease of the people...then I believe that person must be none other than you. I know that if you ever asked for aid, I would gladly be there to heed your call and lend my hand. And there would be many others who would answer the call as well. Garfiel would surely stand at the head, and I would of course be there, too. You would do well to remember that."

This was an oath sworn out of an incredibly powerful sense of trust.

"———"

Subaru lost his bearings, shocked to his core, and he struggled to breathe at the level of trust he'd been granted.

Swiveling his head, he saw Anastasia. She nodded.

Turning again, he looked to Garfiel. He flashed a toothy grin and held out his fist.

Julius's eyes had never left Subaru. Turning to face Subaru head-on, he nodded elegantly.

—How badly can you overestimate someone?

"———"

He had felt this way before as well, when interacting with Wilhelm and Crusch and Reinhard. They were misunderstanding who he was. They were badly mistaken. They were all far more worthy of praise. They worked far, far harder than he did. They were indescribably nobler.

And the way they all praised Subaru, reached out to him, and treated him as a friend as if it were the obvious, natural thing to do—that had always tormented him. These people he respected, people who treated him as an equal, people whom he could never hope to match… He didn't want them to acknowledge him like that.

It made him anxious. He was sure that, at any moment, his real self would slip out and he would just end up disappointing them. He would only disappoint them and make them regret everything when they realized that the real Subaru was pathetic, weak, helpless.

He had always believed that. And yet…

"—General."

Garfiel, Anastasia, and Julius were all expecting so much from Subaru. Even though he was always so desperate, always on the verge of being crushed under the weight of their expectations, they were adding more and more to the load, as if his desperation was not enough.

That…that was the path Subaru Natsuki walked.

The path of a boy who had once sworn to be a single girl's hero.

Somewhere along the way, he realized that he couldn't stay just her hero. He'd needed to—

"—If you're not sure, then just leave it be, Bro." Subaru's face tensed as a gruff voice called out.

Looking up, Subaru was greeted by a gloomy gaze.

"You're spoutin' that crap now of all times?!" Garfiel exploded.

Rushing in, Garfiel grabbed Al's thick neck, as if to say he could snap it at any time if he wanted, glaring daggers at him all the while.

"You shut your damn mouth! What do you know about the general?! Nobody asked you!"

"I could say the same to you. Is saying 'General' supposed to cast some magic spell? That the name of some superman who can solve any problem?" Al fired back coldly.

"—!"

Al touched Garfiel's arm. Garfiel's expression suddenly changed, and he quickly pulled away. Garfiel was clearly not sure why he had reacted that way as Al leaned into his face, headbutting Garfiel with his black helm.

"Looks like you're leaning on him pretty hard, but is he really all that special? You could beat him in a straight-up brawl, and when it comes to smarts, he wouldn't beat that young lady or her knight over there."

"Who asked you? Don't talk about the general that way! You don't know just how much he..."

"If only he could just put the whole world on his shoulders and keep on rollin'. Now, that would be somethin' to see. Awe-inspiring, even. Just what you'd want from the star at center stage. But your average background character can't carry that kinda weight. I can't, and Bro can't, either. And now you're forcing him to take on this massive burden...for what? You ever think about how he must feel?"

That last line caused Garfiel's expression to tremble. He had seemingly realized something, and the powerful momentum he had been riding dissipated.

Al pulled back and looked over Garfiel's head at Subaru.

"Hey, Bro, that girl is the most important thing to you right now, isn't she?"

There was a hint of disappointment in Al's voice. As if he knew the answer already and had no expectations of Subaru at all.

"——"

Anastasia and Julius were silent, watching the two of them. They had already said what they had to say. All that was left was to leave it to Subaru's judgment.

"I—I...I... Ge-gen..."

Garfiel looked up and then immediately back down again, unsure what to say. He was hesitating. He'd started to call Subaru General like always, but he could not finish saying it when he thought about the meaning it held.

And the one person there who had no expectations of Subaru at all continued.

"I'm gonna do what I have to for my princess, for Priscilla. I'm just gonna leave everything else for later. If I can just protect her and myself and Schult, then that's enough for me."

"Al..."

"You should do the same, Bro. Just focus on that little lady... Save Emilia, and that'll have to be enough. The cultists are just vermin that'll pop up again somewhere else even if you go out of your way to exterminate them here. They're like a demon that just keeps coming back to haunt you. Getting involved with them'll only make things worse," Al said, his voice wavering a little uncontrollably, as if he was clinging to something.

Al's suggestion was one possible answer. Subaru was in complete agreement with him about the cultists being vermin. There was nothing to be gained by getting too deeply involved with them. There was no denying that. But that was not the choice before him. The cultists had already gotten involved with them. Subaru was going to have to act in order to deal with the sparks they had set off.

From Al's point of view, though, that would just lead to the question "Why?" Naturally, it was true that the situation was bad with Emilia held captive. But even if she was not involved, Subaru would not be able to choose to run away. That was because...

"I wouldn't need a reason to pull a kid back to the sidewalk if they wandered out on a red light. I wouldn't even think twice... It's probably something like that."

"______"

Al caught his breath at that. Only Al, though. The meaning was lost on the other three, but Subaru was satisfied that he had gotten his point across.

"I'm not going to worry about the little things. I'm here, so I want to do the most I can to help. I know full well there are lots of things I can't do. But still."

It was surely something Subaru Natsuki should not do.

"—If you're going to do this, Bro, then you're going to be carrying the full weight of that heroic delusion."

—Heroic delusion.

Al had said that when he had first entered the room.

He kept his eyes on Subaru to the end.

"You can't afford to lose. You *have* to win. You'll be fighting while carrying everyone's hopes and expectations, all while leading them to some happy future. If you make that choice now, you'll have to follow through."

"...Not being able to afford to lose is how it's always been for me."

"The weight ain't the same at all. If you lose, then it won't just end with your loss, Bro."

He couldn't understand what Al was getting at.

It was always like that for Subaru. Every time he fought, losing meant risking far more than just one fight. It meant losing everything that he wanted to protect. It was like that every single time. There was never a time it had not been like that.

If he could lose without losing anything, then he would never fight in the first place. The reason he still fought was that there were things he could only protect by fighting. And right here and now, those things were many and enormous.

"That's all? That's how it's always been."

"______"

Exhaling, Subaru made up his mind.

His heart, which had been pounding badly before, was calm, and his eyes were clearer than ever. Al caught his breath. Subaru could tell he was dumbfounded even without seeing his face.

"You don't have to hold back, Garfiel. Just call me what you always do."

"—Ah."

"It was embarrassing at first, but at this point it just feels right. I can't promise I'll be able to live up to your expectations, but I'll do everything I can." Subaru smiled at Garfiel, who was floundering in front of him.

For some reason, it felt like he was smiling particularly naturally. Seeing that, Garfiel caught his breath.

"General… Ahh! General! You are definitely my general…!" Garfiel's fists clenched, and his fangs trembled as he repeated the nickname like an incantation.

"You aren't making any sense at all."

Smiling wryly, Subaru turned back to Anastasia and Julius.

"Let's do this, Anastasia. If you think my voice can reach the people, then I'll do it."

"…You sure? If you choose to be the symbol of hope all by yourself…"

"It won't change what I'm going to do in the end. *Hero* has a nice ring to it. Well, actually, it's embarrassing as hell, and calling yourself a hero is sort of…"

Subaru scratched his nose in a show of bashfulness.

"But if it's playing the role of the hero, then I already decided to do that a year ago. If I don't follow through now, I could never show my face to those people looking up to me. And I wouldn't be able to keep up with the person I'm trying to catch."

"—If you say so. No helpin' it, I guess; boys are always tryin' to look cool."

Anastasia smiled hopelessly and held out her fist in front of Subaru's chest. He answered in kind by holding out his fist and bumping it against hers. It was proof they were on the same wavelength, even though they had messed it up once downstairs.

"Don't laugh if I screw up the lines. And don't sigh, either. In fact, you'd be doing me a huge favor if you just don't listen at all."

"I won't laugh, nor will I sigh. And I shall listen closely until the very end," Julius shot back.

"Tch."

Then Subaru turned his head to Al.

"Thanks for worrying about me, Al— Thanks to that I was able to find my resolve."

He said nothing more. And Al probably did not want to hear that thanks, either. But Subaru had felt it was necessary to at least say that much, so he had.

"———"

Subaru turned to face the subject of all that debate: the metia waiting in silence at the other end of the room. He thought about what he should say while standing in front of it.

Naturally, he did not have the contents of the speech in mind yet. He didn't even know if there was a right answer. But for some reason there was no unease or confusion. It was all rather mysterious.

Perhaps because in his mind it really was the same as always.

—Because he knew that he was just going to have to try to look good, like always.

5

—A gloomy silence had fallen over the shelter.

"______"

The air was filled with faint, stifled sobs and the restless rustling of people unable to hold still.

A girl hugged her knees and looked down as she heard those noises unpleasantly breaking the silence.

She was a small girl with blond hair. Resting her chin on her white knees, she drew closer to the weight beside her—the young boy leaning against her left shoulder. He was her younger brother and had been sobbing just moments earlier. Now he was exhausted and had slipped into a fitful slumber.

She started to caress her brother's head, but she paused, afraid of waking him up. She was sure that if he could sleep, then it would be better for him to get some rest. Staring into her brother's tearstained face, she prayed that he could at least find peace in his dreams, because the world outside of dreams was far too cruel for her brother, who was still so young.

It had been half a day since the broadcast announcing that the control towers for Pristella's floodgates had been captured. She and her brother had been out in the city plaza that morning when they heard the announcement. The announcement itself had been hard to believe, and the voice making the proclamation had sounded almost like it was chanting a hideous curse. Scared for their parents, the girl had taken her frightened little brother by the hand and fled to a nearby shelter with the adults in the plaza.

Faced with the unexpected, they had done as they had always been told and sought shelter. That was the result of the instructions that were broadcast every morning. If she was being honest, the little girl never really listened closely to anything in the morning broadcasts other than the Songstress's singing, but she was astonished at the adults' foresight and planning.

But everything that had happened after they had fled to the shelters had been too unpredictable even for the adults.

—The appearance of the Witch Cult. Occupation of the control towers. Cryptic threats and demands and then the flooding that came not long after.

The vicious woman's voice had riled up unease and hatred in the hearts of all the people cowering in the shelters. Her unbearable voice and unsettling words had been more than powerful enough to sink the whole city into despair.

They were locked away in a gloomy shelter with no way to contact anyone outside. There were no signs of anything getting better, and one of the floodgates had even been opened for a second, forcing them to hear the sound of all that water crashing over the city.

The shelters had originally been constructed as a countermeasure against intermittent flooding, so there had not been many injuries or deaths due to the earlier flood—but that meant very little to the people still cowering in fear.

The voices that had encouraged everyone at first had gradually weakened and then started to grow uneasy and angry at the silence, and before long there had been people making no effort to hide their rage, which had spread, creating a mood of aimless disagreement and annoyance, becoming a silent madness that scratched at everyone, spreading everywhere like wildfire.

And then the flooding had snapped the last thread of their nerves, bringing on the collapse. A swelling, violent mood filled the air, a dangerous atmosphere that could quickly devolve from people glaring at one another to their yelling at one another to their hurting one another to their even killing one another, all with just a single spark.

"Agh."

The only reason it had not exploded yet was that right as their nerves were strained to their limit, the girl's little brother had started crying.

The seething adults had still had the good sense and pride not to be violent in front of a sobbing child.

—But even then, they had come dangerously close to the edge.

In the end, though, the explosion had been delayed by her brother's crying. And the girl had cried softly as she patted her brother's head, hugging him from behind. After that, there had been no more quarrels in their shelter. But that was only holding thanks to a fragile equilibrium. Everyone knew it was just a temporary respite.

If another buildup began, a child's tears would not be enough to keep the peace. And because they knew that, the people in the shelter who should have been working together were all staying away from one another, trying to protect themselves by not provoking anyone else.

For their own sakes—for everyone else's sake, it was best for everyone to not draw any unwanted attention, to remain apart and isolated. They waited for time to pass, desperation on their faces. Trusting themselves to the faint, fragile hope that something, anything might get better.

"______"

The girl suddenly looked up, noticing an omen of that change.

Waiting quietly, eagerly for news of any development, the girl noticed a slight change in the air.

Several people around her looked up for the first time in hours, too, noticing the same thing she had. It was a familiar feeling to anyone living in Pristella. The precursor of a broadcast by the metia at city hall.

Sensing that, the girl tensed, holding back the urge to vomit welling in her throat as best she could.

She had wanted a change, but she'd meant a change for the better. A broadcast could only mean the terrifying Witch Cult was about to say something again.

What new impossibility would that earsplitting voice demand of the city while spewing so much bile?

But the girl's—the people's—pessimistic prediction was—

"—Um, can everyone actually hear me through this? Mic test, mic test. One, two. One, two."

—turned on its head by the voice of a young man who sounded almost like he was playing around.

"______"

Unlike in the last two broadcasts, this was the voice of a boy who sounded unsure of himself. Not the familiar, famous man from the daily broadcasts or the boisterous Songstress—this was a voice she had never heard before.

The girl's eyes widened, and so did the adults' as they glanced at one another, wondering what was happening.

But not noticing their reactions, the boy spoke several more times, making sure that his voice was heard by everyone across the entire city, before finally clearing his throat once he was confident it was working. And then—

"It looks like this is actually broadcasting, then. First of all, let me apologize for surprising you. I imagine a lot of you were worried or steeling yourself wondering what you would be told next. But please don't worry. I'm not a member of the Witch Cult."

"...It's not the Witch Cult..."

The volume of the boy's voice was wavering slightly as he used a metia he had never handled before. But the shock at what he was saying easily outweighed that, and no one bothered dwelling on that small point. The people's gloomy expressions started to change as they looked up at the broadcast echoing down from on high.

"A-are we...saved?" someone murmured, as the faint seed of hope they had been holding on to started to grow.

The hope conveyed by that murmur spread to the whole shelter—to the whole city.

It was natural. If someone who was not a cultist was using the metia at city hall, then that meant that someone had to have taken back the building from the invaders. If there was someone who could reconquer city hall, then they could seize the control towers, too—

"Run all of those hooligans out of here...!"

"And I'm sorry for getting your hopes up, but the cultists are not gone yet. We've taken back city hall, but they still hold the control towers. Their demands have not been met yet, and there is still a danger of the city being flooded. I'm sorry, but you deserve to know the truth."

"———"

However, their fragile hope was shattered by none other than the boy on the broadcast.

The way he spoke, it was almost like he was reading the minds of the people in the shelters. It seemed a cruel thing to do, to smother the seed of a faint hope so immediately. The eyes that had been filled with hope clouded again as they were told that their belief that they would be freed from their fears was mistaken. And soon, their anger was pointed not at the cultists, who were like a natural disaster, but at the boy speaking to them.

"—I'm sorry."

But he had also anticipated the masses' venting at him.

"Where are you all right now? I imagine most of you are in the shelters, but there are probably some of you who didn't go to the shelters. I'm sure you are all feeling worried and anxious. I can understand feeling scared and wanting to just curl up. And I'm sure there are some of you wondering who I think I am, going and getting everyone's hopes up for nothing."

"______"

"I'm just a regular guy. I've been tossed around by this crazy situation just like all of you. I'm on the verge of being crushed by the madness of it all. Just like you. My knees are quaking in fear. Just like you. That's all I am. I actually had a bit of an argument with the people telling me to do this before I agreed to talk to you like this. I still think this is too big, too important a job for me. If I'm being honest, I think there are probably other people who would have been more suited to talking to all of you like this. In fact, I'm sure of it."

His voice was wavering as he spoke, as if showing that he really did understand how they all felt in a sea of fear and unease. He was open and honest, sharing his timidity, his insecurity. Everyone listening, the girl included, was past the point of suspicion or disappointment and could only feel confused.

Everyone wanted a little hope. Even if it was fake, even if it was fragile, they wanted something to hold on to. So why was he the one standing in front of the metia? He'd said it himself, hadn't he? There must be someone else better for it. So then, why was he—?

"But right now, it's just me. I'm the one here speaking to you. People way more special than I am told me that I should do this. That there was a meaning in me doing it… My voice is trembling, isn't it? I'm not the sort of guy meant to be standing in front of a crowd. I don't have the words or the charisma to lead everyone. I'm weak, pathetic, and even in a moment as important as this, I can't help wanting to run away..."

His tone gradually sank, drawing everyone listening gradually to the depths of despair. His weak, hoarse voice grated on their hearts, which were already tortured by fear, causing their stomachs to constrict. If he had been somewhere they could reach, they would have wanted to shut him up as soon as possible.

"Sister..."

At some point, her younger brother had woken up, and he called out to her.

She hugged her brother tight and held him close. Desperately clinging to him so that the weak, penetrating voice from the metia would not reach his ears, so that he would not be crushed by that hopelessness and despair. And while she was protecting her brother, her own ears were exposed, forcibly swept along on the path of the boy's weakness as he continued.

"...and hoping that I can just plug my ears and ignore everything while someone else takes care of everything because I don't know what to do..."

"Nooo..."

The girl closed her eyes tight, shaking her head, trying to keep away the grief and despair.

The boy's words described exactly what everyone in the shelters, everyone in the city cowering in fear of the cultists was feeling in the depths of their hearts. That was the weakness eating away at the girl's heart and the cowardice that had taken root in the depths of the adults' hearts and the fear that plagued her little brother's mind. This was the despair that no one would be able to fix.

She could not bear the boy's voice forcing her to face the unresolvable reality in front of her. It was so unbearable, so terrifying...

"—But even so. Even with all that, I can't run away from this. So I'm going to fight. That's the sort of person I am."

She could hardly believe what he said, his voice still wavering.

"—Eh?"

She opened her eyes and looked up, sure that she had just misheard him. She could not see the voice's owner. But she did see other faces around the room looking up with the same shock she was feeling.

There was a beat of silence as he chose his words and got his voice under control. And then—

"Let me ask you again: Where are you right now? Did you flee to a shelter? Are you hiding in your home? Are you all alone and scared? Is someone else there with you? Is that person someone precious to you? Even if you didn't know them before, are they familiar now after all these harrowing hours together?"

"———"

"I know it's not my place to say this, and it might be difficult for you, but please try not to wall yourself off. When you are all alone, it's easy to fill your head with all sorts of meaningless thoughts. I know, I've been there, too. So please try not to be by yourself. Stay together with someone else. And also—"

He inhaled, a faint hesitation in the back of his voice.

"If you can, try to look that person in the eye."

"———"

As if led on by his words, the girl slowly looked down into her arms. Her brother was looking up at her. She met his quavering, uncertain green eyes.

"Whose face did you look at? Was it someone special to you or someone you had never met before a few hours ago? Or maybe it was a friend… They probably look terrible right now. Was their face teary? Pained? I doubt anyone is smiling right now. No, maybe there are some people. Trying their best to put on a smile to keep you from worrying. If they are, then they are truly amazing people. If someone precious to you smiled for you like that, you should be proud. And then you should compare their expression now to the smile you remember."

Her brother's eyes were wet and weary. He was all rumpled and looked like he might burst into tears again at any moment. And seeing herself reflected in her brother's eyes, she saw that she had become expressionless and had a vacant look on her face.

"—Are you really okay with things staying like this?"

"...No..."

A soft reply slipped from the girl's lips.

It was weak and faint. A voice she could barely hear herself. And yet...

"I'm not. I can't forgive it. I don't want to accept it."

The boy's voice continued strongly, almost as if he had heard her.

"I have people I care about. I have comrades who mean the world to me. And I can't forgive the people who made them suffer and feel so sad. And I don't want them to force themselves to smile for me, either. It's enough to make me want to scream. I'm not stupid; I know her real smile is way more beautiful than that."

"Sister..."

"I can't just let it end like this. I could never live it down if I just gave up now. There's no way I can let things stay this way. They're the ones who are wrong, and I'm not going to sit back and let the bad guys win. I don't want to admit I lost to them."

"Fredo..."

She gently pulled her brother closer as he called out to her, pressing her forehead to his. It was warm. The warmth of life. She could not tell whether the heat was coming from her brother or her, but she could feel it nonetheless.

"I want to run away, but I can't. I want to cry, but I can't just cry. The enemy is dangerous, but I don't want to just lose. So I'll fight. I know full well that I'm weak, that I'm not smart. But I'll still fight. Because they are the ones who are wrong. I'll fight to prove to the people I love that the ones who made them so sad were wrong. That's why I'm fighting—and I want you all to fight, too."

"—!"

Her breath caught in her throat as it became tight. She felt pathetic for her moment of weakness.

Because the tremor in his voice disappeared, and she could hear in his voice the path that he was pointing to.

She understood his feelings. The meaning of his words was painfully clear to her. That was exactly how she felt, too. She wanted to fight. She wanted to run the bad guys out of the city if she could. But she and her little brother were small and young. They couldn't do anything.

They were powerless, ignorant, weak, so there wasn't—

"—Please don't misunderstand me, though."

But the boy's voice provided shelter as she berated herself for her weakness.

"When I say I want you to fight, I don't mean rush out into the streets with whatever weapons you can find. In fact, please don't do anything so rash. I don't mean you should form a mob and go running around looking for cultists to fight. What I want is for you to keep your head up."

"Keep my…head up…"

"Nothing changes when you stare down at your feet. You can't burn a hole in the ground no matter how long you look at it, and even if you could, that wouldn't help anyone… So please, keep your head up. Keep your eyes in front of you."

Raising her head, she looked not at her knees or her brother's blond hair but at the shelter. And as she looked around, she met the gazes of others who had also been struck by despair. They had all instinctively looked up at the boy's urging, just like she had.

"If you look around you, I'm sure you'll meet someone else's gaze. They are feeling the same unease, the same desire to just run away from it all, but…they also don't want to lose. Your loved ones, and the person whose eyes you just met, and if you count yourself, that's already three people. And depending on where you are, it might be even more people than that."

Like he said, when she looked up, she could see several different people's faces. The feelings in their eyes were complicated and muddled, and her eyes probably looked the same to them. But somewhere along the way she'd stopped feeling like she was just cowering in fear.

"I hope you understand now that you are not alone. That feeling is a powerful thing even all by itself. Not wanting to see the sad face of someone you care about. Not wanting to look lame to the person whose eyes you just met. I can't be the only one who's that shallow and stubborn, can I?"

"______"

The voice was pleading with them, calling out to them, trying to raise their spirits and inspire their courage, and yet it sounded to the girl almost like the boy was looking for something to cling to himself.

And finally, she realized. His heart had not changed at all from the very beginning of the broadcast. Even as he hated his own weakness, even as he regretted the things he lacked, he had not given up. He talked about himself—that was the only weapon he had. And he spoke to everyone about the things he was sure they all had in common.

"I want to believe. I'm weak. And pathetic. But I haven't given up yet. Please let me believe that I'm not the only weakling who doesn't know how to give up."

It was a cowardly voice and a cruel request. In a situation where everyone was pleading for help, here he was, shamelessly pleading with them, begging them all to give him something to believe in—

"Or am I really the only one?"

His voice faltered and lost confidence.

No, there had never been any confidence in his voice from the start. Irritation welled. *Stop it!* Even if she did not know what to shout—

"…No…"

It was as soft as a gnat's buzz, just a faint voice that barely crossed her lips.

She would not reach him with a voice that soft. Louder. She had to answer his question.

For the weak guy on the other end who was also afraid of being alone—

"Am I the only one who can still keep going…? Who still wants to fight?"

"—NO!!!"

The girl's eyes flared as she screamed.

The voice carried through the shelter. And her voice was not the only one.

"______"

She and another person who had raised their head had responded.

Their cries struggled against the sadness, the weakness, and the fear that rested in their hearts.

If that had been what the boy was planning, then they had played right into his hands. But why should she care?! If that weak, trembling voice, that unreliable rebuke, that meager encouragement, and that trust desperately clinging to faith alone had been nothing but a cheap performance, if he really had played them that perfectly, then there was no reason to feel bad about falling for it.

—But if it wasn't an act, if that had been what he truly believed, warts and all, then they couldn't let him stand alone.

"I'm not, right?"

"NO!"

"You can still fight, right? You won't let the weakness consume you, right?"

"I won't lose… I don't want to lose!"

There was a fire in her chest now. Her jaw clenched as an emotion different from anger welled up inside her. And she was not the only one.

All around her were people swallowing that same feeling as it turned into an inferno of emotion.

Just minutes earlier, all of their hearts had been consumed by unease, but now a different, fierier emotion was uniting them.

"If the person beside you is special to you, then hold their hand and have faith. If your neighbor is someone you don't know, then give them a nod and do your best to stand together. Do your best to fight so that neither you nor they break. And as long as you all don't give in, I'll keep fighting without giving up, too. I'll fight…and I'll win."

"______"

They were in a shelter far away from city hall, after all. No matter how much they raised their voices and shouted, there was no way their yells would reach him. And yet it sounded like there was a sense of relief in his voice, as if he had heard their cries, and his voice quivered as he made that declaration.

—I'll fight…and I'll win.

No one doubted he could do it. They absolutely trusted he could make it come true. Just like he had trusted that they would not give in to despair. They believed that the boy would be victorious in the most dangerous battle to come.

How could they believe that? Because his voice was sure—

"—I am Subaru Natsuki, the spirit user who defeated the Witch Cult Archbishop of Sloth."

There was a stir when he revealed his identity.

It was a proclamation that the girl did not understand, but the people around her did. The shock was enormous, but not in a negative way. First was astonishment, and then understanding—and finally hope and trust began to spread explosively, swallowing up the girl's heart in the swell of emotions.

"My comrades and I will take care of the cultists in the city! So please, trust us and keep fighting, too. Hold the hand of someone precious to you and give that feeling of weakness a good thrashing. And as for the rest…"

"———"

"…just leave everything else to me!"

Voices cried out as a singular hope multiplied and spread.

Looking down at her brother cradled in her arms, she could see hope lighting up his green eyes, too. Confirming that, she hugged him tight. His arms timidly wrapped around her waist, too, and she looked up at the ceiling as she felt the warmth of his hug.

The boy who could not hide his own fear, his own unease, who could not hide anything from them, had sworn he would still fight, carrying the hopes and expectations of all the people in the city on his back until the very end.

She did not know his face, but in her heart, he was a picture-book hero, and she closed her eyes as if praying that he would be blessed with every good fortune she could imagine. Because he would surely break if she didn't.

—Because he was just your average, everyday boy who was struggling against the outrageous for someone precious to him.

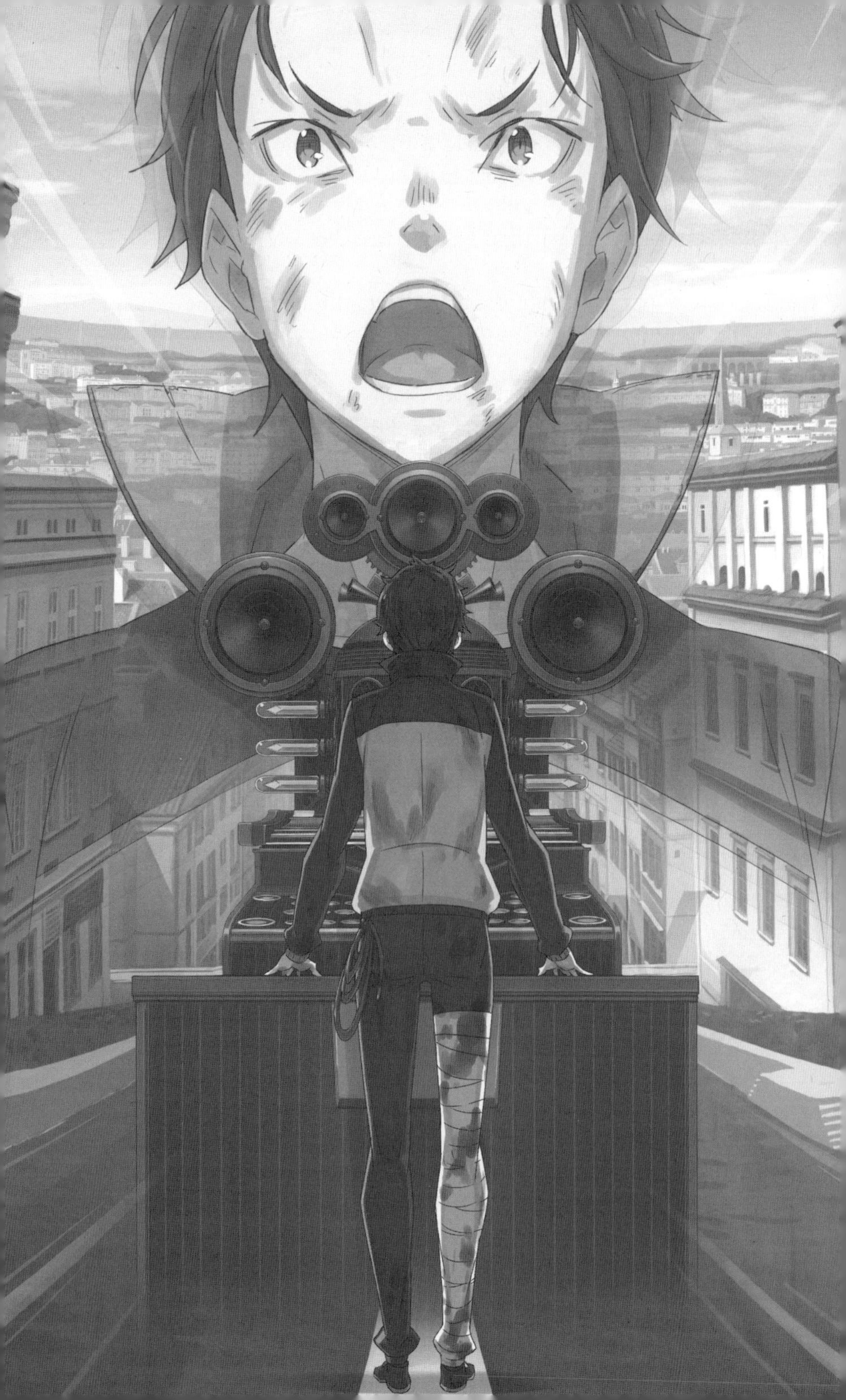

6

"*—Haaaaah.*"

Moving away from the pipe organ–shaped metia, Subaru took a deep breath.

Wiping away the sweat on his brow, the expression of all his worries and nervousness, he suddenly realized his legs were trembling and his jaw was tensed, and he hoped that his current mess of emotions had not come out in his voice.

"Ahhh, that was rough…"

Subaru sighed as he rolled his neck at the unexpectedly heavy exhaustion.

Honestly, he had lost himself in talking partway through and could not remember the details of what he'd said. It was not all gone, but parts of it were fuzzy.

Had he actually conveyed everything that had been in the draft note that Anastasia had given him?

"Huh?"

As he contemplated what he had done, he suddenly realized that the room was awfully quiet. The people who had been watching in the room, Anastasia and everyone else, were silent.

"______"

Anastasia, Garfiel, Julius, and Al had all been watching, and somewhere during the broadcast, Ricardo had joined them. They were a group not known for being short on words normally, and yet they were all silent.

Subaru could only assume he must have really badly screwed up the broadcast.

"—Natsuki."

"Ugh! I'm sorry! I swear I'll do better next time!"

"Huh? Why are you apologizing? You really are an oddball."

All wound up from self-doubt, Subaru reflexively started to apologize, but Anastasia just laughed in confusion as she elegantly touched her hand to her cheek.

"It's a bit of a strange question to ask after that, but are you by any chance—?"

"Am I what?"

"A former con artist or something?"

"Where'd that come from?! As you can see, I'm just your average, everyday schoolboy… Well, I guess in a sense, I'm not even that!"

"Ah, that's not what I mean. I didn't mean it as an insult. The way you wound them up was just too perfect… Bringin' the audience down low and then liftin' them up to a new high. You had the process down cold like you've been doing it for years," Anastasia said, waving her hand as she nodded in a combination of admiration and praise.

"Huh?" Subaru cocked his head. "I don't know anything about that. Honestly, my head went fuzzy somewhere in the middle, and I had no clue what I was saying. I only remember up to when the note started looking blurry, and I stopped trying to read from it."

"You pretty much totally ignored my draft from that point on. And you even started going on some tangent that was totally different from what we discussed beforehand. Do you have any clue how much I was worrying watching you from over here…?"

"Ugh… I'm really sorry about that! But wasn't it basically the gist of the draft? If it was that far off, you would have stopped me, right?"

The note that he had forgotten in the heat of the moment had been filled with Anastasia's negotiation techniques—and the little mood-lightening jokes and witty remarks that Subaru had put in to clear away the fear the people of the city were feeling. Even if he had messed up reading it back, it should be fine as long as he had hit the high notes—

"Not much point in dwelling on it now, but you didn't really even touch on anything we wrote down. Not even a little bit."

"Eh?"

Anastasia breezily denied Subaru's optimistic view.

Subaru stiffened, and he looked around the room for confirmation from the others. But the four other people all confirmed what Anastasia had said in their own ways.

"Lady Anastasia is correct, Subaru," Julius said, stepping out and tilting his chin austerely. "Your speech was certainly not what we discussed beforehand. In particular, I was of a mind to press you on why you did not reveal that you had defeated Sloth until near the end, when that was supposed to be shared early on."

"Wait, really?! If I didn't even say that much, then I was just some nobody for most of that! If it was that bad, you should have stopped me! Even if it messes up the mood, if you thought it would be better to start over, then you should have stopped me!"

"Start over? That would be absurd."

Subaru could only judge that he had screwed up badly enough to ruin the whole point of the broadcast, but Julius shook his head with a serious look on his face.

It almost seemed like he was feeling some sort of respect for Subaru.

"It was a splendid speech."

"...Huh?" Subaru stared at him dubiously.

"Forgetting the contents of the draft was not a problem at all. You managed to come through even better than we could have hoped when you put it in your own words. I have nothing but praise for your performance. I cannot help but see in you the same Subaru I witnessed during the battles with the White Whale and Sloth."

Julius hailed him with praise that was far more than he deserved. It was unlike him, and Subaru could sense a silent excitement radiating from the Finest of Knights. And when he realized that, it immediately felt absurd to him.

"Don't make fun of me. For a while now, it's felt like your jokes aren't funny at all."

"If it sounds like a joke to you, then it is because you think too little of yourself. But that is also part of why you were able to give the speech that you did. That was something that no one other than you could have done."

"You really are just taunting me, aren't you?"

Julius's unbending stance even in such an urgent situation annoyed Subaru. He was used to Julius's sarcastic jabs, but this was not the time for another pointless back-and-forth. If he had screwed up the speech, then they needed to do something else quickly.

"That was supposed to quell everyone's fears, so it would be a problem if it made everyone even more unsure. Someone else should do the next one..."

"There should be limits to how self-deprecating you can be, right? It's not like anyone else enjoys hearing it," Anastasia cut in, annoyance blazing in the backs of her eyes as she glared sharply at Subaru. "It looks like you really don't remember it at all, so I'll come out and say it for you—your speech was perfect. Much better than what I thought up. You're a natural demagogue."

"The lady's right! Yeaaah, that was sure somethin'! You really have a way with words! That was smooth, Bro! With a gilded tongue like that, you could get all the ladies or talk a kid out of his snack."

"I would never take candy from a baby! And 'demagogue' sure doesn't sound like a compliment, either!"

Subaru's eyes flared at Anastasia and Ricardo's explanations. But the two of them just glanced at each other and then shrugged, seemingly without any ill will. It half looked as if they had practiced their timing, but they also did not seem to be messing around with Subaru.

It was clear from Garfiel's expression, too, from the way he was holding his breath and peering at Subaru's face.

"What did you think, Garfiel? How was the broadcast?"

"...That's why you're my general. I wasn't wrong to follow you out of the Sanctuary. That's what I thought."

"...Your expectations are always just a little bit too heavy for me..."

"But it's 'cause of what you always do to earn them," Garfiel said, breaking into a toothy grin.

"Then I guess I should quit trying to escape responsibility," Subaru said, scratching his head. Everything that had happened since he started speaking into the metia still didn't really feel real. "I sort of feel like I said something along those lines during the speech, too."

"You did." Anastasia laughed, rubbing her scarf. "If anything, I'm worried you inspired them too much, and people might try to do something unwise. Even we felt the effects up here, thanks to Wrath's ability."

"When you put it that way, it sounds more and more like a lie... If it were true, that would be some blessing of eloquence–level performance," Subaru joked as he looked over at Al, who had started moving to the corner of the room at some point.

Noticing his gaze, Al silently looked away and made a point of slumping his shoulders. Al had been against the broadcast, so if he was reacting like that, then that had to mean Subaru really had pulled it off like everyone was saying.

"It will be a big help if the people can calm down a little bit now. Is there anything else we can do?"

"If you want anything more than that, all that's left is to get rid of the source of all this. They're gonna know we're coming, after your great performance."

"Even so, they're still just going to do whatever they have planned out. I guess we'll have to count on their irrational thinking when it comes to that, but we have to try to settle things as quickly as possible."

Regardless of how well the broadcast had gone, the cultists still had the ability to destroy the city.

—We have to kick their asses for sure this time before they can do what they came to do.

"And in order to do that, we need to take down all four control towers at the same time, huh?"

"There are four Archbishops and two powerful people helping them. There's the demi-beast problem to deal with, too, so we're gonna have to figure out how to divide our forces to deal with 'em."

The key to saving the city was capturing all four control towers simultaneously, which meant concentrating all their fighting power in one group like they had during the first raid on city hall would be hard. If they targeted the control towers one by one, then one of the other Archbishops could just open the floodgates.

Subaru could not imagine them managing to successfully pull off that gamble four times in a row.

There were six people on the enemy's side. Meanwhile, Crusch was down for the count. They were low on cards and pieces to play—

"Then how about adding a trump card to the field?"

"———"

As Subaru was going over the numbers they had, a voice suddenly interrupted him. Spinning around, he saw a figure standing in the doorway. Subaru's eyebrows rose, and then he exhaled and flashed a wry smile.

"Disappear for a few hours and now you think you're a trump card?"

"Certainly not in comparison to the man who took on the task of addressing the masses… And here I was, sure that I didn't have any heroes for friends. I guess that was an oversight on my part."

"I don't think that really fits me, either." Subaru shrugged and walked over and gave the newcomer a high five.

As he saw their lighthearted exchange, Garfiel's eyes gleamed.

"Bro!! You were okay?!"

"I was running for dear life, but somehow I managed to get out alive."

It was Otto Suwen, their missing friend—looking worse for wear but seemingly uninjured.

Otto held his hand up for another high five as Garfiel dashed over, but Garfiel leaped into him at full speed, wrapping his arms around Otto's waist.

"Wah?! Wh-what?! Wh-what is it, Garfiel?! Were you really that happy to…? Owww! Ow, ow, ow! Too strong!"

"Aahhh, thank goodness… Not that I was worried about you at all, though…!"

"Y-you aren't very convincing… Ngh…"

Just like with Subaru, Garfiel rejoiced with all his might at reuniting with Otto. After a little bit, and after Garfiel released him, Otto steadied his breath and then flashed a wry smile.

"Still, though, I'm glad to see the both of you safe. You are both far more stubborn and resilient than I am, so I wasn't too worried."

"You don't say. Actually, I wasn't that worried about you, either. I wonder why?"

"Hard to say. I guess that's just Otto's natural virtue?"

"Come on, it doesn't have to be as much as Garfiel, but you should have been at least a little worried about me, Mr. Natsuki! I was running around headlong into this dangerous emergency situation all by myself!"

But there was not really much weight to what he said, either, since he actually had managed to join back up with everyone safely. Still, though, as they were enjoying their happy reunion, Anastasia broke in, clapping her hands and saying, "Yeah, yeah."

"What a relief, what a relief. I'm glad you made it out alive, Otto. There's a lot I'd like to ask about what you were doing during all this, but before that..." Her tone shifted as she looked Otto in the eye. "What you said earlier sounded rather important... Would you care to explain what exactly you meant by that?"

"You mean the trump card, right? It's quite simple, really. I brought someone with me, though if he'd entered first, the celebration of my safe return would have gotten completely drowned out." Otto explained the sad fact as he stepped aside, clearing the way.

Taking that as a sign, the person who had been patiently waiting on the other side started walking in. And when that person stepped into the room—

"—My apologies for being late."

Just that one line was enough for them to feel like a whole army had just shown up at the gates.

"______"

It almost felt like a breeze was blowing, fanning a flame that had suddenly ignited before them.

What's more, he really was that strong. The fighting power they had been desperate for, the ultimate support, had finally arrived, and it set their hearts ablaze.

"Reinhard van Astrea of the Sword Saint lineage— It is late, but allow me to join you as well."

Saying that, the fire burning bright, the Sword Saint announced his desire to join the battle.

CHAPTER 4

THE STARS ETCHED INTO HISTORY

1

"I am sorry for being unable to aid you at the crucial moment. I have no excuse for my failure."

Reinhard apologized as everyone's attention focused on him. And as the Sword Saint lowered his head, no one could muster an immediate response. It would be simple enough to smooth the awkwardness over on a surface level, but they could not hide their true feelings with something so half-hearted.

It was still true that during the few hours when they most desperately needed every last bit of fighting power, Reinhard had been nowhere to be found. They could not help wondering what would have happened if he had joined the assault on city hall.

Because of that, none of them could assure him that it was all water under the bridge.

No one except—

"You got that right, you jerk. Do you know how much trouble we had while you were gone?"

—Subaru, who followed that up with a pointed little jab to the Sword Saint's chest.

His only reaction was to look at Subaru apologetically. Subaru simply snorted.

"And if you were gonna come at all, you should have done it fifteen minutes earlier. I ended up having to give a performance way outside my comfort zone thanks to you. That was supposed to have been your job."

"Forgive me... However, that was an excellent speech worthy of your reputation. Even if I had been asked to do the same, I would not have been able to manage a broadcast that stirred the people's courage so magnificently. You were the right choice for that task."

"I think people would be looking for different things if it was you and not me."

Subaru jabbed Reinhard in the chest once more for good measure after receiving his wry smile and praise. And then, as the hero still looked apologetic, Subaru held his finger out in front of Reinhard's face.

"Reinhard, forget a hundred other people. I'd take you over a thousand soldiers. So how 'bout it, can I pin that much hope on you? I'll be counting on you."

"——"

Even that did not even begin to describe how reassuring his presence was. Having Reinhard's help was like knowing a full army of reinforcements stood at their back.

Reinhard blinked his blue eyes at how open Subaru's anticipation was. But his surprise soon faded as the Sword Saint's lips curved into a smile.

"Yes, you can count on me. If that is what you want, then I'll live up to your expectations."

"Oooh, so reliable... I can feel my heart fluttering." Subaru flashed Reinhard a smile, putting him at ease before turning to the others and pointing back at him. "All right, we've got Reinhard with us now. You guys should say whatever you want to say while you can. At times like this, it feels way worse to be all awkward and careful around one another. Besides, it isn't every day you get a chance to tell off the Sword Saint when he's practically begging you to be mad at him. Let him have a piece of your mind."

"——"

"And once you're done picking on him, let's get down to business and figure out how to save everyone," Subaru announced with an easy wink.

He could hear some startled breaths but saw that Otto and Garfiel simply broke into grins at Subaru's familiar tough act.

Well, it was fine as long as at least one or two people could tell how he really felt.

—He had just done a whole speech about not shouldering everything yourself, after all.

2

Afterward, everyone voiced their own complaints with Reinhard (details omitted), and then they got settled in the conference room and prepared to discuss the best way to retake Pristella.

Otto and Reinhard had rejoined the party—and while Otto's fighting power was negligible, Reinhard's assistance was a game changer.

With that in mind, Subaru wanted to move the discussion along, but before that—

"By the way, what happened to Felt? She was with you when all this started, right?" Subaru asked Reinhard before they broached the first subject.

Reinhard's expression darkened a bit at that. Though he had been looking like that most of the time since getting there.

"To be clear, I'm not blaming you or anything. It's not like I think you just holed up somewhere safe to protect Felt or anything...," Subaru said, softening the blow.

"Agreed," Anastasia added nonchalantly, "but I would like to know what you were doing and where you were doing it while we were out of communication. It's not like we're playin' house here, after all."

She petted her fox scarf as she looked Reinhard directly in the eye.

The focus of her question was what Felt's faction had done that morning—the group had apparently gone to see Reinhard's father, Heinkel, to discuss something—and what their members had done since.

Wilhelm obviously didn't get along with him, but it seemed like everyone in the Astrea family found interacting with Heinkel rather awkward. Subaru was probably not the best person to say it, but it almost felt like—

"It's like a family that gives the cold shoulder to a kid who holed up for years and turned into a professional NEET..."

"Apologies for interrupting while you indulge in your odd imagination, but if Mr. Reinhard is finding it difficult to speak on the matter, perhaps I can elaborate?" Hoping to set aside Subaru and the alien analogy he was entertaining, Otto offered to clear things up. The way he looked at Reinhard almost made it seem like he already knew what had happened.

"Oh yeah, you were with Reinhard, but don't tell me that was from before all this even started?"

"Not since it started. I only met up with them at the very end of it all... Even so, I have a general grasp of the situation."

"Thank you, Otto. But it is my family's problem, and it involves Lady Felt as well. This is a difficult subject for me, but I should be the one to explain." Reinhard shook his head, and then, after pausing for a second, said, "First of all, I've said it many times already, but allow me to apologize once more. I should have been the first person to come your aid, and yet it was only at this late hour that I was able to join you. You have my deepest apologies."

"...On that point, I do believe our position is unchanged. It is difficult to wholeheartedly forgive your absence, but you are nonetheless essential to the coming battle. If you wish to make amends, I ask you do it with your sword," Julius responded, nudging Reinhard forward in his own way.

Reinhard's expression softened at his friend's words, and he added a soft "Thank you" before continuing.

"When the Witch Cult carried out their first broadcast, Lady Felt and I were leaving the second district to go speak with Vice-Captain Heinkel."

Reinhard's voice was wooden as he referred to his father by his official title. That alone was sufficient to show just how strained their relationship must be and how wide the gulf between them truly was.

"It's not exactly my place to comment, but she really decided to go talk to him after everything that happened at breakfast?" asked Subaru.

"She is not so irresponsible as to shirk what must be done out of mere personal discomfort. She set forth fully intending to negotiate with the vice-captain. And naturally, I accompanied her in that."

"Incidentally, I suppose I shouldn't ask how the negotiation went."

"That does involve internal matters, after all. But it would be fair to say that discussions were not overly favorable."

Reinhard's tone obliquely indicated how much of a struggle the meeting had been. And even without that clue, it had been a negotiation between Felt, who was still impulsive and straightforward by nature, even if she had grown, and Heinkel, who made no effort at all to hide his base vulgarity. It was not hard to imagine things getting complicated fast.

And while they were going at it—

"That was when the first broadcast occurred. I could hardly believe my ears, but I immediately thought to act. I had actually made certain arrangements beforehand in the event of an emergency. In fact, I even prepared a way for Lachins and the others to reach me if the need arose."

"Ah, yeah, I know. I…well, I had a chance to talk to Lachins."

Subaru was familiar with the magic signal that Reinhard could use as a beacon to home in on after spotting it in the sky. Lachins had actually used it during one of the loops when Subaru asked him to summon Reinhard. Unfortunately, the "just call Reinhard" plan had been put on hold because of Sirius's nasty ability.

But Reinhard had not been exaggerating about intending to come immediately if he got the signal from one of his allies. And yet he had not been able to do anything for hours while the cultists had free rein. What could possibly have stopped him—?

"—Lady Felt was held hostage by Vice-Captain Heinkel."

"———"

For a second, Subaru failed to understand. And it was not just him, either. Everyone in the room was at a loss for words at the absurdity of that statement.

"It was an irrevocable failure on my part. And with Lady Felt at sword point, I failed to find an opening to counterattack and remained held there."

As he gritted his teeth at the shameful memory, Reinhard's expression was etched with the regret burning inside him.

Hearing that, Subaru realized why Reinhard's face had darkened when he was first asked what had happened. The master he had sworn to serve had been taken hostage by his own father, of all people. And because of that, he had been unable to leave. It was shocking to think about how troubled he must've been and how much heartache he must have endured.

And it had not ended there, either. There was an even darker possibility.

"...So then...what? Was he an agent of the cultists?"

Reinhard's shocking admission opened the door to a cruel and terrible possibility.

Subaru had heard that cultists sometimes wormed their way into local governments undetected, but he didn't want to imagine what it might be like to discover someone in your family could be one.

Particularly not after learning about all the different terrible, nauseating Archbishops who existed besides Petelgeuse.

"—I don't know. If he was, then..."

But Subaru's theory seemed to be provoking complex feelings in Reinhard. Subaru himself looked dubious, as did half the people around the table, but Anastasia, Julius, and Otto all seemed to have reached a different conclusion.

Reinhard furrowed his brow and slowly shook his head.

"I have no intention of defending him on the basis of our blood relation, but the vice-captain is almost certainly not connected to the cultists. At the very least, there is no reason to suspect that based on what he said after taking Lady Felt hostage."

"That's absurd. Why would he take her hostage, then? What would be the point...?"

That was when Subaru noticed it. Given Reinhard's melancholic expression and the matching miserable looks that Otto, Anastasia, and Julius all sported, there was a reason Subaru could think of for

Heinkel to do that. It was a terrible reason, utterly beyond redemption, but not one that he could simply laugh off as unthinkable.

"You can't mean…he stopped you from leaving…in order to protect himself?"

"—. He said so himself. 'Your precious master and the father whose blood runs in your veins are both here. Would you really abandon them to save some strangers you've never seen before?'"

"What kind of father would say something like that?!" Subaru's anger boiled over, and he slammed his fist into the wall.

He had been weathering extreme flashes of emotion all day, ever since morning, but he never would have guessed such rage would be caused by someone not connected with the Witch Cult.

If he was going to end up hating people, it would've been preferable to limit it to just people connected to the Cult.

"Lady Felt said that he was just bluffing. That she would be fine and that I should go fight. But I disobeyed her command and stayed. I'm the one to blame."

"Like hell you are! There isn't anyone here who doesn't know exactly who's to blame!"

"Even so, that choice was mine. I am the one who made it."

Reinhard would not yield responsibility, no matter how much Subaru might shout. He could only regret that stubbornness verging on a perverse, meaningless obstinacy.

"In the end, it remained a stalemate. I was unable to act in the aftermath…and the situation remained unchanged during the second broadcast as well… I'm sure Lady Felt was disappointed in me."

He could not hide his own disappointment in himself. It was practically dripping from his expression, which just made it all the sadder that he did not realize how hurt he looked.

Based on what he had seen that morning and the night before, it looked to Subaru like Felt and Reinhard's relationship had changed quite a bit over the past year. And it seemed the insertion of his father into all of it had brought about another major shift.

"So then, what happened to Felt?"

Anastasia directed the conversation forward again, not touching on the look on Reinhard's face.

She was the only royal-selection candidate present, as well as having been entrusted to decide the fate of the city by Kiritaka, a representative of the Council of Ten. At the very least, she was keeping her sympathy to herself while prioritizing the smooth continuation of the discussion.

"You're here now, so is it safe to assume the problem was resolved?"

"Yes, Lady Felt has met up with her retainers, and at her judgment, she is currently standing by at a shelter with the vice-captain, who has been placed under arrest."

"Under arrest? As in you caught him?"

"His arms and legs have been bound, and he has been gagged. Lady Felt contented herself with meting out that much punishment. Was it not for Otto's help, it might have been much more difficult."

"Wait, that's when Otto showed up?" Subaru was surprised, given there had been no sign of Otto making an appearance before this.

"It's true," Otto himself said as he adjusted his hat. "Though it was sheer happenstance that I stumbled upon them. Having seen their interactions at the inn, though, I quickly grasped the gist of the situation."

There had been the incident in the morning that had touched on the deeply rooted problems of the Astrea family and the territory managed by Felt's faction. Having seen all that and then actually bearing witness to Heinkel holding Felt hostage just to keep Reinhard from leaving, a person didn't have to be a genius to guess what was happening.

"I judged it the worst possible situation for Mr. Reinhard to be unable to act while the cultists were freely running around. Just the thought of it was bone-chilling, so I knew I had to do something."

"And that's when you pummeled Heinkel and saved Felt?"

"Wait! Wait! Don't just nod along like that's obviously how it would go! I wouldn't do something that rash! I merely distracted him with a simple spell to create an opening for Lady Felt to escape." Otto sighed as he corrected Subaru's mistaken guess. "Thankfully, there was no difficulty finding everyone, what with your big performance. It would have been nice if I could have helped sooner, but I had quite a lot on my plate."

There had been a few digressions, but Reinhard was nodding, acknowledging that Otto had indeed come to their aid.

Otto had really put in a lot of work behind the scenes, like always. He was the ultimate behind-the-scenes talent.

"Still, though, what were you doing up until then, Bro? Honestly, given your strength, wandering around out on the streets would be suicide."

"I was a little surprised at how vigorous your concern for me was earlier, but I really did endure all sorts of twists and turns… I suppose I should elaborate."

Clearing his throat, Otto pointed outside the tower.

"This morning, as I had planned, I headed to the Muse Company alone in order to reinitiate negotiations with Mr. Kiritaka. However, I had some time to spare, so I got off the dragon boat early to walk the rest of the way… That was where I encountered the Witch Cult."

"You mean the broadcast? No, wait, that would've been too early."

Capella's first broadcast had been after the noon bell. Even with a leisurely detour, there was no way Otto wouldn't have reached the company before noon.

Otto nodded.

"Correct, it was not the broadcast. On the way to the Muse Company, I encountered the actual Witch Cult… In fact, I encountered someone who called themself an Archbishop. Near the second district's control tower."

"An Archbishop appeared before the broadcast went out?!"

Subaru was shocked, but it was not that unbelievable a story when he thought it through. Sirius and Regulus had also been doing as they pleased at the time tower before the broadcast. Other than Capella, who was occupying city hall, the Archbishops had apparently been free to wander the town and take in the sights.

And the one he had encountered could not have been any of the aforementioned three.

"So then, the one you met was…the Archbishop of Gluttony, huh?"

"…Yes. At least that was how they identified themself. And I cannot imagine any reason to lie about it, so I am certain it's true. They looked like a child, but I doubt actual age has any bearing on their appearance."

Otto's description matched with the Roy Alphard Subaru had seen. He didn't want to know the standard for selecting Archbishops, but Gluttony had been a child. A child whose arms and legs were not fully grown and who had clearly never finished maturing…a child with a hideous, scornful grin.

"I assumed it was some thoughtless child's mischief at first, but when I tried to draw the attention of the person guarding the tower…he was pulverized. Literally. With a splat."

"______"

"After watching someone's entire body get smashed flat, I had no choice but to believe. The nearby guards and the city's security forces quickly surrounded the Archbishop…but they did not stand a chance."

The way Otto's face paled spoke to how gruesome the encounter with Gluttony had been. An average person could not hope to lay hands on Gluttony, and Otto had been powerless to do anything.

Dragged into the battle without any choice, Otto had given it his best shot, but—

"In the end, the control tower was captured, and I could not say whether anyone else managed to escape."

"You did well coming away from something like that still in one piece. You were facing an Archbishop, after all."

"That was through no action of my own. It was only thanks to the people around me. Members of the White Dragon's Scale who joined the battle recognized me and gave their all to allow me a chance to escape."

"…Them again, huh?"

Kiritaka's personal troops had played a crucial role there, too. They were the cornerstone of Pristella's defenses, and the majority of them had gone missing, together with Kiritaka himself. And now it was clear that at least some of them had given their lives fighting Gluttony in order to fulfill their duty.

"I fled into the waterways during the confusion. Hearing the cultists' broadcast later, I realized I could no longer act carelessly, so I moved discreetly…which is when I encountered Mr. Reinhard's group."

"So that's how you met up."

And then resolving the stalemate over there brought them back to the present.

Subaru's face twisted up as he listened to the tightrope walk that Otto had endured to survive and meet back up with everybody. His path had been no less trying or death-defying than anyone else's in the room.

"And there were even people who sacrificed themselves to buy you time to escape. That's rough."

"Truly—it pains me as a merchant to be unable to repay my debts."

Otto bit his lip, mortified by the weight of what he was bearing. Debts must be settled—Anastasia had said it, too, but it was a pet saying that Otto had a habit of pulling out. Under that creed, he had to do something to make good on his debt.

"So I shall pay it back by guaranteeing the fate of this city—and judging by your performance earlier, I suppose I can count on you to do enough work for the both of us, Mr. Natsuki."

"Damn it, Otto…"

Subaru's anxious nerves relaxed a bit at the sudden change in tone as Otto gave him a wink.

The tightness in his shoulders went away—tension that had been there ever since he began his speech.

"———"

What Otto was getting at was that he had his own reasons to fight. And by conveying that, he was letting Subaru know that he wouldn't let his friend shoulder the fate of the city alone.

He was trying to tell Subaru there was no need to get too worked up.

"Ngh…"

Subaru's face felt hot, an intense embarrassment welling up at having his tough-guy act seen through.

Who did Subaru think he was? Someone who could decide the fate of a city? A symbol of hope and the people's wishes? It was ridiculous to even imagine.

The city and the people who resided within it were not so insignificant and light that Subaru could shoulder them all by himself. How had he forgotten that until Otto pointed it out?

"If you take your little bit of strength and add in my little bit of strength and top it off with Garfiel's stupid amount of strength, it all adds up to something quite sizable. Why not think of it like that?"

"'None can lift the quain stone alone,' huh? Every once in a while, you're kind of amazing, you know that?"

Subaru pulled out one of Garfiel's inscrutable sayings and found himself amazed yet again by Otto's steady hand. Otto was always saving him. He suspected that even if he tried his hardest, he would probably never be able to pay him back for everything he'd done, so he decided to do whatever he could to be worthy of his friend.

"Ain't that a nice group you've got there? Really know how to keep things moving, don't ya? It's heartwarming."

"Ah, my bad, we kind of started talking like it was just the two of us."

"It's fine, it's fine. Besides, it looks like Natsuki's finally relaxed a bit," Anastasia teased, welcoming the change.

She had noticed how tense he really was. Scratching his head sheepishly, Subaru quickly changed topics.

"Now that we've covered what you two were doing, the next topic we should be discussing is…"

"—I would like to address the four demands that the Witch Cult made," Julius proposed.

His golden eyes narrowed as he pointedly held up four fingers and looked around the room.

"They are not to be negotiated with, of course, but it is crucial to know what they are after. We know the silver-haired maiden, and we know about the Witch's bones from what Mr. Kiritaka told us, but…"

"An artificial spirit and the book of knowledge…" Reinhard furrowed his brow. "I've no clue as to what that book might be, and as for the former, the very idea of an artificial spirit sounds dubious as well. Does such a thing even exist?"

His doubts were shared by many in the room. No one outside of

Emilia's camp would have heard of either of those things before. Other than Anastasia, whom Subaru had told earlier.

"______"

Subaru glanced over at Anastasia. She was just looking at him, and as if sensing his intent, she nodded. Subaru decided that he would have to explain the two demands to everyone as well.

"—Sorry to interject yet again, but if I may."

But before Subaru could say anything, Otto raised his hand. Seeing that, Subaru guessed he was thinking of revealing that Beatrice was an artificial spirit. He had been about to explain that himself anyway, so he wasn't against it, but—

"If it's Beako, then I can..."

"No, this is about the book of knowledge, not Beatrice."

"Hn?"

Subaru's eyes widened in surprise.

Not looking at Subaru, Otto sighed slightly in resignation.

"I'm sorry—I'm the one who brought that into the city."

3

Everyone in the room was utterly shocked by Otto's explosive confession.

They weren't sure such a book even existed, and yet the person in possession of it had just announced himself to them all. Surprise was a natural reaction, but Subaru's shock was immeasurable because he had been so sure that he had already seen the last of that book—that both copies were burned and gone from the world.

"Wh-why did you?"

"First, I should be clear to prevent misunderstandings. While I did bring the item that would be called the book of knowledge into the city, I am not the one currently in possession of it. And the cultists' demand was a bolt out of the blue for me as well."

"That's a roundabout way of puttin' it. What exactly do you mean?"

Noticing Subaru's troubled reaction and Otto's studiously calm response, Anastasia cocked her head.

"Allow me to explain." Otto nodded. "I suspect that most of you are not aware of the book of knowledge. Put frankly, it is apparently the origin from which the Gospels that cultists possess are derived—those suspicious magic tomes that record the future of their owner. Its passages are also supposedly far more precise than the Gospels."

"The origin of the Gospels? When put that way, it makes some sense that they would want it. It is a blasphemous comparison, but I suppose it is similar to the Dragon Tablet?"

"Unfortunately, it's a bit difficult for me to say, because the book of knowledge was largely burned by the time I obtained it and was little more than charred scraps."

"Charred scraps…"

Otto's words also described the fate of the two tomes in Subaru's memories.

Beatrice's book had been burned in the fire along with all the rest of the contents of the forbidden archive. Meanwhile, Roswaal's book had been burned by Ram and lost in the Sanctuary.

As he had told Anastasia before, both of the books had been burned to ash. Which meant that if Otto had picked up the charred remains of one, it was most likely to have been Roswaal's copy.

"Ah, I think I know what you were after, Otto. The restorer Darts, right?"

"…There's no hiding anything from you. Yes, that was it precisely."

Otto nodded in resignation at Anastasia's quick thinking. And Julius and Reinhard both seemed to understand as well from that exchange.

"Wait up there. Don't go leaving me behind as the only one not getting it. What's this 'restorer' thing about?"

"Exactly what it sounds like. A specialist in magic who restores items. Darts is particularly well-known for his skill when it comes to this craft. If it's him, then he could even restore a book from its mere ashes."

"From its ashes?! Wait, that's actually possible?!"

"On the strength of that reputation, I secretly requested the restoration of the book of knowledge. So unless he took it during the evacuation, the book is currently being kept in Darts's workplace," Otto said, revealing the location of one of the objects the cultists demanded.

"...When did you have time to ask him to do a job like that, Otto?"

"After the negotiations at the Muse Company collapsed and I parted ways with everyone yesterday. Darts is deeply curious about ancient and rare items, and he was quite enthusiastic about taking the job..."

When he had heard the cultists' demand during the broadcast, Otto had probably been thrown for a loop. And his story explained how the burned book of knowledge could be in the city.

But what Subaru could not understand was what Otto's real reason for restoring the book had been.

As had been made eminently clear, Subaru did not think highly of the book of knowledge. And considering the pent-up grudge he bore against the Witch who'd made it, he had honestly felt pretty good about its being burned to ashes. So why had Otto wanted to restore that devil's book?

"I will have to ask that you allow me to leave out how I came to be in possession of it and what my goals were in restoring it. I merely wanted to make clear that the book actually exists and where it is currently. Any further, and it becomes an internal matter."

"At the very least, one of the factions in the Witch Cult has named the book of knowledge as its goal. Where do you believe that the blame for that lies?" Julius pressed.

"I believe that there is no point in trying to pin responsibility for the actions of the Witch Cult on anyone other than the Witch Cult themselves. If I were to be hounded regarding that, though, then I would have no choice but to respond with similar boorishness," Otto fired back, his eyes narrowed as he looked at Anastasia.

Between the lines, he was clearly asking whether blame should also be placed on the one who had invited the royal-selection candidates to the city in the first place; whether blame was not to remain solely with the cultists.

Seeing that, Julius shook his head.

"Apologies, that was wrongheaded of me. Naturally, I did not mean to blame you. Their crimes are their own, of course, and they are the ones who must atone for those crimes."

"I agree." Otto nodded.

Then, faced with Subaru's doubts, Otto looked him in the eye and said, "We can discuss it later."

He meant he would reveal his true goal in due time. That meant he was asking Subaru to set aside his doubts for the moment and come back to the topic later in private.

"Either way, it is clear that the book of knowledge actually *does* exist. In which case, we should assume for the sake of our planning at least that the artificial spirit also exists," Reinhard said, shifting to a new topic with the previous one more or less settled.

And that meant the topic that Subaru had started to bring up before Otto's unexpected confession.

"On that note, Anastasia, I was thinking of telling them..."

"Mm. Yeah, I guess we should."

"?"

Anastasia's gaze seemed distant for a moment. Feeling odd about her reaction, Subaru clapped his hands to get everyone's attention.

"Can I have your attention? Sorry for always talking, but I've got something to say about the artificial spirit."

"Are you sure, Mr. Natsuki?" Otto checked, realizing what Subaru was going to say.

It was a topic that touched on Beatrice's origin, so he probably judged it to be a delicate subject, but Subaru had decided that it was necessary to explain. Everyone in the room was an ally, and the conflicts among different camps could be set aside for the moment.

"I'm not going to hold anything back here. The artificial spirit they're after is my partner Beako—Beatrice. Right now, she's recuperating with the injured."

"Lady Beatrice? I see. That makes sense..." Julius nodded in acceptance.

"Makes sense?" Subaru cocked his head.

"Ah." Julius touched his hair. "I knew that Lady Beatrice was a powerful spirit, but I felt a somewhat mysterious signal coming from her. Upon my learning that she is not a natural spirit, it makes sense."

"...Is that just something that any decent spirit user would recognize?"

"I'm not sure what you are getting... Ahhh, you are worried about her. I see."

"If they could tell at a glance, or by getting close to her, that would be a problem."

Currently, the cultists had demanded an artificial spirit, but they had not named Beatrice specifically, so it was unclear just how much information they really had about the artificial spirit.

If the enemy did not know what she looked like or her name, then they could simply keep Beatrice's true identity a secret and not let anyone else find out. But if the enemy had a way of checking, then it would be a lot harder for Subaru to leave Beatrice's side.

"You need not worry," Julius said to put Subaru at ease. "The reason I felt an oddity was because I have been blessed with so many opportunities to interact with spirits due to my blessing. It would be safe to assume that most people would not be able to notice under normal circumstances."

"I see... Gotcha. That's...yeah, that's a relief."

Hearing that, Subaru exhaled the weight that had built up in his lungs. Reinhard and everyone else nodded, indicating that they had not noticed Beatrice was a special spirit in that regard. At least Subaru would not have to worry about her drawing all sorts of dangerous attention.

"Still, though, that crazy book, and the spirit thing, too—basically everything comes back to your place."

"...You don't have to tell me that. I'm starting to despair for the world. Maybe I got cursed somewhere along the line or something."

"Despair for the world? That's a riot!"

Ricardo opened his mouth wide, and his booming laugh shattered the mood building in the room. That unrestrained laughter helped Subaru right himself just a bit.

"_____"

The truth was just like he said, though. The cultists were coming straight for Emilia's faction with their demands. Otto and Julius's back-and-forth had ended with an agreement that no one was to blame for what the Witch Cult did other than the Witch Cult itself, but with so many things overlapping, it was entirely possible that the others would start to turn a cold eye on Emilia's camp. But by making a point of saying it like that, Ricardo nipped the friction in the bud. He rarely fussed about the details, or perhaps was just plain careless, but as expected of the leader of the Iron Fangs, Ricardo could read the room and set the mood like the best of them.

Although—

"If anything, I'm almost startin' to wonder if you're actually human yourself! You lived through gettin' washed away by the flood, after all. You hidin' anything from us?"

"You *are* reading the room, right? That was intentional, right? It's starting to feel like that was just natural, which is a scary thought."

"You're best off not thinking too hard about it. By and large, he's not thinking anything at all when he does that."

Subaru was starting to regret his admiration for Ricardo's rude act, which seemed less and less like an act, but Anastasia just shrugged it off before continuing.

"Anyway, the artificial spirit definitely exists, too. Naturally, just like with what Otto was sayin', we aren't gonna give 'em anything they want. Right, Natsuki?"

"Damn straight. I'm not giving up Beako until I die of old age. And I'm gonna cuddle up with her to sleep even when I'm an old man. So there's no way in hell I'm gonna let the likes of them get their hands on her."

Seeing Subaru's unyielding determination not to give in to the cultists' demands, Reinhard nodded firmly.

"Understood. We cannot afford to accept even one of their demands. Depending on the situation, the wedding ceremony could perhaps have been overlooked, but—"

"No! That's a hard-and-fast *nay*! Because the person that white-haired asshole is trying to marry is my Emilia-tan!"

"—?! I had a bad feeling about it, but it really was Lady Emilia, then! I had assumed her not being here was because she had taken shelter…!"

Reinhard stared in wonder, and Otto turned pale in shock. Seeing that, Subaru apologized for not explaining sooner.

"I'm ashamed to admit it, but she was taken away right before my eyes. That 'silver-haired maiden' is Emilia. But I'm not going to let that happen. I'm the one who's gonna marry Emilia." Subaru pounded his chest with an eruption of righteous indignation and love.

"———"

Otto clutched his head at Subaru's out-and-out proclamation, and Reinhard's eyes widened.

"…Huh? Did I say something weird?"

"Not weird so much as… I'm surprised to hear you actually say it out loud. I was astonished by your performance over the metia earlier as well, but I just felt it again now. You're a real man's man, ain't ya, Natsuki?"

"What's with that tepid response?! I really did say something weird, didn't I?!"

Anastasia shook her head no as Ricardo obviously snickered. And Garfiel's nodding with arms crossed and Otto's slumping were just the usual responses.

"Even you're looking at me weird, Reinhard."

"I was surprised—and astonished like Lady Anastasia—I suppose. I had, to some extent, sensed how you felt, but I would not have expected you to express your feelings toward Lady Emilia so explicitly and confidently."

The surprise fading, Reinhard's cheeks softened, and from the look in his eyes he appeared to be genuinely moved. Subaru could hardly believe he was getting teased by someone as honest and forthright as him.

Which would mean Julius, that paragon of knightly chivalry, must be pretty annoyed—

"———"

"Julius?"

However, when Subaru nervously turned around, Julius's reaction was nothing like what he'd expected. Julius's golden eyes were narrowed, watching Subaru with what almost felt like jealousy. An earnest yearning that stirred the depths of his heart.

"——" Julius returned to his senses after a moment. "Apologies. I was just thinking about something. Did you need something?"

"No, it's fine... Ah! Anyway, moving on!" Realizing he had lost track of the conversation for a moment, Subaru spun around to take in the room. "I'm going to get Emilia back with my own two hands, and I'll kick Greed's ass to do it. There's no room for negotiation on that."

"Very well, then that's what we shall do. If that is how it is, then he is not someone who can be overlooked or forgiven."

As he agreed with Subaru's determination, Reinhard's eagerness for battle welled up. Getting goose bumps from that, Subaru continued, "Also, it looks like you're feeling pessimistic, Otto, but it isn't all bad. Even after she was caught, Emilia-tan didn't just sit around waiting for us to make our move, either. She managed to get in contact with Al once and pass us some info on the enemy."

"Lady Emilia did something that sophisticated?! Is she all right?!"

"You could at least comment on how dangerous that must have been, man... Anyway, can you fill them in on what she told you, Al?"

It was clear from his reaction just what Otto had expected of Emilia, but Subaru lobbed the conversation to the man leaning against the wall in the corner of the room.

"——"

Al slowly raised his head and stepped away from the wall sluggishly.

For some reason, he had been like that ever since Subaru's speech. Between that and the intense exchange before the speech, everything about him seemed very different from usual. It was really starting to bother Subaru. But Al just nodded listlessly as Subaru focused a concerned gaze on him.

"Yeah... That little lady wasn't discouraged at all about being behind enemy lines. Maybe she was confident she wouldn't be killed since Greed wanted to marry her."

"Yeah...I'm not so sure about that part."

Subaru tilted his head as Al scratched at the seam of his helm.

It was not that unreasonable a thought, but in Emilia's case, Subaru suspected she would have done basically the same thing even if the situation had been drastically different. For better or worse, she always prioritized others over herself. That side of her made Subaru happy, but it was also incredibly worrying at times. He had wanted more information about her and wanted her to be safe while she was captured, so even just knowing that much was fortunate, but…

"…Emilia let us know which control tower is controlled by Greed and which one is controlled by Lust. And from Otto's story, we can be fairly confident which tower contains Gluttony, right?"

"Correct, it was the control tower in the second district. And from Emilia's timely intelligence report, we know Lust is in the first district and Greed is in the third district, which makes the fourth district Wrath by process of elimination. That's valuable enough information to merit her doing something rash," Anastasia summarized.

"So there you have it," Subaru said with a light snap and a wink. Greeted with wry smiles, Subaru, undiscouraged, turned his finger to Al.

"And we're grateful to you for bringing this information back, too…so what are you sulking about, Al? Is it just 'cause I didn't listen to your warning…?"

"I ain't sulking. An old guy like me gettin' bent out of a shape like that wouldn't be cute anyway."

"Cute's got nothing to do with it… I don't really want to admit it, but we got our asses kicked pretty hard the last go-round, and I don't want to fall into the same trap as before." Subaru spread his fingers, holding out his hand to Al.

Al looked down at the hand through his visor and then looked back at Subaru dubiously.

"I want you to help us out this time. Fight the good fight so I can save my love."

Subaru papered over his more earnest feelings with a joke as he waited for Al's response, trusting that in the end he would just crack wise and give in.

But—

"—If that's really how you feel, then I'm not against helping out."

There was no intimacy in Al's voice as he brushed Subaru's hand away in seeming annoyance.

"_____"

"Uh..."

Subaru felt a chill down his spine. The tone that was so clearly different from normal and the gaze he could not read behind the pitch-black helm caught him off guard. In that moment, Al pointed a wild, frayed rage right at Subaru. Subaru recognized that mysterious, almost violently aggressive feeling as something he had encountered before. But he could not remember where he had sensed it or the form it had taken then. He simply couldn't connect the two.

And while he continued struggling to make sense of it all, their awkward stare-down continued—

"Hark. Please lend me thine ears— Thine eyes evoke a heated, racing heart."

"Ugh—?!"

"Eep?!"

Totally caught off guard by the sudden interjection, Subaru spun around, sending the newcomer flying with a shocked gasp. She went rolling backward for some distance before dramatically crashing into the spare tables lining the wall.

"Ugyah! My elbows! My knees! The pain of every bone in my body breaking! All six of my ribs just snapped! I'm sure of it!"

The small figure curled up under the tables, writhing in pain with an earsplitting scream. Subaru's eyes widened as he turned around and caught his breath. The girl rolling around on the floor, unleashing every last bit of her quirky personality, was—

"Liliana?! Wait, if you're here, then that means..."

"—Naturally, I brought her here myself, commoner."

"Oh."

Right after confirming Liliana's presence, the owner of that voice, the walking embodiment of arrogance, stepped into the room. Footsteps rang out, luxuriously and magnificently, emphasizing the overwhelming aura of the brilliantly red woman. Her bloody crimson eyes lorded over the occupants as she pulled a fan from her voluptuous cleavage.

"The actors have all gathered. I suppose I should praise your prudence in waiting for the guest of honor to assume her seat. Be sure to maintain that diligent attitude going forward."

Smiling and apparently in a very good mood, the crimson beauty Priscilla Bariel joined the fray.

4

"P-Princess! You were safe!"

Everyone, Subaru included, was surprised by Priscilla's sudden appearance. But among them all, the quickest to snap back to reality was her retainer, Al, who quickly dashed over to her.

"I was worried, since I couldn't find you anywhere I looked… Gragh!"

"You fool."

The joy at reuniting with her lasted but a moment, though, as she smacked Al upside the head with a splendid crack. The sound echoed in the conference room, and Al was sent flying, only coming to stop after landing in a heap next to Liliana. Knowing from personal experience just how powerful that fan could be, Subaru reflexively groaned.

"Explain yourself, Al. Not only did you fail to accompany me, but I find you here playing around with these commoners. You and Schult have a duty to watch me, heed my voice, bask in my scent, and obey my every command. Nothing more and nothing less. And you, Schult: making your master personally search for you? Does your impudence know no bounds?"

"Ugh. My humblest apologies, Lady Priscilla…"

As she mercilessly kicked Al, a young, pink-haired butler peeped nervously out from behind her back—Schult, the person she had been searching for.

"So you really did manage to follow through on that… That really is some amazing tenacity."

Priscilla had led Liliana and Schult through a city filled with menacing demi-beasts where violence and chaos could erupt at any moment thanks to the cultists' devious machinations. The way she carried herself and her general sense of absolute confidence easily surpassed Subaru's wildest expectations yet again.

"It was like that at the inn this morning, too. You really like to surprise people, don't you?"

"You commoners merely collapse into shudders when faced with my peerless beauty and presence. If you would then bow your head in that awe, I might grant you mercy, but every last one of you is utterly lacking in charm. Of particular note..."

Priscilla and Anastasia did not seem to get along particularly well, and they engaged in a bit of verbal fencing, but after that, Priscilla turned her eyes to Subaru as she trailed off. The pressure made him a little claustrophobic as he managed to ask, "What?"

"...That clumsy broadcast earlier. That was your voice, was it not?"

"...And what if it was?"

"Hmph. There is no need to be so tense. I am fair in judging results. I simply call it like I see it—and currently, the eyes of the masses have turned to you. And I have decided to take them back with my own hands."

"...Ummm, so in other words...?"

"Do not make me spell everything out for you. My noble lips do not need the pointless labor."

Her eyes narrowed confrontationally as she sat herself down in one of the seats around the table, leaned back with a squeak, and crossed her arms, emphasizing her buxom figure.

"So report the current situation and be quick about it. You will become my hands and legs and fulfill thy roles. And be grateful, for I shall reward you by joining your plan."

"W-wait, Princess! Are you seriously planning to go at it with those cultists?!"

"Would you have me flee, Al? If so, *impudence* would not begin to describe your transgression."

Al tried to argue with Priscilla, who had sat down and announced her participation in the plan, but she glared back at him, causing the iron-helmed man to tremble.

"It was I who decided to visit this city, and it will be I who decides when to leave this city. I will brook no other person's directions. Particularly not the mad ramblings of zealots."

"———"

"—Everything in this world exists for my convenience. As my retainer and jester, you should know as much, Al. My very existence is the embodiment of the will of the world. My actions themselves are divine providence."

There was no breaking Priscilla's steel will—no, *diamond* would probably be more accurate. And Al should have known that better than anyone else there.

"Um, uh, that is just how Lady Priscilla is, so…"

"…Yeah, I know. Sorry for worryin' ya, Schult."

Al shrugged his one arm weakly and smiled wryly at Schult, who had struggled to find the words to comfort him. The prickly air he had directed at Subaru moments earlier disappeared.

He had made up his mind—Priscilla's domineering personality had finally done the job.

"Otto, maybe we could step out for a real quick moment?"

"Yes, of course."

Al lost out to Priscilla's demands and started calmly explaining the situation to her. Taking advantage of that lull, Subaru led Otto out into the hall to pick up a certain topic—the restoration of the book of knowledge—and to press him on what he had been thinking when he'd decided on that wild course of action.

"Garfiel, call us back once the conversation's moved on," Subaru said before leaving the room.

They stood across from each other out in the hall. Otto looked at Subaru quietly before starting in.

"It was one year ago. Immediately after cleaning up the problems in the Sanctuary. After the marquis's snowstorm melted away, while I was looking around the village, I found it by chance… No, it was not by chance. I was explicitly searching for it due to what Ms. Ram had said."

"If you found it there, then that would mean there's no mistake that it was the remnants of Roswaal's book."

"Yes. His was the one whose contents I wanted to confirm. And for once, I was in luck."

It was a bit of self-deprecating humor about his naturally poor fortunes, but Subaru was not in the mood to share a laugh when it came to these books. There was already a bad taste lingering in his mouth from talking about them, and when he saw that, Otto's smile disappeared as well. And then he took a deep breath and sighed heavily.

"What do you honestly think of Marquis Mathers?"

"Of Roswaal?" Subaru thought about it for a moment. "I think I can't let my guard down around him. And there was the thing a year ago, too. But his real goal is clear now, and as long as our goals are aligned, he isn't a threat. Right now…he's more of an accomplice."

"—I cannot find it in myself to trust Marquis Mathers in the least," Otto responded bitterly, almost seeming to write off Subaru's thoughts as far too easygoing.

The sharpness of that response made Subaru catch his breath.

"'The thing a year ago'? Yes, that's right. There was the situation last year in the Sanctuary. And before that, he seems to have schemed many different things as well. Though when it comes to this topic, both you and Lady Emilia seem to have been content to easily forgive him."

"…I haven't forgiven him at all. I'm still pretty pissed about what he did, and it still bothers me. But that doesn't change the fact that we need him. I just think that getting all up in arms about it won't help anything, and Emilia's the same."

"And I'm saying that that, that right there, is naive. I did not, however, say that it was a bad thing."

Otto glared at Subaru as if he was looking at something incredibly vexing. Subaru could understand the irritation he was feeling, he really could, but…

"It is all right. You and Lady Emilia can be that way. There is no need for either of you to change at all. Because I will be there on guard where you are not."

"Be on guard?"

"My job is taking care of internal matters, so I have had many opportunities to interact with the marquis. And during the past year of observation, I have not noticed any signs of schemes or suspicious artifice. However, that is only in the present tense. I cannot speak to what he might have done in the time before that. Say, for example, if he had perhaps arranged some sort of long-term scheme."

Subaru was at a loss for words. He could feel the weight of how much Otto was watching out for them, constantly thinking and planning and observing. The doubts he had regarding Roswaal were well-founded. And it was only natural that every action would provoke a reaction. For better or worse—if anything, precisely because it was bad.

"If he was obeying the directions for the future laid out in the book of knowledge, then by looking at the book, it should be possible to determine what, if anything, he arranged. And that will surely be beneficial at some point in the future."

Otto explained with clenched fists, as this time Subaru experienced irritation welling up inside himself.

Just like Otto had said, he had been the one best able to observe Roswaal from up close during the past year. And Otto had watched his each and every move without letting down his guard the entire time. And having done that, he'd judged that there had been no traces of hidden machinations over that time. That was a relief, but an inability to let it go at that was Subaru's worrisome friend's bad habit.

—In his own way, Otto wanted to trust Roswaal. But regardless of how he felt about the current Roswaal and his future actions, he could not just easily forgive the past schemes that might or might not even exist.

"So what you wanted out of the book of knowledge wasn't anything about the future."

"It was what was recorded in the past. I wanted confirmation that no one else inside our camp will be hurt. That is why I retrieved the book and sent it out to be restored… I'm sorry for my selfish actions."

Otto lowered his head and apologized. Subaru had nothing to say, since he or Emilia also should have noticed the things that Otto had been worrying about. He was struck again by just how much Otto was saving him day in and day out without his even realizing it.

Why would he go so far for—?

"I'm not going to talk about that. It would just be boring."

Realizing what Subaru must have been thinking from his expression, Otto raised his head and cut him off. In the end, the discomfort just deepened as Subaru scratched his head and sighed.

"I understand now. And I can understand why you picked up the book. I'm not mad, either…but them wanting the book is definitely a problem. What are we going to do about it?"

"Regardless of the result, I was thinking of recovering the book now, whatever state it might be in. It's quite possible that Darts has been injured in all of this, and I don't want it to fall into the cultists' hands even by chance. It is my responsibility."

"…Taking back the four towers is our top priority. We can't afford to divert any fighting forces for that."

"Need I remind you that I managed to make my way through this dangerous city and even bring the Sword Saint with me? And while I may look like this, I'm particularly skilled at finding a way to survive by relying upon the aid of animals around me," Otto explained, pointing to his lips in a veiled reference to his blessing of language.

In actual fact, when it came to just staying alive, Subaru trusted Otto more than anyone else. And with the enemy's main forces holed up in the towers, Otto's chances of success were not terrible.

"That's not enough to remove all doubt, but that's the same for everyone simply by being here in this city, and you have to put all your effort into recovering Lady Emilia. We both have weighty responsibilities."

"I know. I'll slap Greed down and marry Emilia. Those are my jobs here."

"Feel free to do your best on the latter if you'd like, but that's the spirit, at least."

Seeing Subaru steel his resolve again, Otto turned back toward the meeting room. Nodding at his suggestion to return, Subaru started to turn toward the door as well—

"—Sir Subaru."

A soft voice called from the stairway, stopping him in his tracks.

Turning back, he was met by Wilhelm's gaze. The same Wilhelm who should have been by Crusch's side.

"You go back first, Otto."

"Understood. I'll keep the discussion on track."

Nodding to Wilhelm, Otto returned to the meeting room. Meanwhile, Subaru headed over to Wilhelm, who bowed slightly.

"My humblest apologies for not joining the meeting. I've caused you all nothing but trouble."

"It is what it is, Wilhelm. No one thinks badly of you for it. And um…how is Ms. Crusch?"

He had heard that she was in a poor state—in fact, he had practically been told she had been hurt badly. Badly enough that it would be difficult for her to be seen like that, given her beauty.

Seeing the concern that Subaru could not fully hide, Wilhelm averted his blue eyes.

"She opened her eyes just moments ago. It is still too early to say for sure, though…"

"She woke up?! That's a huge relief! I was so worried."

"—Lady Crusch asked me to call for you. Could I perhaps trouble you to accompany me?"

Subaru rejoiced at the good news, but he cocked his head at Wilhelm's next statement. Of course he would gladly welcome the chance to talk to Crusch. And he wanted to be able to confirm with his own two eyes that she was safe. But—

"She has requested it herself. Still, please understand that Ferris is by no means excited about it."

"…No, he wouldn't be, would he?"

What Ferris had said before was still eating away at his heart.

Subaru had been the only person in the position to save Crusch during the battle with Capella on the top floor of the tower. Ultimately, he hadn't been able to give her any reliable help, and Ferris likely hadn't forgiven him for that yet on an emotional level, even if he understood the reasons.

And Subaru could understand that feeling so badly it hurt.

"Ferris might say something impolitic, but please do not heed it. And if possible, I would ask you to forgive it. He understands, but there are some feelings that he just cannot help."

"I can understand hating everyone around you when you can't do anything to help someone precious to you. I don't want to assume that one moment's darkness is all there is to a person."

If venting like that could help him calm down a little bit, then who could blame him? Subaru had the resolve to stand there and take it if that was what he needed.

"...This way."

Closing his eyes at that, Wilhelm led Subaru to his master's room.

For a moment, their two sets of controlled footsteps echoed in the hallway.

"Sir Subaru, there is one thing I would like to report from the battle at the tower."

"What? Something other than Crusch...?"

"It is about the cultists who accompanied the Archbishop...those two fighters."

Subaru caught his breath slightly. It was a problem he had imagined. Mimi had received a wound that would not close, and Wilhelm's old wound had reopened. The two extraordinarily powerful swordsmen that the cultists had brought with them—

"One of them is Eight-Arms Kurgan. A general of the Empire of Volakia and a swordsman who desired to be the strongest above all else. He was an eight-armed greatsword user who wielded four different greatswords. He died over ten years ago."

"If he died already, then, um, doesn't that...?"

"And the other one..."

Wilhelm continued, cutting Subaru off. He stopped walking and Subaru stopped as well. His back to Subaru, Wilhelm remained silent. Subaru instinctively took a step forward, coming up beside him—and immediately regretted it.

That was something he should not have seen.

"—The other is the previous Sword Saint, Theresia van Astrea. My wife, who should have fallen to the White Whale and died in the expedition fifteen years ago."

His voice remained calm. That alone spoke volumes about how sturdy his mental fortitude was. But it didn't matter one bit when Subaru saw how painfully warped the Sword Devil's face was. Rage and pain and a swirling, dark emotion that could not be described in a single word were threatening to tear the man apart.

"Is there any chance that your wife and the empire's general are somehow both still alive…?"

"…No, it is not possible. My wife and Kurgan are both dead. That is an indisputable fact. However, there is a fool somewhere on this earth who has disgraced their memories in death."

Wilhelm gritted his teeth as he confirmed that his wife really was dead. Subaru thought about that.

—A blasphemous desecration of the dead.

In other words, a type of necromancy. Some sort of magic to manipulate corpses was a staple of fantasy genres. Naturally, in a fictional world, it would not be that odd for a magic for reviving the dead to exist, but there was no convenient magic like that in this world.

The dead could not be revived. That was an unwritten ironclad rule that Subaru had learned over the course of the past year and change. So Kurgan and Theresia's being there was not the result of resurrection, but of someone using magic in order to turn the dead into puppets.

"There were once those who could manipulate the dead using a forbidden technique. During the Demi-human War decades ago, several people joined the demi-human side during the kingdom's internal struggle and became the kingdom's greatest enemies by raising a host of corpses to add to their ranks."

"The kingdom's greatest enemies, capable of raising a host of the dead…"

"The hero of the demi-humans Libre Fermi, the great strategist Valga Cromwell, and—" Wilhelm paused for a second. "The witch Sphinx. A being most foul who caused an ocean of blood to be spilled by both humans and demi-humans alike without even batting an eye. The one and only witch other than the Witch of Envy who left her bloody name in the kingdom's history."

5

Wilhelm named a witch Subaru had never heard of before. The witches Subaru knew were Envy—Satella—and the six others associated with the deadly sins, whom he'd met in Echidna's tomb. That there were more witches came out of nowhere.

"Then, do you think that that Sphinx is connected with this situation now?"

"No. My apologies, I was not clear enough. The witch Sphinx was destroyed back during that war and is most certainly dead. She is surely not connected to the current incident."

"She's dead? You're sure, right? A witch pretending to die in order to be able to act freely sort of fits the mental image I have of them."

There was the way Satella appeared whenever Subaru came close to the taboo of revealing his Return by Death ability, and there was the way Echidna was living it up in her domain after having died, too.

"They don't die no matter how many times you kill them, almost like cockroaches..."

"I cannot speak to the sort of impression you may have of witches, but Sphinx was merely referred to as a witch out of convenience. The more important point is the magic that Sphinx used."

"Which is a magic to raise the dead...?"

"At the time, they were commonly called corpse soldiers. That taboo technique is the most likely culprit behind the current situation."

Corpse soldiers was a blunt, easy-to-understand, and brutal phrase. A dead person, someone who had been lost, was moving again, and calling them a corpse soldier hammered home the reality of the situation.

And Wilhelm's beloved wife was being used as one of those corpse soldiers. Subaru could not even begin to imagine what he was feeling.

"My wife passed away. I was unable to protect her."

"———"

Subaru regretted his bitter expression, because it had made Wilhelm feel compelled to say it again.

His foolish inability to keep his emotions from showing had forced Wilhelm to repeat it.

There was nothing he could say as he watched the older swordsman's face. Not a single thing.

"Apologies for keeping you here so long. I mustn't make Lady Crusch wait any longer. Please proceed inside."

Wilhelm bowed and pointed to the door at the end of the hall.

The farthest room. That was where Crusch was waiting for Subaru. His feet were heavy, like the bottoms of his shoes were clinging to the floor.

That was surely an expression of the weakness of his heart as he started to feel daunted.

"—It's me. Subaru Natsuki. Crusch?"

Knocking on the door, he called out hoarsely. There was a moment's silence, and then the door slowly opened inward.

"Subawu…"

Ferris appeared on the other side. His gruesome appearance made Subaru catch his breath. His eyes were swollen and red from crying, and his chestnut hair was an absolute mess. His body was covered in spatters of blood that belonged to other people, and perhaps because he had not even spared a thought to wipe them away, there were even dried blood spots on his cheeks and neck.

"…Ah, I was…I was told Crusch asked for me…"

"Mm. She's in bed… Don't you dare pull anything."

His voice was strained, a hint of hatred seeping into the warning. But the hatred was not directed at Subaru. It was an all-encompassing hate. What was consuming Ferris was an aimless rage, a hatred of everything in the world.

Taking a deep breath, Subaru continued inside behind Ferris. The room was not very large. Originally it had been a break room, and it was divided into several little spaces with beds for naps. And Crusch was in the one farthest to the back.

The woman lying on the simple bed noticed Subaru.

"…Sir Su-baru?"

Her lips moved, calling his name. In trying to respond, Subaru felt his throat clench. Steeling himself and feigning calm, responding in such a way as to keep her from worrying—he could not even do something as simple as that.

"A-pologies for my un-sightly appear-ance..."

"...No, no... That's not...that's not it...at all..."

Seeing Subaru stiffen, Crusch apologized weakly, but Subaru desperately spoke up, trying to smooth things over, flustered by her pained demeanor.

She had been afflicted by a horrific black curse after having been bathed in Capella's blood. Her neck, arms, legs—huge swathes of her skin—were covered in a mottled black pattern. It was not hard to imagine that it was the same for the skin that was not showing as well. The network of black veins spreading across her body pulsed unnaturally, like a venomous snake constricting itself around her slender body.

The hideous curse was an insult to her hale, unblemished skin.

And of course the affliction did not stop at her neck. Her dignified, sharp beauty, which brought to mind the keenest of blades—the whole left side of her face was enveloped by a mottled splotch of black. The right side of her face remained clear, almost as if by malicious design, forcing Subaru to constantly compare the two sides, evoking an anger that something so noble had been so deliberately defiled.

Her left eye was covered by an eye patch, and he was hesitant to even imagine what the eye underneath looked like. He could understand why everyone had so adamantly insisted on his not seeing Crusch in her current state. The sheer difference between how badly they had been affected—it was just too cruel.

"Is this...is this really the same dragon's blood curse as I have?"

If so, then what could possibly explain the cruel difference between their conditions?

The same black pattern was covering his right leg, but beyond the appearance, there had been no effect on his leg at all. It did not hurt, and nothing about it felt off. But it was clearly different for Crusch. Her pained wheezing, the way she trembled every time the network of vessels pulsed as if she were experiencing tremendous pain...

"Ferris..."

He turned to Ferris, one of the best healers in all the kingdom, to ask if he could do anything, but that did nothing more than rub salt in the wound as Ferris bit his lips at his own powerlessness.

He dug his nails into his arms as he looked down. He regretted his powerlessness more than anyone else ever could. Given what he knew about their relationship, Subaru could be sure that Ferris had tried every possible method to help her—far more things than Subaru could begin to imagine.

"Crusch… Why…?"

Why had she called for him when she was clearly suffering so much? He doubted she could do anything. Was there something she wanted to say? Did she want vengeance against Lust for doing that to her? To curse Subaru?

He placed his ear close to Crusch's lips as she wheezed painfully, not wanting to miss anything she might say.

"…Th-ank good-ness you are safe…"

"———"

"I heard…you were exposed to the blood…like I was…"

She seemed relieved. There was a gentleness to her voice.

The next moment, Subaru realized what he had really been feeling and almost wanted to die from anger at his own pettiness.

He had been thinking that it would be so much easier if she just blamed him. Because of that, he had looked down on her noble spirit and doubted her virtue. She had simply been worried for him, worried that he was suffering the same excruciating pain that she was.

"I'm sorry… I'm so sorry…"

For doubting her, for her having to suffer like that, for being unable to do anything to relieve her pain: It all melded together into one great ball of remorse. He instinctively reached out, taking Crusch's limp hand. Her hand was covered by the mottled blackness. It looked distorted and was slick to the touch, which only emphasized the terrible state she was in. But—

"Gh, ahh?!"

For a moment, an intense pain coursed through his veins, like he had grabbed a red-hot iron. Pain shot through his hand, and he reflexively let go of Crusch's hand and looked at his own.

—His hand, which should have been normal, now had the same black pattern.

"Let me see your hand!"

Ferris took his hand, examining it as he stared in shock. The light of healing magic enveloped the dark veins, but there was no trace of pain nor sign of the black affliction fading.

But Subaru realized what had happened instead.

"Ferris! Crusch's hand!"

"What…?"

Spinning around, Ferris widened his yellow eyes. The reason for his shock was Crusch's right hand, the one that Subaru had held. The swollen blackness on her right hand had faded ever so slightly.

"Did it shift to my body from hers…?"

There didn't seem to be any other way to explain the way their bodies had reacted. The stark difference in what their hands looked like now was proof.

The curse afflicting Crusch's body had shifted to Subaru.

"B-but nothing happened to me! I touched her countless times while caring for her… See? It isn't moving! I—I…"

Hearing Subaru's hypothesis, Ferris touched the black flesh and tearfully shook his head. He was overwhelmed with anguish not by the possibility of a treatment, but at his own inability to do anything. The stark reality before him—his own inability to save his master—was just a never-ending series of difficult-to-bear blows.

"Even though I can't help her…"

"Move aside, Ferris… I need to test this…"

He felt bad for Ferris and the shock he must have been feeling, but verifying what was happening took precedence.

Setting Ferris aside, Subaru faced Crusch again. She looked confused at what was happening as she looked up at him, her right eye tearing up. Subaru held out his hand, touching her cheek so that his hand covered her left eye, the one masked by an eye patch.

"Gh-gaaaaaaaaah!"

Immediately after, it felt like his brain was being seared and magma was flowing through his veins. The curse afflicting Crusch's body traveled through his fingers, seemingly burning, melting, and bursting his nerves as they went.

Was this what Crusch was feeling with every moment that passed? She had been bearing something like that and even still had been worried about him? In that case, he would—

"—Ahhh."

Before realizing it, Subaru fell back to the floor, his mouth puckering and sputtering like that of a fish out of water. Beside him, Ferris, who was watching Crusch…

"That's…"

Had it had at least a little effect?

Crusch's right eye was blinking in shock. The sign of the curse, the black pattern running across her left cheek, had faded somewhat. Seeing that, Subaru knew he had gotten some response. Lifting himself heavily, he prepared to try again.

If it could change that much from one time, then if he repeated the action enough, she could be saved—

"You mustn't, Sir Subaru… Have you not noticed?"

"What?"

But it was Crusch herself who stopped him. Her amber eyes were focused on his outstretched hand. Following her gaze, he noticed what she was seeing and belatedly understood what she was saying.

His right arm was covered by swollen black masses just like his right leg. That part was fine, though. He had successfully taken the curse from Crusch. That change was exactly what he wanted. That alone would not shake his resolve. But the amount of curse he had gained was also clearly not commensurate with the amount that had been taken from her. He had just lessened the curse on her left hand and part of her face, but his right arm from his elbow down to the back of his hand was covered in the black mass. It was not a one-to-one exchange. It was one to ten, maybe even more.

"That's not enough to stop me."

The instant he absorbed it, it hurt. But once it was inside him, it showed no sign of hurting or eating away at him. Unlike Crusch's, his pain only lasted for an instant. And there was no question which of the two of them was better suited to bearing the hideousness of the curse.

If it would save Crusch, then he could put up with parts of his body getting hideous-looking welts.

"You mustn't, Sir Subaru… I cannot accept that."

"Don't be stupid. I'm fine with a little bit of pain. This is way better than getting an impulsive tattoo, anyway. So…"

"There is no guarantee it will remain that way… If the both of us are unable to fight…that would be fatal given the current situation…"

Crusch was worried more about the people of the city than about her own fate. That was a logical point, but Subaru didn't think everything could be decided so logically.

"Ferris, stop Sir Subaru…"

"I—I… Lady Crusch, I…"

"Please. Right now, the people need him more than they need me…"

Ferris hesitated precisely because Crusch was absolutely the most important thing to him in the entire world. And no one could blame him for that hesitation and doubt. No one in the room was wrong. But merely not being wrong did not make them right.

"Do not be swept away in a burst of emotion. Please, Sir Subaru…"

"I understand what you're trying to say, Crusch, but I still—"

"You said it, did you not? 'Just leave everything else to me.'"

"—!"

His desire to prioritize the ones closest to him was broken by Crusch's plea. The words she chose, the strength with which she spoke, had he really said that himself? And, having heard him say that, Crusch was now telling him to follow through, to keep his word?

"Say it to me, too, please."

"———"

"'Leave everything else to me.'"

She waited for Subaru's response with a pained smile.

Catching his breath, moving his tongue inside his dry mouth, Subaru quietly closed his eyes.

Having been scolded for clinging to the chance to save someone right in front of him without thinking of what would come later, having been told something he should not have needed to be told, then at the very least—

Then at the very least, for that one moment, he should do what she wanted—

"Crusch, please take your time and rest."

"...Sir Subaru..."

"You can leave everything else to me."

"—Thank you."

He could at least fulfill the role asked of him, say the words that she wanted to hear from him.

"——"

Hearing that, she exhaled a deep breath, as if relieved. Then she weakly closed her eyes—proof that she had only been carrying on as she had through sheer force of will. Her breathing became shallower, and she was soon too busy battling the encroaching curse again to pay attention to anything else.

In order to free her from that even a minute sooner—

"Sorry, Ferris, but I have to go."

"...What should I do?"

Adjusting Crusch's blanket, Subaru stood up and spoke softly. Ferris looked exhausted as he turned to Subaru for some sort of consolation.

Honestly, he wanted to just tell him to stay by Crusch's side. But Ferris's abilities would not allow that, given the situation.

"We need your strength. There are sure to be more people hurt going forward. There are going to be a lot of people we won't be able to save without you. So please."

"...But I couldn't even save the one person I most wanted to save..."

"Ferris..."

"Sorry, that was stupid of me... Let me stay here with her a little longer."

Turning away, Ferris sat down in the chair next to the bed. Subaru tapped his shoulder lightly, glanced at Crusch's resting face, and then left the room.

When he entered the hallway, he was greeted by Wilhelm, whose head was lowered just like when he had left. Perhaps realizing what had happened inside, he thanked Subaru.

"You have my gratitude for answering Lady Crusch's wish."

"It's not anywhere near as noble as you make it sound. If anything, she lit a fire in my belly… What the hell is going on with my body, though?"

Absorbing Crusch's curse, and also seemingly weakening the effects of the dragon's blood, and then the resistance to the Witch Factor, and his ability to Return by Death… It was all incredibly shady.

Would he ever get a proper answer to all these questions?

"Either way, I'm going to have to try this again with her after everything else is all cleared up."

"Is your right arm truly well?"

"Yeah, though I know it looks terrible. Guess I'll have to stick to long sleeves and maybe some gloves, too. But if a couple of permanent scars are all it takes to save a pretty girl, then you won't find me complaining."

It was his body, and he did feel a certain amount of reluctance. But his flippant statement was also fairly close to how Subaru truly felt about it. If there was no other solution, then he would be fine with bearing her curse for her. Even if it ended up covering his whole body in that nasty mottled black, he could just apologize to Emilia and Rem and Beatrice and ask for their forgiveness.

"That's something to worry about once we get through all this. Let's head downstairs. They should be getting to how to attack the towers around now."

"—Reinhard is down there now."

As Subaru started to hurry to the conference room, he was stopped in his tracks by Wilhelm's murmur.

For a split second, he flashed back to the scene at the Water Raiment Inn. The reconciliation between grandfather and grandson, and the way it had been ruined and their chance at reconciliation stopped in its tracks—

"Please do not misunderstand, Sir Subaru."

However, Wilhelm shook his head, allaying Subaru's fears.

"I do not feel any resistance to fighting together with Reinhard. But I have one request for you."

"A request?"

"—Could I ask you not to reveal the identity of the corpse soldiers to Reinhard?"

"______"

Subaru was at a loss, unsure what the meaning of Wilhelm's soft-spoken request was.

He had only just heard about them from Wilhelm: a technique that desecrated the dead and had been used in the city this time to—

"Do you mean don't tell him about your wife…about his grandmother?"

"Yes. I don't want him…I don't want my grandson to have to deal with my wife being turned into a corpse soldier. He would surely blame himself. And it is no one's fault but my own."

"Your fault? It's—"

He wanted to say it was not Wilhelm's fault at all. But he could not say something like that so thoughtlessly. Recalling the scene from that morning, he also remembered what Heinkel had said. Something that should have had no credibility at all—but even so, Wilhelm had not denied it.

He'd said that Wilhelm had blamed Reinhard for his wife's death. It was hard to believe, but neither of them had denied the charge.

"Sir Subaru, are you aware that the blessing of the Sword Saint is a unique one?"

"…Not particularly. Mostly just that it's a blessing that all the people called Sword Saint in history had and that having it made them super powerful."

"At a high level, that is not mistaken, but there is one point where the blessing of the Sword Saint is notably different from all other blessings. That point is that it is an inherited blessing."

"An inherited blessing?"

Wilhelm nodded as Subaru exhaled. The old swordsman's eyes were closed, his expression twisted as if he was remembering a painful past.

"It was inherited through the generations, passed down from the original Sword Saint, Reid Astrea. The blessing resides in the Astrea family's bloodline, and the next Sword Saint always arises from a descendent of their house. My wife inherited it from the last Sword Saint, and Reinhard inherited it from her."

"A blessing inherited among family… I see, so that's how it was. So when you lost your wife, it was inherited by Reinhard."

Something caught in Subaru's head as he tried to understand the situation.

The previous Sword Saint had fallen to the White Whale, and as a result, Reinhard had inherited the blessing. It was a painful past, but in a sense, it was just the natural order of succession as well. But the argument that the Astrea family had had earlier that morning did not fit with the official story.

Wilhelm's grief, Heinkel's scorn, and Reinhard's silence—all of them seemed to be arguing against the legitimacy of the blessing's inheritance in some shape or form.

And the reason for that was—

"It occurred in the midst of the battle with the White Whale."

"———"

"—Reinhard inherited the blessing while my wife was in the middle of the hunt. She lost her blessing during the fighting and became nothing more than a single regular woman, which left her unable to support the rear guard alone."

—That was the origin of the rift in the Astrea family.

The blessing had been transferred to the next generation while she was right in the middle of fighting during the White Whale hunt. This would have left the former Sword Saint on the battlefield without her blessing. And entrusted with the rear guard of the enormous force, she'd fought to protect the lives of the many soldiers who depended on her and breathed her last in the course of duty.

"It was none other than I who stole the sword away from my wife. It was I who made the woman beloved by the Sword God abandon her sword. And that was what invited her doom."

"Wilhelm…"

"The Sword God did not forgive my wife for her betrayal. Imagining what she must have thought, having her blessing go away on the battlefield, leaving her nothing but the sword I had made her abandon to rely on…I could not accept it. It is true that I berated Reinhard for inheriting the blessing. Fool that I was, I could not forgive my young grandson, who was grieving his grandmother's death and struggling with the far-too-heavy fate he had been burdened with. I assure you—I regret it deeply."

The regret he had shared with Subaru the night before—this was the mistake he had made.

Reinhard was not at fault at all, but despite understanding that, in his grief, Wilhelm had refused to acknowledge the fact. As a result, a fatal fracture had split the Astrea family, dividing them.

"I do not want to go through that pain again. Because Reinhard was not to blame at all for her death. There is no reason for my grandson to shoulder that burden at all."

Because of that, he wanted to resolve it with his own sword, without revealing the truth to Reinhard.

Subaru could understand those feelings, that regret, and that resolve so badly it hurt. In which case—

"Crusch and Ferris, and your wife and Reinhard… If you try to carry everything by yourself, you'll be crushed under the weight of it all. And even if I keep quiet about the corpse soldiers, they'll still show up somewhere."

"That is an unnecessary concern."

"Eh…?"

Subaru was trying to warn him that it was an unrealistic gamble with poor odds, but Wilhelm merely smiled. The Sword Devil's expression warped into a fiercely valiant grin.

"—There is no way that my wife—that Theresia won't come to meet me."

6

"______"

The mood tensed when Subaru returned to the conference room.

The reason was Wilhelm. He and Reinhard traded glances, and

after a silent exchange of sorts, they adopted positions standing on opposite sides of the room. Subaru could not help the complex feeling he had knowing what Wilhelm had on his mind, but there was nothing he could say, so he reclaimed the empty seat at the table between Garfiel and Otto.

"Sorry for the delay. Where are we at?"

"The explanation is more or less done. How were things up there…? What of Lady Crusch's condition?"

"…Not great. Not hopeless, either, though. There might just be something we can do for her, but it'll have to wait until we've dealt with the cultists first."

"I see. That, at least, is a bit of good news."

Otto straightened himself up, and the others sitting around the table looked a little bit relieved.

Unfortunately for them, Subaru was not going to explain exactly how he could help her. He knew that if he did, someone was sure to try to stop him, so he would just ask for forgiveness instead of permission if things came down to it. Though the best thing would obviously be if they could beat Lust and find a way to get rid of the mottled blackness entirely.

"Either way, it is unlikely Crusch will be rejoining the fight. And Ferris wants to stay with her, so that means the relief squad and the people from the Iron Fangs will probably need to stay here. How's that sound to you guys?"

"City hall's right in the middle of the city, so it makes sense to set up our command post here. It's not going to change the basic plan for a simultaneous attack on all four of the control towers, either. But…"

"But?"

"There's someone who's got her own thoughts about that plan." Anastasia glanced over the table at the person sitting across from her.

It didn't take much imagination to guess whom she meant without even needing to look. Even in their current predicament, the crimson candidate casually fanned herself, showing no spirit of cooperation at all.

"Priscilla? What crazy idea do you have now?"

"It sounds as if you presume to know me, commoner. Then tell me, could you predict this? I shall go to the control tower in the fourth district to behead that Wrath or whatever resides there."

"Wh...?"

Priscilla looked smug as her majestic declaration caught Subaru entirely off guard. He was well and truly taken aback by her plan. Anastasia nodded when she saw the shock on his face.

"See? She's been like that the whole time. I've been trying to figure out what to do about it."

"We have to stop her, obviously...is what I'd like to say, but..."

Ordinarily, her suggestion would be unbelievably rash, but when he thought it through coolheadedly, there was a certain merit to her plan, too.

Crusch had joined the attack on city hall earlier, so he could not reject Priscilla's suggestion just because she was a royal-selection candidate. And there was no way to argue that she was lacking in strength. At the very least, she was powerful enough to easily slay the ferocious demi-beasts roaming the city. She did not pale in comparison to Crusch in her swordsmanship, either. As an amateur who had observed dozens of experts, that was how Subaru rated her strength.

"This is asinine. I possess both strength and beauty. So what reason is there to hesitate? Do not think me a fool who renders herself useless in the opening scenes or some weakling who never had the strength to stand and fight in the first place."

"I do not believe I can allow that to pass without comment. I am certain you could not possibly be referring to my master as a fool, could you?"

"It sounds as if you have someone in mind, old man. Being forced to leave the stage during a warmup before the main performance even starts could hardly be called the action of a person fated to play a leading role. I suppose it was just a misjudgment on my part to have expected more."

Priscilla and Wilhelm were clashing dangerously from word one. Ordinarily, it was a situation to just let something like that go, but for various reasons, Wilhelm was not quite composed enough to let it slide. And Priscilla was so totally unchanged from her normal self that it was hard to imagine her ever not behaving like that.

"Yeah, yeah. I'm the weakling and the fool, so let's just move on. Quit arguin' among ourselves."

"I'm not so kind as to unconditionally lend an ear to the prattling of a weakling, she-fox."

"Being weak isn't the same as being incapable of winning. And how are you going to get the people around you to act how you want without a little show of magnanimity? We're all pissed off here, so just have a little patience."

"Hmph."

Subaru was amazed at Anastasia's mediation skills as he watched her talk the both of them down and silence their squabbling. They both still looked annoyed, but Priscilla retracted her prickly attitude, and Wilhelm sheathed his sharp aura.

Of course, the mood could hardly be called harmonious. Given the situation, they had to prioritize moving the conversation forward regardless of how some people felt about one another.

"Then, would that mean Sir Al will be accompanying you to slay the Archbishop of Wrath?"

"Spare me your nonsense. Bringing that jester would only darken my glorious procession. And obviously, I will be leaving Schult here as well. He is only with me to be a pet."

"...In that case, were you perhaps actually intending to go there by yourself?" Julius pressed in a sharp tone, as if to say there was no way that that could be acceptable.

"Yeah, Princess," Al responded, agreeing with Julius. "Even you can't just declare you'll be fine alone. At the very least, take the Sword Saint with you..."

"Don't go giving away our strongest trump card with a cheap 'at the very least'! And you, do you actually have some plan that makes you think you can win?"

"Of course. And in the first place, don't jump to conclusions. I never said I would be going alone. The diva there and I shall hunt the Archbishop of Wrath together." Priscilla snapped her fan closed and pointed it at the corner of the room.

"The diva…"

Liliana was sitting cross-legged on the ground there, dozing off with her lyulyre in her arms. She snapped back to reality at suddenly being called onstage. Her jaw dropped as she responded.

"Y-you chose me?! And for what reason would you suddenly do that?!"

"Commoner, there was no lie in the previous conversation, correct? That irksome chaotic presence proliferating throughout the city was something evoked by the Archbishop of Wrath's impudent Authority?"

"Y-yeah, there's no mistaking it…"

Remembering how the residents in the shelter had been set free by Liliana's singing, Subaru inhaled sharply.

He had considered using Liliana's music to counter Wrath's Authority as well, but the problems were the danger of bringing her to a battlefield and her reluctance to use her singing as essentially a weapon—a tool to counter that Authority—

"Can you explain, Subaru? What is the connection between Miss Liliana and the Archbishop of Wrath?" asked Anastasia.

"…You heard about how Wrath's Authority works, right? It creates a resonance between the hearts and minds of the city's residents, which has been causing unrest and panic to spread unchecked. We used the broadcast to amplify and spread courage, but Liliana's singing can do the same thing. Honestly, it can probably do an even better job."

After all, they only had to hear Liliana's singing. There was no need for the tightrope walk that Subaru had carefully navigated after carefully choosing his words and mustering what little courage he had to offer. Her music was the real deal—just her singing could captivate people's hearts, and experiencing that pure passion firsthand was enough to free people's hearts from Sirius's Authority.

"How much did your singing move the masses' hearts when we were going around between the shelters before? You need only do the same again. Merely steal away the hearts of the vulgar masses."

"Wh-what a violent logic! B-but I only encouraged people with my singing. I don't have any confidence at all that I can meet such a weighty expectation…"

"I see. So then you do not have faith that the music you have inherited from your forebears in eras long past will succeed."

The way Priscilla sniffed expressed such disdain that it caused Liliana's eyes to change instantly. She had been trying to beg out of the fight with a servile, polite smile, but her expression suddenly turned serious.

"What do you mean by that?"

"It should not require deep thought to understand. Those are the songs you have so devoutly continued singing, and yet in the moment when people's hearts are crying out for salvation, you shrink back and fall silent? I have no need for such a craven, whipped dog. At least a wild mutt still howls freely. Hark, a eulogy for a whipped dog."

"A-ah, ah! You said it! There are some things you just shouldn't say! Fine, then! I'll do it! I'll let you hear it! If I remained silent now, I would lose everything! If I hesitated now, Mr. Kiritaka would spin in his grave!"

Priscilla's tremendous instigation brought on a terrific explosion from Liliana. Her face was bright red as she fired back, plucking the lyulyre's strings at high speed.

"I was of a mood to sing a requiem for the fallen Kiritaka, but nay! A scramble to steal away hearts? I say let them come! The songs that I have inherited would never lose to some mysterious ability no one has ever heard of! Because the power of music is even more mysterious!"

In a fit of excitement, Liliana leaped atop the round table and played her lyulyre while lying down. Flustered by her performance, Otto and Schult quickly pulled her back down to the floor. Subaru ignored Liliana, who was starting to compose a rock ballad in the corner of the room, as he looked Priscilla in the eye.

"I know full well that both her singing voice and her stupidity are on the level of national treasures. And I also agree she could be a perfect counter for Wrath's ability. But there's no proof it will work as planned, either."

"I would never embark on a fight where I had any chance of losing. The very logic of this world proceeds only in the manner that is most convenient to me. And there is no one who values her singing more highly than I. I shan't allow her to suffer a single scratch above her shoulders."

"...Singing starts with the diaphragm, so I'm pretty sure it won't mean much if there's anything missing from her waist up."

Priscilla was showing no sign of yielding, but Subaru wanted one final nudge. If there was at least some proof they could point to that Liliana's singing would work against Sirius, then...

"Hey, Reinhard, by any chance, do you have some kind of ability to see the power that people have—right, blessings? Do you have some kind of ability to see blessings or something?"

"There *is* a divine protection called the blessing of judgment that allows one to know people's blessings. I see. If she truly does bear a songstress blessing, then that could serve as evidence to accept Lady Priscilla's contention."

Reinhard rested his hand on his chin in thought. Subaru had turned to him because he figured he might as well try, but it was only natural that Reinhard did not just magically have the solution to something like that.

"Don't worry about it." Subaru waved him off. "That was too much to hope for. Anyway, if we could just get a little bit of data about how much effect Liliana's singing has..."

"There is no need for that—I was just blessed with one."

"Huh? Blessed with what, a child? You've got to be kidding me, right?"

That was the first thing that came to mind at that turn of phrase.

Smiling awkwardly at Subaru's reaction, Reinhard looked closely at Liliana. Liliana seemed to writhe under his gaze, but he ignored her reaction.

"That is surprising. She is indeed a bearer of the blessing of telepathy."

"I'm more surprised by you than her blessing, honestly. Huh? Wait, what did you just say? You were granted something?"

"This isn't the time for joking around. Put simply, the telepathy blessing is one that allows the bearer to convey their feelings to others. Ordinarily, it just acts on a level that allows one to share one's thoughts with another who is particularly intimate, but…singing? I had never considered that possibility before."

Reinhard was purely admiring the power of Liliana's songs, but Subaru still had not scooped up his jaw from where it had dropped when Reinhard started explaining the blessing. He had called Reinhard's strength a cheat and beyond superhuman before, but this was just too much. He was way too beloved by God, the world, or fate. Whatever was responsible, simply granting the blessing the moment Reinhard desired it…

"———"

When he thought it through that far, Subaru noticed something tripping him up.

There was not really any way for him to describe what had just happened other than by saying Reinhard had received the blessing he desired on the spot. In and of itself, that was an incredibly envious position. But it also felt like something was tremendously wrong about it in a way that he couldn't quite place.

Either way, though—

"Nay! Please entrust this task to me! I shall surely follow through. Have no fear. I shall do nothing but sing. Nothing but…sing. Just singing…right? There's nothing else, right? Right? Right, Lady Priscilla?!"

"Where'd that concern come from all of a sudden…? Anyway, for now I suppose we can leave the Archbishop of Wrath to Priscilla and Liliana? And we've got Reinhard's seal of approval that she should be able to counter Wrath's Authority."

"I guess I can accept that. Everyone else okay with it?"

Ignoring Liliana, whose face was blinking back and forth between stop and go, Subaru checked around the table, with Anastasia responding for the group. There was still some reservation on everyone else's face, but they all seemed ready to accept it on a theoretical level.

The only one who looked entirely at ease was Priscilla herself.

"How absurd. I'm the one whose life is being staked on this diva's voice. Do you really believe I would risk my fate on something I did not trust completely? Her singing is worthy of that much."

When she put it that way, Subaru really didn't have anything else he could say. It was true, after all. Priscilla was the one who had seen the potential in Liliana, and she was the one who would be fighting Sirius while entrusting her fate to that potential. There was no mistaking that she was heroic in her own right and excelled in ingenuity and prudence despite how she spoke and behaved.

"Still, though, I want to do whatever I can to reduce the risks..."

"Why? It would never happen, even hypothetically, but were I to die it would only benefit your master. Her greatest obstacle would disappear without any effort on her part. Shouldn't you welcome that?"

"Don't you dare assume that."

"———"

Subaru immediately shot down Priscilla's intimation with a cold look. Trying to win by increasing the odds of another candidate's dying in order to boost Emilia's chances would be the lowest of the low. He didn't want anyone to die. And he would certainly not welcome that result if it truly did come to pass.

"You got what you wanted, right, Princess? Let's just let it be now... Princess?"

"...It's nothing, I was just caught unawares by a thought I had not considered."

"———"

"What, are you sulking? How cute for such a hulking man."

"...It's not that at all."

Looking away, Al propped his head up on his arm as if it was no concern of his. Priscilla harrumphed and leaned back in her seat, done speaking.

Finally the discussion could move on to the next topic.

"After several twists and turns...as for the other groupings...I have a suggestion. The first district, where Lust is waiting, the one we all have a bone to pick with—that is probably where the enemy's greatest concentration of forces will be. The Archbishop as well as two cultists. And possibly a slew of demi-beasts, too."

"You suspect that they are all Lust's personal forces?"

"Given how the demi-beasts look, it seems a safe bet they are connected to Lust. As for the two cultists..."

"—They are most likely sword masters being manipulated by a technique to control the dead: corpse soldiers," Wilhelm interjected.

Subaru was a little bit surprised that he'd volunteered that information himself.

"Corpse soldiers," Julius murmured to himself. "I've seen note of them in past records. The result of a deplorable, forbidden technique from the era of the Demi-human War. The witch Sphinx's taboo magic."

"She has claimed to be a member of the royal family who is long dead and claimed to have the dragon's blood that is locked away in the castle. Even if the claim about dragon blood is in fact merely a bluff, she does appear to have an extreme obsession with the kingdom and its history. It is possible she is capable of employing forbidden techniques that have been sealed away in the kingdom's dark past."

"It feels as though that logic is a tad of a reach… Can you truly be sure?"

As expected of Julius, he was latching on precisely where Subaru would rather he not dig too deeply.

He could always just say that one of the corpse soldiers was Theresia, and that would be proof enough, but that was exactly the point that Wilhelm had asked him not to bring up around Reinhard. This meant Subaru was stuck trying to figure out a way to get out of it without saying that too explicitly.

"—If they were corpse soldiers, then the one I was duking it out with had to be Eight-Arms Kurgan."

And it was Garfiel sitting right next to him who came to the rescue. Garfiel had his arms crossed and was scowling with his teeth bared.

"A swordsman that strong with eight arms…there ain't anyone else it could be. Not that I can think of, at least. You got anyone else, Finest Knight?"

"You fought with them personally, so if you say so, then I would defer to your experience. Among the many-armed tribes, it is exceedingly rare for one to be born with eight arms. If that someone was also extraordinary strong, then…"

"There ain't anyone else it can be. And that other woman's gotta be on the same level as him."

"Corpse soldiers, you say? And going so far as to use a woman as well. Lust is a rather detestable opponent."

Miraculously, Garfiel and Julius had managed to advance the conversation just enough without dwelling on Theresia's true identity. Reinhard's brow furrowed a bit at the point about one of the corpse soldiers being a woman, though—

"There's no mistaking they are using corpse soldiers. Fortunately, they don't seem to be able to turn the whole graveyard on us. There's either some kind of limit on numbers, or maybe Lust just prefers quality over quantity."

"And the taboo technique of corpse soldiers that disgraces the dead is a fitting technique given the Archbishop of Lust's self-avowed interests. I see. It is painful to wrap my head around the possibility, but there is a logic to it. I can accept it."

"The convincing piece of evidence being how terrible her personality is is a pretty grim indictment, though," Subaru said, grimacing bitterly.

There were similar expressions around the table as they all nodded in agreement.

Capella was the one who had conducted the citywide broadcasts, so she was the one cultist everyone could immediately recognize as being utterly twisted and rotten to the core. And as luck would have it, that shared recognition was enough to convince the room.

"Anyway, back to what I was going to say before… I wanted to leave dealing with Lust to Wilhelm, and if possible Garfiel as well."

"Wh—? General?!"

Once he decided the room was ready, Subaru put forth his original proposal: sending Wilhelm and Garfiel to deal with Lust.

Their reactions were polar opposites. Wilhelm nodded quietly, having already expected this, while Garfiel, who was completely caught by surprise, opened his eyes wide in shock. From his perspective, that was a natural reaction—

"You're going to go save Lady Emilia, aren't you, General? In that case, I should…"

"I'm grateful you'd say that, and trust me, it'd be incredibly reassuring to have you with me. But I think this is our best answer from a force-distribution perspective… Besides, you have your own scores to settle, right?"

"______"

Garfiel fell silent. That line hit right where it hurt.

Wilhelm was not the only one with a connection to Lust and her troops. The man who had been changed into a black dragon by Lust's Authority was someone Garfiel knew. And also, Lust's subordinate, the corpse soldier Theresia, had—

"Mimi got it bad, and her two brothers shared it, too. All three of them have been unconscious since fighting to get away from the Muse Company— You get it, right?"

The blessing of the grim reaper was extraordinarily powerful. Just a single wound would continue eating away at someone until their life force gave out. There was no escape from that death without defeating the person who possessed the blessing. Garfiel had his reasons to be fighting on that battlefield just like Wilhelm did.

"As you are all aware, my master, Lady Crusch, is currently suffering due to the effect of Lust's contemptible ability. As Lady Crusch's vassal, I have a duty to fight for my master."

"If possible, I was hoping to learn more about this supposed link to dragon blood from Lust. Was that also part of why you're rarin' to go there, Mr. Wilhelm?" asked Anastasia.

"It is as you suggest. Because of that, I would like you all to leave the slaying of Lust to me…"

Wilhelm's swirling bloodlust filled the room. Everyone hesitated to argue with his unshakable resolve and his loyalty to his master.

All except for his one blood relation.

"—I am against this proposal."

"…Reinhard…"

"You are not calm and collected, Grandfather. I can understand your hostility toward the Archbishop who so grievously harmed Lady Crusch, of course. However, that anger will only cloud your sword strikes."

"…You would argue that I cannot adequately serve Lady Crusch while insufficiently calm?"

"Out of concern for Lady Crusch, we cannot afford to fail to defeat

Lust. In that case, it should be I who takes that role. At the very least, I will not fall behind the enemy in terms of composure."

Reinhard's logic was sound and based in a desire to resolve things in the surest way possible. And it was true enough that Wilhelm was not entirely coolheaded about the fight that lay before him.

But when Reinhard said it, Wilhelm's—no, the Sword Devil's lips curled into a sneer. It was by no means a kindly old man's smile—it was the grin of a ferocious beast.

"My not being calm and collected is only natural, Reinhard."

"Yes, but…"

"Who do you think I am? What do you think your grandfather is? I am the man hailed as the Sword Devil. A hopeless man stuck in the middle of transforming himself into a mere blade, and unable to follow through with conviction, ended up falling in love with a woman. But it is precisely because of that half-heartedness that I never once held back in the slightest in the face of what needed to be done."

His fierce grin had banished his gentle expression. And now that he had broken free of that facade, what appeared was the face of a devil starved for blood and the clash of steel. The devil who was bewitched by the blade, his blue eyes only ever seeking a single other light—

"When I've decided to bare my sword, my heart burns with an unbearable heat. Not coolheaded? That is how I always am on the battlefield. And yet I've still lived to this ripe old age. I have no interest in rotting away without fulfilling my duty to my master. Your concern is neither needed nor desired."

"That argument is mere idealism…"

"Conviction is nothing but idealism backed by a resolve to see things through to the very end. Having persisted fourteen years, my rusted blade was still sharp enough to claim vengeance for my wife—it is too soon for me to sheathe it for the last time."

It was Wilhelm's conviction that had avenged Reinhard's grandmother in the Battle of the White Whale. And there was nothing Reinhard could say in response to that. However, he averted his eyes, still unable to fully accept it.

"The battlefield that needs you is elsewhere, Reinhard," Wilhelm continued.

"And where exactly might that be?"

"—Please take Reinhard with you in the battle you are about to embark on, Sir Subaru." The Sword Devil looked Subaru in the eye. "You will have to face Greed in order to recover Lady Emilia. Please have Reinhard be your blade for that battle."

"Wilhelm..."

Subaru scratched his cheek and sighed softly at Wilhelm's proposal. He then turned to face Reinhard and met his blue-eyed gaze.

"I was going to get to that next, but...yeah, I want you to help me fight Greed. There's no way we can beat that crazy narcissist without you."

It was possible to generally guess the Authorities of the Archbishops from the phenomena that happened around them, and based on that, the Authority that Regulus had was on a whole other level in terms of lethality. There was no way to explain what happened as being the result of anything other than something absurd like invincibility. He didn't want to believe it was *true* invincibility, with no weakness or opening of any kind, but—

"We need someone strong enough to fight Regulus head-to-head in order to figure out how to defeat his apparent invulnerability. In terms of offense and defense, if we compare them head-on, he's almost certainly the most powerful of the Archbishops by far. So I want you to lend me your strength."

"———"

"If you frame it as me planning to slam invincibility and the most powerful force into each other to see what happens, that makes it sound like some weird test of strength."

Pair the illogical with the illogical and the absurd with the absurd.

Even if he wanted to fight fire with fire, that was not usually an option, so the one time he actually got the chance to do it, Subaru was not going to be picky about it. He was sure that that was the best choice.

"An opponent who is unaffected by attacks of any kind, you say?

Certainly, if there were a monster like that, then I would be the best choice. But..."

"—I'm asking you, too. Could you please help the general and Lady Emilia?"

Reinhard was still unsure, even after hearing about Regulus's invulnerability, but to his surprise, Garfiel stood up and lowered his head. He kept his forehead pressed to the table as he bowed low in order to plead with Reinhard.

"I'm a failure as a guard. Since coming to this city, I haven't been able to carry out any of the roles I was given, the things I had to do no matter what. Because of that, on the biggest stage of this huge fight, I'm here desperately trying to repay the debts I owe other people instead of being able to fight for my own camp...so please!"

Garfiel's fangs were trembling as he accepted his own weakness and the results of his own failures.

"Garfiel..."

The red-haired Sword Saint fell silent for a moment—

"—Then give me your word. Just as you have your expectations of me, I will hold you to the same standards. Give me your word that you will surely follow through on your end as well."

"Ah...yeah. Yeah, leave it to me! Between me and the Sword Devil, there ain't no enemy that can stand in our way!" Garfiel straightened up, his fangs grinding.

"Okay. Then I will trust in your and my grandfather's victory—and I shall become Subaru's blade." Reinhard nodded.

"——"

And like that, the Sword Devil and the Sword Saint—grandfather and grandson, two fellow swordsmen—exchanged gazes and shared a firm nod. With Reinhard finally agreeing to join his fight, Subaru was sure he wouldn't feel more confident even if he had an army a million strong at his back.

"Sorry for the selfish request, Reinhard."

"It's fine. I don't mind. No matter the battlefield, I will always do my best. So if I can help you and Lady Emilia in the process, then all the better."

"I really am sorry for always relying on you. I know I've already relied on you far too much because of how strong you are, but…I'll do my best to make up for anything you might be lacking, so you can count on me."

"———"

For a second, Reinhard fell silent, and his eyes widened. Subaru cocked his head at the odd reaction, but Reinhard just shook his head and chuckled softly.

"No, it's nothing to you, I imagine— Yes, I'll be counting on you to take care of whatever I cannot."

"—? Yeah, feel free to get your hopes up, 'cause I know I've got high hopes for you."

With that, they had confirmed the groups that would be attacking the first three control towers. That left just one—

"—By process of elimination, Ricardo and I will be tasked with Gluttony." Julius spoke stiffly, drawing everyone's attention.

As he said, of everyone who had gathered in city hall who could fight, the only ones left who could face Gluttony were he and Ricardo. But—

"…Are you all right, Julius? You've seemed a bit off for a while now."

"My apologies for worrying you. However, I am well. If we are talking about physical condition, then I cannot really complain with Subaru here."

"Hey, what's that supposed to mean?"

"Naturally, a consideration for the state of your right leg. Please don't snap at me like that. I had no intention of getting into it with you in this moment."

"Mrgh…"

Subaru felt a little sad getting parried so flatly.

Anastasia was not the only one who felt Julius was acting rather strangely. Subaru did as well. But he couldn't tell what the source of the strange behavior was. And Julius declined to answer the deeper question as he nodded gracefully, a resolute gleam in his eyes.

"Ricardo and I shall take the remaining Archbishop, Gluttony, an opponent we encountered at city hall and have a connection with— In other times, he is an opponent you or Sir Wilhelm would have preferred to have drawn, but having been entrusted with him anyway, rest assured that we will prevail."

"...Yeah, I guess so."

Julius said aloud exactly what Subaru had been thinking.

—Defeating the Archbishop of Gluttony was precisely what Subaru had wanted to accomplish himself. And Wilhelm, with Crusch suffering on the floor above, was in the same position as Subaru.

Gluttony's Authority, the ability to consume memories and names—when Subaru thought of how Rem had suffered due to that power and was even now in a wakeless slumber, he wanted nothing more than to crush Gluttony with his own two hands. Punch, kick, stomp, and make that cultist regret everything until there was nothing but tearful pleas for forgiveness—that was what he wanted to do.

And he was yielding that chance to someone else—

"I really don't want to leave it to anyone else. You know I wanted to bring Rem back myself. I believed that was my role."

"——"

"But still, if I don't get a choice about it, if I have to leave it to someone else, then I want to leave it to you. Don't get the wrong idea, this was process of elimination... Still, you are the person I trust with this. As much as I don't like it, you are one of the few people I could bear to have take my place."

Rem's memories and her very existence were still being held hostage.

Emilia was being held hostage and was waiting to be rescued.

They were both precious to Subaru, both people who had to be saved no matter what. He wanted to be able to show off for both of them.

—Because Subaru was Emilia's knight and Rem's hero.

"I'll defeat Greed and bring Emilia back, so I'll let you beat the crap out of Gluttony this time... Don't screw it up."

"—I shall live up to your expectations. This time, this time for sure."

Julius nodded deeply, accepting Subaru's faith in him. The Finest Knight then looked to Wilhelm and nodded slightly.

"Sir Wilhelm."

"Sir Subaru managed to say most everything that I wanted to say. It is true that I cannot forgive Gluttony for what happened… therefore I shall entrust that to you as well, Sir Julius. There are just slightly too many rogues in this city at the moment."

"Agreed. I shall accept your thoughts."

Bathed in Wilhelm's keen battle aura, Julius quietly closed his eyes, taking encouragement from it.

And watching their exchanges quietly, Ricardo opened his toothy mouth wide.

"Man, y'all sure like to talk like I'm not here! Not that it really bothers me, though! And I can't say you're wrong about this bein' the best deployment, either."

"You're the kinda guy who's down for just about anything. And there's nothin' cute about a guy as big as you gettin' all pouty… Take care of Julius, though."

"Don't you worry. You ever known me to tell a lie, Lady Anna?"

"…Could you quit with the names already? I *am* your master."

Ricardo guffawed as Anastasia's cheeks puffed out in a cute pout. Ricardo's black eyes were filled with a pained kindness as he looked down at Anastasia.

"In that case, all the matchups are settled."

Looking around the table, everyone nodded at Subaru's concluding statement.

"The fourth tower, Wrath, will go to the Priscilla-and-Liliana pair. And Al will stay behind for defense… That's all right with you, yes?"

"A fool who would dare try to control people's hearts while I remain on this earth? Absurd. I will grant that empty-headed dunce a fitting punishment."

"I shall sing, sing, and sing, for I am but a mass of flesh whose purpose is naught but to sing. I shan't regret my life, but I shall regret my stage. All right, I can do this. I can feel it now! I've got this!"

"——"

Priscilla was fanning herself as Liliana focused her all on a mysterious sort of auto-suggestion. Al's expression was hidden, but it was clear as day that he had not really come to terms with the situation yet. And it was just as clear that Priscilla had no intention of paying his discomfort any heed. There were still a lot of questions about how their pair was going to work, but they were the ones most confident of success.

"Next is the first district, Garfiel and Wilhelm taking down Lust."

"Yeah! This is gonna be like *Mezoreia's panorama*. I'll grab it all with this fist of mine."

"Please leave it to us—we shall settle things with the corpse soldiers as well."

They had a difficult battle ahead of them, but the two of them probably had the strongest spirits. The Sword Devil Wilhelm fighting out of fealty to his master and for the sake of the beloved wife he had never forgotten. And Garfiel in search of a resolution to the shapeless emotions rumbling around in his soul. They were both setting out for a battle with things they could not concede hanging in the balance.

"And the second district. Julius and Ricardo, you two are taking on Gluttony."

"It is the role I've been entrusted. If I cannot live up to that trust, then I can hardly call myself a knight."

"My family got hit real hard by those bastards. I'll knock 'em around 'til they're beggin' for mercy."

When it came to connections with the cultists, the two of them had been relatively far removed from them until today. But having people close to them fall in battle and having been entrusted with the feelings of Subaru and their other comrades, they had more than enough reason to fight. They would be able to wield their swords freely.

They were comrades with whom Subaru had walked the fine line between life and death before. He did not need a reason to be able to trust them.

"And finally, Reinhard and I will take Greed in the third district. I'll be counting on you."

"—Yes, leave it to me. And I'll be counting on you as well, Subaru."

Reinhard nodded easily. However, that alone was more than enough reassurance, proof that his mind was already clear and focused even before the fight began in earnest.

As they were about to take the fight to the cultists, they couldn't afford any mistakes. Subaru pointedly straightened up and stood tall. And with the deployments all confirmed, Anastasia clapped her hands.

"In that case, if everything's decided, all that's left is handing out the conversation mirrors… We have three. Assuming I keep one here at the base, who's going to take the other two?"

"If possible, I'd like the Wrath team to have one. As for the other… either the Lust or Gluttony team would be fine."

"Why's that?"

"Wrath's Authority is affecting the entire city. That being gone or not changes the situation in a big way, so it would be best to get that report as soon as possible."

Hearing that, everyone nodded. As for the remaining one, he figured it was fine for either of the two remaining non-Greed teams to take it.

The reason for that—

"Put bluntly, Reinhard is handling Greed. His Authority seems to be some kind of conditional invincibility, so while I don't want to be overly optimistic, there is a nonzero chance of us finishing up with him real quick. If that happens, I want Reinhard to be able to join up with whichever team needs the most help."

"And depending on how the conditions in the city change, we can give directions to the general populace from here using the broadcast metia. That's another thing that becomes a more viable option once Wrath is down," Otto added.

"That's quite prudent. You're gettin' awfully reliable, ain't ya, Natsuki?"

Anastasia smiled in admiration before tossing the mirror in her hand over to Priscilla, who deftly caught it with her fan and rolled it over to Liliana.

"Wh-wh-wha—?!"

"You take it, diva. I do not carry anything heavier than silverware."

"You lazy… As if that fan of yours isn't heavy enough with all those decorations."

"Don't be ridiculous. Can you not appreciate its elegant design?

Do you not comprehend the beauty of this chasing and engraving? It does not begin to compare to that shoddy item lying there. Do not dare hold it to the same standard as mere silverware."

"So it *is* heavier than silverware..."

Priscilla's obstinacy aside, it was decided that Liliana would take the conversation mirror. After watching her slip it into the bosom of her small outfit, they gave the last one to Wilhelm. It was Julius who made that decision, sliding it across the table to the older gentleman.

"In consideration for the differing number of enemies in both locations, it would be best for the Lust team to have a means of instant contact. I don't believe either of you is likely to fail, but please report in if you deem the situation to be dire."

"Understood. Though I agree that such a situation is unlikely to occur."

Wilhelm slipped the final mirror into his breast pocket in accordance with Julius's suggestion.

With that, they had divided up the squads and distributed the items they had to pass around. They had made their preparations for the decisive battle.

"Let's wait a little bit, and then all of us should leave at once. This is the official start of our plan to take back the city," Subaru said.

There was tension in everyone's face as they all nodded. There was a quiet weight closing in on them that felt wrong to Subaru.

"Do you guys not get the feeling that us looking all serious and depressed like this is just going to lead to everything going wrong?"

"That's another odd thing for you to say, Mr. Natsuki. What are you talking about?" Otto responded with a bitter expression.

"It's not odd at all. It's important. It's an iron rule of life that no matter how many or how few people you manage to bring together, a group with no morale and no unity is just a mob. So what do we do to keep that from happening? Maybe have everyone say something all at once or something? Even if it's just for show."

Subaru stood up and clapped his hands together loudly. Then he held his fist up for all of them to see.

"Let's do this, guys! We're gonna throw everyone who gets in our way out of the city! We'll show those cultists who's the boss and get our happy ending back!"

"______"

Hearing that, everyone looked at one another, and then, a half beat later, they held their hands up one after the other.

"Ooooaaah!"

They all raised their voices, and Subaru's lips cracked into a smile as he felt the electric excitement crackling over his skin.

Their cries were all over the place, they felt aimless, and it was hard to say those gathered were really united given the mixture of fists and palms raised in the air. But these were Subaru Natsuki's comrades. The people he would fight alongside in order to retake the city. It was hard to come by a group as fine as they.

They had been beaten up good, cornered badly enough that for a moment there it had looked like they were not going to be able to recover. But they had returned to fight.

—The final decisive battle for the Water Gate City was beginning.

"—We're gonna win this fight!"

And the meeting of the round table ended with that final, fittingly Subaru-esque line.

7

—Having finished her secret conversation with Al, Emilia had returned to the bedroom and disposed of the ice sculpture that she had used as a body double. Nothing seemed to have been disturbed, so it appeared her absence had gone unnoticed. Or else they had been thrown off by the finely crafted ice sculpture.

Emilia regretfully returned the sculpture to mana as she appreciated her handiwork.

"...I'm surprised. I did not expect you to return."

"Eep!"

All of a sudden, a voice called out from behind her, causing Emilia to jolt in shock before turning around. When she did, she saw #184 standing at the entrance, looking right at her.

She had last seen her cleaning up the room Regulus had destroyed, but there she was, her eyes narrowing as she watched Emilia panic before letting out a small sigh.

"You went to such effort to leave a replacement behind. Did you have a change of heart?"

"What? A replacement? I'm not sure what you mean. I've been resting here the whole time since I was tired. Right here in bed... Ah, it's cold! Ah, I mean it's not cold at all!"

"——"

The bed was absolutely freezing from having an ice sculpture lying on it the whole time she was gone, so it was practically rejecting her body warmth. But admitting that would only confirm her lie, so she resolutely endured the cold and went to lie down in the bed.

"See, I've been here all along. I would never have done something like run away."

"...Yes, of course. My mistake. But that would truly be odd. Why did you not simply run away while you could?" #184 asked quietly.

"...If I did that, it would have been bad for you and the other wives and the people in the city," Emilia responded, sticking her legs out of the covers and sitting on the edge of the bed.

#184's eyes were cool and emotionless—but something about her felt off to Emilia. At first it was just a vague feeling of unease, but it gradually came into a fuzzy focus. The emotion hidden deep in her eyes looked almost like a desperate plea.

"Did you by chance want me to run away?"

"——"

"But why? If I did that, then it would be bad for you and the others."

Thinking back on their exchange, Emilia started to wonder if #184 had noticed the ice sculpture left on the bed but chosen not to report it to Regulus. By doing that, she would delay the realization that Emilia was gone, which would've given her more time to get away.

In reality, Emilia had had no intention of fleeing, so her effort had gone to waste, but—

"No, if you hadn't hidden it for me, Regulus would have found out I was sneaking around investigating. So thank you anyway..."

"Please don't thank me. In the end it did not amount to anything—I had intended to muster just a little bit of bravery at the end of my life, but even that was meaningless."

"———"

With that, #184 tightly clenched her arms. Her hands were visibly trembling. Emilia realized that her delaying the report she was supposed to give had taken every last bit of her courage.

Regulus had casually tried to kill #184 out of nothing more than a mild irritation. If that was an everyday sort of occurrence, then she and all the other wives were living day in and day out with death hanging right over their heads. How much courage had it taken to endure that level of terror that had become an everyday phenomenon?

"Why did you come back?"

"—Um."

"It would have been better if I had just been consumed by his anger after you never returned. Whatever became of the city, whatever became of us. This just means it will go on and on. This unchanging, never-ending time will just continue until it all ends."

#184 spoke fervently, half clinging to Emilia, half cursing her. Biting her lip, Emilia stood up.

"In that case, if you could stand up once, then let's try again together. I haven't given up yet."

"I can't. I gathered what little willpower I had left and got nothing in return. Just thinking about trying again makes everything inside me freeze... Anything more is impossible."

#184 shook her head desperately as Emilia watched, unable to say anything. Her eyes locked on to Emilia as she continued, the light in her eyes frozen—no, dead.

"You are free to decide that you will not give up. However, I will never have that choice ever again. And I'm sure the other women in this hell are the same."

"———"

"I was just a normal girl living in a small village in a mountain valley with my family. In order to marry me, he eradicated my mother and father, my siblings, my neighbors, and all the villagers who merely knew my name and face. All his wives have experienced similar fates."

Her eyes dead and dull the whole while, #184 spoke of what had happened when Regulus demanded her hand in marriage.

It was a horrific, almost unbelievable story, but the only ones who could laugh it off as a joke would be those fortunate enough not to know Regulus. He was more than capable of committing such heinous acts. That was unmistakably something he would do. He had created a paradise of his own making, served by the wives he had forcibly wedded.

"...Regulus said there were two hundred and ninety-one..."

"Yes. And two hundred and thirty-eight have already passed away, leaving only the fifty-three here in this city."

"Those wives who passed away..."

"Do you really need me to spell it out?"

Her hoarse response scoffed at Emilia's question. No, it was more self-deprecating than that.

#184 was exhausted with existing and with the curse that had consumed their lives. She had reached the present day at the cost of her very will to resist. And after trudging her way through those terror-filled days, she'd stumbled upon evidence of Emilia, the one whom Regulus had chosen to be his new wife, running away. What had #184 felt in that moment?

Her statement that she would never have the will to resist again had surely been true in a far deeper sense than Emilia realized.

Emilia had only just begun to scratch the surface of what it took to spend a life with Regulus, but for #184—for all the women here, it was something that had already shaved away pieces of their very souls.

"——"

Though it had not been intentional, Emilia realized just how important a thing she had shattered, and realizing that, she lost sight of what she could possibly say to #184. Even if she said something baseless in the heat of the moment, it would never reach this woman. She frantically searched for the words, anything she could possibly say to reassure or bolster #184.

She was desperately, desperately searching, but she could not come up with anything. There didn't seem to be a right answer. No ideal or essential wisdom.

No matter how she looked, she could not find the words to tell #184 the thing she most wanted to convey. Emilia was terrified from the depths of her heart, as if it would all slip away from the palm of her hand. A cold despair crept into her heart.

And at just that instant—

"—Um, can everyone actually hear me through this? Mic test, mic test. One, two. One, two."

—the voice Emilia most wanted to hear rang out from above, as if extending a hand to her.

8

It was a faltering performance. Even if a listener was inclined to be generous, it could not be called impressive.

"It looks like this is actually broadcasting, then. First of all, let me apologize for surprising you. I imagine a lot of you were worried or steeling yourself wondering what you would be told next. But please don't worry. I'm not a member of the Witch Cult."

Even though it would have been fine to lie, it was brutally honest even where it did not need to be, not even hiding the sort of thing that would cause the people listening to feel more anxious. And yet, at the very end of it all, it said, as if to kick away everyone's unease—

"—But even so. Even with all that, I can't run away from this. So I'm going to fight. That's the sort of person I am."

It was a shock and almost certainly exactly what Emilia wanted most in that moment. It was the thing that the people of the city most wanted in that moment.

"I want to believe. I'm weak. And pathetic. But I haven't given up yet. Please let me believe that I'm not the only weakling who doesn't know how to give up."

Ahhh, it really is not fair at all.

Trembling and meandering but obviously his best effort, it made anyone listening almost want to cry. It almost felt like the speaker's pulse could be heard through his voice, even though that was obviously impossible. It nearly brought tears to her eyes.

"Or am I really the only one?"

—No, no you're not.

"Am I the only one who can still keep going…who still wants to fight?"

—No, I'm okay. I can keep going.

"I'm not, right?"

—No, you're not. Absolutely, from the bottom of my heart, you're not alone.

"You can still fight, right? You won't let the weakness consume you, right?"

—I can hear your voice, so I'm okay. It's fine. I'm not scared of anything.

"—I am Subaru Natsuki, the spirit user who defeated the Witch Cult Archbishop of Sloth."

Just hearing that alone was enough to blow away all the cold despair encroaching on Emilia's heart.

Even though just a little while earlier it had felt like she had fallen into an inescapable dark abyss. Even though she had been unable to move forward or backward, cursing her own powerlessness. Just hearing that voice had relieved her. Had satisfied her.

Because he had said it. Emilia's knight had said it.

"—Just leave everything else to me!"

He had said to leave it to him. So no matter how dark things might seem, he would blow it all away. No matter how impossible or absurd, he would overcome all the odds. There was no doubt he would succeed.

That was why—

* * *

"...That voice just now..."

"—That was my knight. He's always *really* trying his best."

The broadcast ended as suddenly as it had begun, leaving a stunned #184 in turmoil. And standing before her, Emilia held her hand to her heart and smiled softly.

"______"

Looking into Emilia's eyes, #184 opened her own eyes wide, and she was at a loss for words. It was because of how Emilia looked as she spoke about her knight, but Emilia did not realize it. She then looked #184 in the eye as she continued.

"I won't run. I won't disappear and leave you all here."

"—! Why?"

"You shared your painful past with me, as well as what you're feeling now. But as scared as you must have been, you still tried to help me."

Even if it was only once, even if she felt broken down and lost, she had fought back; she had conquered her fear even if only for an instant. So Emilia would do the same—she would do her best not to bend or break.

"I want you and everyone else to be able to find happiness. A wedding is a ceremony to bring happiness to two people who love each other very much. The bride has to be happy, too."

When she thought of marriage, she imagined a scene of blissful happiness between two people who adored each other. In the back of her mind, she saw the image of Fortuna and Geuse—they had not been married, so they never became husband and wife, but that was what Emilia wished for them. For their sakes, Emilia dearly wanted them to have been able to be married. Their relationship, the way they loved each other—that was surely what a proper marriage should be like.

"I know people who loved each other but weren't able to get married. And to this day, it makes my heart hurt to think of them."

That was why—

"—I can't stand the idea of a marriage that isn't happy. I don't want that sort of relationship for anyone."

Just thinking of it made her stomach roil. She hated the very idea of it. Emilia fundamentally refused to give in to something like that, so she would not give up on the city or on #184 or any of the women here. She would carry them all in her own hands. And if that was not enough, she would borrow someone else's hands, too—someone like her knight.

"Th-that is a lovely thought, but…as I said before, if there were anything to be done, it would be for you to escape alone."

"Alone…? No, that isn't what we should do at all."

Emilia shook her head, gently rejecting #184's statement.

#184 had revealed she was alone in the world, with no one left to turn to—but that wasn't true. Not any longer. It was none other than Emilia's knight who had revealed that when his voice could be heard all throughout the city.

But she had no intention of just leaving everything to him.

"I was never alone. That was dangerous; I almost forgot that."

"What are you planning?"

Even though she was insistent that it was none of her concern, #184 was still asking what Emilia's plan was. Seeing her riled emotions, her frozen emotions stirring into life, Emilia could not help an odd feeling that that was the same sort of thing Subaru saw.

To #184's shock, her response was—"We're going to hold a wedding ceremony."

CHAPTER 5

THE PERSON I ONE DAY FALL IN LOVE WITH

1

The preparations for the ceremony in the chapel continued apace as planned.

Fortunately, Regulus's irritation had not exploded in the chapel, and the austere, dignified building was still standing. The gleaming decorations for the ceremony were safely in place.

Having decided to face the wedding ceremony, Emilia was in the wardrobe room getting her hair styled to look the part of a bride by #184 and a couple of Regulus's other wives.

It had been a long time since she'd had her hair set in a style this complex. Puck used to tweak her hair every morning, but she had neglected it ever since he had vanished. She mostly went without doing anything complicated to her hair, excepting the rare occasions when Annerose did something fancy for her.

Her long silver hair was braided and carefully done up. Her outfit was adorned with accessories to accentuate the beautiful, pure white of her dress without verging on ostentation. With that, Emilia's bridal makeover was complete.

Seeing herself in the mirror, she was amazed by their skill.

It was quite different from her usual appearance. She mostly just kept things simple and tied her hair back without much effort unless

Subaru was helping out that day, and she usually made a point of not wearing accessories in order to be able to move more freely, but her current hairstyle and accessories were solely focused on enhancing her ladylike allure.

"It feels like this is all just wasted on me, though..."

The women who had helped her change all sighed heavily at that.

Just like #184, they had all said nothing more than the bare minimum necessary while helping her change. Feeling inadequate when she heard their heavy sighs, Emilia straightened her back. Her silver hair shimmered like moonlight streaming against her slender back.

"Let's go. Be careful to not upset our husband," a tall, red-haired woman said before taking the lead, with Emilia following behind her. #184, who had been ordered to accompany the procession, was helping carry the train of her dress.

"——"

She intentionally kept her expression motionless, but there was a faint unease in her eyes. As the only person who had heard Emilia declare she would face the ceremony in her own way, she had especially turbulent emotions. She had no idea at all what Emilia had in mind for the coming ceremony, but she had apparently chosen not to mention her unease to Regulus. And that was enough. Her simple presence was enough to support Emilia's resolve.

—In the chapel, the guests present were already gathered, waiting for Emilia's arrival.

"——"

There was a red carpet over the central path, with the guests beautifully arrayed along either side of the carpet. They were all Regulus's wives—fifty women—every last one besides the three in Emilia's procession. And waiting in front of the altar at the end of the carpeted aisle was Regulus, standing calmly in a white tuxedo.

The red-haired woman led Emilia directly to him. Emilia glanced at the expressions of the women lining the aisle but found nothing more than calculated, practiced, expressionless faces.

Beneath the gaze of this masked audience, Emilia approached the altar. The women in her procession stepped away, taking their places among the women lining the aisle. All except for #184, who moved to the opposite side of the altar, a faint tension on her face as she began officiating the wedding ceremony.

Her body still facing #184 and the altar, Emilia turned to look at Regulus.

"I'm surprised. The previous dress was magnificent, but this wedding gown is truly unmatched. My eyes were not mistaken when I first saw you. We really are the most fitting pair in the world."

Regulus nodded to himself, satisfied with Emilia's appearance. He brushed back his white hair.

"Still, seeing this, I can see I was right to leave the seat of #79 open. I had a feeling that there would someday be someone worthy to take it. And the confidence and decisiveness to trust in that decision and follow through are quite amazing, if I do say so myself. Believing in yourself through thick and thin is not something just anyone can do."

"About that number… Why was there an open seat?"

Now that she had entered the chapel and was standing before the altar, the first words out of Emilia's mouth were a question. Her question clashed heavily with the mood of the ceremony and didn't complement Regulus or his self-satisfied, flowery rhetoric. But the question didn't dampen his mood. He merely cocked his head.

"Hmm? Ah, that. Previously, there was another woman I set eyes upon who I thought would be fitting for that number. Unfortunately, before we could be wed, I judged her to be unsuitable. But when it came to the most important point of appearance, she was incredibly close to my ideal. I left the seat unfilled in order to remember her, out of a sense of lingering attachment, I suppose…but thanks to that, I was able to meet you. Truly, ours was a fated encounter."

"Before…"

As Regulus spoke of fate, Emilia was hung up on another part of what he'd said.

Something that felt very off. A clear oddity that came whenever she interacted with him; an invisible unease that was gradually coming into view, but one she still could not quite pin down.

And as she was thinking that, Regulus adjusted the collar of his matching tuxedo.

"Well then, shall we exchange our vows? Unfortunately, we will have to settle for a shortened ceremony without official witnesses, but you don't mind, do you? Such an important ceremony is not for fussing over details but for cementing our binding love. Fretting over appearances only to neglect the substance of it all is truly nonsensical, and yet, it is a rather trite and common mistake. Naturally, I would never stoop to such folly."

#184 began her preparations behind the altar as Regulus's torrent continued unabated.

#184 performed the preparations that the officiant was normally supposed to take care of with a practiced ease that indicated this was not the first of Regulus's weddings that she had presided over.

"Obsessing over appearances and losing sight of the point is just absurd. Form over substance? It's all the more unsightly because people like that don't even realize that everyone is laughing at them behind their back. Though I suppose that by living in ignorance, they are happier for it."

Regulus did not even pay any attention to #184 and her sadly practiced ease.

She seemed something like the leader of the wives. And from the fact that Regulus had tried to kill her on a whim, it was clear that he did not view his wives as actual people.

It was a little late to be reaching that conclusion there, but she simply couldn't forgive his revolting behavior.

"—Hey, Regulus. There are a few things I would like to tell you before the ceremony."

Because of that, she had a declaration for him while she was standing there, face-to-face with him.

#184's face tensed at that. There was a slight wave of unease spreading among the wives lining the pews as well.

"That's true. Once we've exchanged vows, we are man and wife. There are things that can only be discussed before that."

But unexpectedly, Regulus responded with an approving nod.

"In fact, I also have something I should disclose about our upcoming married life. It could wait until after the ceremony, but it is important to be mentally prepared when embarking on something this important. It would be a tragedy for a marriage to suffer the fate of 'This wasn't what I had imagined.' In order to avoid that, we should both freely share our thoughts. As future husband and wife and as individuals. Right?"

"Yes, exactly. It's *really* important since we are individuals."

"Yes! Fantastic! It seems like we can truly understand each other. Then, I have insisted on a few promises from my other wives, so I suppose I should start there. Don't worry, the promises are the same for everyone, so it isn't anything too demanding. If anything, you could even say they are almost natural for a wife." Regulus shrugged humorously as he held up a finger.

"The first is—once we have exchanged vows, you are forbidden to smile."

"—Huh?"

Emilia furrowed her brow, clearly failing to understand the point of his demand. Still holding his finger up, Regulus slowly shook his head.

"You see, I like your face. Truly, I love it. I choose my wives based on their faces. A beautiful, sweet, and alluring face is a requirement for my wives. Every last one of the two hundred and ninety-one wives I've wed has had a beautiful face. And your face is lovely as well. That is why I chose to make you my wife. Do you understand?"

"——"

"This is something I've thought about for a long time, but there are many people in this world who simply do as they please. Far more than you would imagine. It is common to hear tales of lovers or married couples whose love has faded, no? They presumably loved each other at some point, and yet when they actually began living together, various areas where they were incompatible were revealed. Food preferences, habits, hobbies, schedules… There is a truly large number of people who are trash and offer up selfish excuses for falling out of love with someone they supposedly loved once. From the depths of my heart, those people are utterly worthless."

Regulus was still smiling, truly enjoying himself as he spoke about such detestable garbage innocently, unrestrainedly, and with a sense of righteous indignation as well as a lack of understanding for people who made light of love.

"They are—each and every one of them—selfish. You loved them? Then why would you drift apart over something as trifling as mere aesthetic differences? Isn't that the height of foolishness? That is why I choose partners based on their faces. As long as they have a face that I love, my love will never fade, no matter what kind of person they end up being. Because it is their face that I love. As long as that remains, my love will be eternal."

"______"

"Whether they are the sort of person who doesn't pick up their clothes, whether they are a serial murderer who only kills children, whether they can't cook even if their life depended on it, whether they were sold off by their family to pay off a loan, whether they don't make any effort to prevent colors running in the laundry, whether they are the sort of off-kilter person who snuffs the life from small animals, whether their sense of style is absolutely appalling, whether they are obsessed with money, whether they don't bathe and smell like refuse, or whether they were genuinely planning to destroy the whole world—I don't mind."

Regulus pointed to the other fifty-three women in the chapel one after the other as he spoke.

Emilia could not say how many people in the building actually fell into any of those categories. But she could at least say that he was not lying. He would love anyone without distinction.

It was impartial. He was talking about an unquestioning love—proclaiming that he loved each and every one of his wives without qualification.

But Emilia could not see the connection between that treatise on love and the requirement he was asking of her.

"What is the correlation between that and not smiling, though?"

"It's simple. There are people whose normal expression is cute and beautiful, and yet when they smile, they become ugly, aren't there? I can't accept that. That's why. I said 'forbidden to smile,' but really any and all changes of expression are out of bounds. Basically, the thought that your lovely face might become ugly is unbearable to me. It would be a net loss for the world. That is why. So don't laugh.

Don't cry. Don't get mad. Don't rejoice. Just stay like this with your beautiful face, always."

"———"

The second part had been a command, with Regulus grabbing her chin and leaning in so close that she could feel his breath on her skin.

That was the promise Regulus wanted. Though it could hardly be called a promise, since it was clear as day what would happen to anyone who disobeyed.

But if it had simply been a command or a demand of obedience, then at least it would not have a hollow ring to it.

"You said you wouldn't fall out of love with someone as long as you liked their face. So what happened before?"

"Hmm?"

"If I hadn't grabbed her arm, she would have died by your hand."

Emilia pointed to #184 on the other side of the altar. #184 froze as Regulus glanced over at her. And after thinking about it for a second, he nodded slightly, as if remembering.

"Ah, that is an unfortunate misunderstanding. That had nothing to do with a change in my love for her. It was merely that she upset my mood because of her inadequate attention. That was why I thought she should take responsibility for it."

"What? If that isn't fickle, then…"

"No, that isn't it at all. I still love her face. Therefore my love is unchanged. It would remain unchanged even if she was to die. It's a common thing to hear, right? Even when someone you love dies, they will still live on in your heart. Your love will continue on without fading. That is precisely how I feel."

"———"

Holding his hand to his chest, Regulus spoke in the clear voice of a stage actor. It was a perfect, flawless logic that started and ended with him. It left no room for other people's thoughts to intrude. It was entirely flawless in its incompleteness.

In the face of how much he had built up and refined his way of life, Emilia felt completely let down.

Even in that moment, she had wanted to believe. She had wanted to believe that even if he was one of the Archbishops of the Witch Cult, there was some way they could get through to each other.

"By any chance…do you happen to have some complaint with me? If you did, that would be just a little bit vexing. I've made so much effort and compromised on so much out of consideration for you, and you won't even acknowledge it? That's one of those things that make you question a person on a fundamental level. If you ask me, that simply wouldn't happen if you would just spend a little effort thinking about others and putting yourself in their shoes."

When he noticed Emilia's silence, for the first time Regulus's brow furrowed suspiciously.

That probably meant that this was the first time he was truly seeing his bride-to-be. But nothing else changed about how he interacted with her.

"Concern for others is the most basic of basics when dealing with people. And negligence in that most fundamental of things is a sign that you don't view the person you are interacting with as worthy of even that much effort. In other words, it is an action that reveals a contempt for me as an individual. A grievous infringement of my rights. That is not something I can forgive."

A dangerous mood radiated from Regulus's whole body as he spoke. It warped the air around him, and a dangerous air filled the chapel that almost seemed to grip everyone else's lungs.

And standing directly in front of the madman responsible, Emilia inhaled softly.

"—I think that marriage is something *really* happy."

"…Huh?"

"It's a ceremony that gives shape to the thoughts of people who love each other and truly want to be together. It is something that happens when a person finds another person that they *really* love out of all the people in the world, and that person loves them back… and I think that is really amazing."

Regulus looked suspicious as he saw Emilia smiling there in her bridal attire. But while he could not read the situation, the expressions of the women in the pews and #184 behind the altar clouded over.

They were expressions that showed fear of the direction the wedding ceremony was taking and concern for Emilia, who stood at the center of it all.

They were wonderful, kindhearted souls who were worried about what was about to happen to someone else.

"Regulus, why do you refer to your wives by number?"

"A fixation on form of address? That's just another mode of obsessing over form. A truly surface-level relationship. It is simply proof of a lack of confidence in your ability to continue your love without unnecessary trappings. I am not swayed by such trivial self-aggrandizement. My love is unqualified and pure, so that truth will remain without any unneeded elements getting in the way. Isn't that just the truth of the matter?"

"It is—but I don't hate it when Subaru calls me Emilia-tan."

"Subaru…?"

Suddenly hearing something that he could not let pass, Regulus raised his eyebrows in displeasure. But Emilia ignored the dangerous change and continued.

"The way he feels is all there in his voice when he calls me Emilia-tan. And when he sometimes just calls me Emilia, it is always obvious that it's a special moment. I don't think that is meaningless at all. A name should have that sort of thought behind it."

"You spoke very eloquently on that subject, but who exactly is Subaru? That's a person's name, right? A man's name, right? Isn't a woman mentioning the name of another man when she's standing at the altar about to be married just a little too irrational? Even if he was someone you had hardly any interaction with, it would be hurtful to your partner. It is hurtful, in fact. You know that, right?"

"He isn't someone I've had hardly any interaction with. Subaru is my one and only knight, the one who calls my name while saying that he loves me."

"What?!"

Regulus's dreadful aura swelled at those words. #184 and all the other wives tensed up at the sudden, violent shift in demeanor.

"Don't move! If you do, I'll erase everything below her head."

"______"

"Let's have an explanation. Be careful with your words and do your best to make sure there are no misunderstandings. I don't want this wedding to turn into someone's funeral. You understand, right?"

Regulus's shoulders trembled as he shouted, biting back the humiliation he was feeling.

Everyone in the pews froze, but Emilia faced his swelling rage with an unchanged, calm expression and a clear state of mind.

The broadcast had given Emilia courage. She wanted to be able to live up to that.

"Marriage is something two people who love each other share together. But I don't have the qualifications for that."

"______"

"I've never once loved a man as a woman before. So when Subaru tells me so insistently that he loves me, I can't give him the answer he is hoping for, or the other answer, either. And I know how hurtful that is and how much it has bothered him. But..."

Regulus fell silent. However, Emilia no longer saw the man standing before her. Everyone in the chapel could tell. Regulus was not reflected in her eyes at all. But Regulus could not accept that fact as he bit his lip.

"I've never experienced falling in love with someone. But I am sure that I will fall in love with someone someday. I will love someone as a woman. And when that happens, I already know who it will be. So..."

Taking a breath, she looked at Regulus while focused on someone else entirely.

"—I will not be yours."

"—! So that's how it is! I certainly don't have any more intention of wedding such a selfish, wanton woman as you! So that's a relief!"

When he accepted Emilia's rejection, Regulus's face turned red as he grew enraged. He extended his fingers in a fit of anger as a chill welled up from Emilia's body and she prepared to attack. Her first clash with his incomprehensible destructive ability—

"—?!"

Just as both of their attacks were about to start, a powerful crack resounded through the chapel. Something flew through the air like an arrow, striking Regulus head-on. What hit him as he stood there in his white tuxedo was a wooden door—one of the two great wooden doors that stood at the entrance of the chapel—sent flying by a tremendously powerful impact. It had flown all the way from the entrance and struck Regulus.

And—

"We both kicked in at the same time, but the results were so different. What are your legs even made of?!"

"Apologies, I failed to hold back. I did at least aim properly at the target, though, so could you perhaps forgive my earlier mistake?"

"Yeah, but our coolness levels are totally different now. My kick opened the door, but your kick turned the door into a direct attack..."

Two figures appeared in the doorway of the magnificent chapel, joking around with each other. A black-haired boy and a red-haired young man.

"—Ah."

Emilia's eyes widened at the sight of them, and Regulus brushed aside the door like it was an annoying gnat. He was wholly uninjured, but there was a tremendous displeasure in his eyes as he glared at the two interlopers.

"That is some nerve, barging your way into a sacred wedding. Who are you and what gifts have you brought, I wonder? Well?"

The two wedding crashers glanced at each other in response to Regulus's bluster and then nodded at each other.

"Subaru Natsuki, a spirit knight whose spirit is currently not present."

"Reinhard van Astrea of the Sword Saint family."

Reinhard took a step forward as he introduced himself. Beside him, Subaru winked at Emilia and then pointed to Regulus, his expression hardening.

"I object to this wedding! I'll be taking that bride!"

2

—The battle that would decide the fate of the city of water—the simultaneous assault on all four control towers—had begun.

Relying on all the information they had gathered, both actively and accidentally, the fighting forces of each camp gathered themselves into their various units and set off for their respective targets, leaving those who remained behind at the base to wait with bated breath for reports of victory.

Or at least, that was the unpleasant fate to which Otto Suwen would have liked to resign himself, but it was not to be.

Instead, he had left city hall alone and was stealthily running around a city roiling with danger around every bend.

"I should be stoppin' ya, but I can't deny wanting to be sure about where the book of knowledge they were wanting actually is— You drew the short end of the stick this time, Otto."

That was what Anastasia had said when she saw him off back at city hall.

She would have preferred that Otto stay put, and she probably had wanted to use him as another set of eyes to analyze the reports that would be filtering in from the battlefield.

With the group at city hall taking the command role for this battle, the more eyes and more heads the better. But Otto had a personal responsibility when it came to the book of knowledge. They were working together with the other factions, but if the situation somehow managed to actually be resolved, it would become a competition again, and he had to avoid any chance the other camps might get their hands on the book of knowledge.

If he was being honest, he would have preferred not discussing exactly what sort of magical book it was in front of everyone else, either, but Subaru and Garfiel were not fond of that sort of covert politicking.

Feeling like he was the bad guy for some reason, Otto heaved a sigh.

"When did I end up becoming the sort of person to run all around like this for other people's sakes…?"

Adjusting his hat, Otto ran into a question that he'd struggled with countless times during the past year. His position was unexpected, his relationship to other people was unexpected, and his own feelings were unexpected.

What would his family think if they saw him running all around with nary a thought about how to turn a profit from it?

"Even Oslo would probably make fun of me, let alone Regin..."

Imagining his older and younger brothers' differing reactions, Otto curled his lips slightly into a wry smile.

Slipping into an emotional train of thought that Subaru, were he there, would surely start raising alarms about triggering death flags and whatnot, Otto ran through the narrow streets of the city, on guard against demi-beasts.

The malformed and grotesque creatures were guarding the control towers being occupied by the Archbishops and were incredibly threatening to any noncombatants wandering the city. But they could be managed with enough caution. That was something Otto had learned during his time out in the city before he joined up with everyone else at city hall.

Because of that, the danger he faced was minimal. If he could not demonstrate the pride of a member of the team who couldn't fight directly in battle now, who knew when he would get another chance?

"...Heh, would have been nice if I could have at least tricked myself."

He clutched his chest, and Otto's expression melted into a self-deprecating laugh as he felt just how badly his heart was racing.

The Witch Cult, Archbishops, cultists—they were all things tied to terrifying memories for Otto. The events that had led to his meeting Subaru and everyone else a year earlier were just the flip side of how he had almost lost his life. He could not forget the fear he'd felt toward the Archbishop then, no matter how he tried. He could not forget the Archbishop of Sloth's sunken, dark eyes in the moment he'd thoughtlessly stolen away someone else's life. He would never forget the image of the mad fanatics who'd offered up their own flesh in accordance with his orders without any thought of pain or suffering. He could not forget the silence that had filled the world around him as he pleaded for someone, anyone to help him.

He had never been more terrified than in that moment. He had never feared the void as he had then. Facing off against Garfiel, running away from the Bowel Hunter, and being attacked by a mob of demon beasts all paled in comparison.

—That was how dark a pall the encounter with the Witch Cult had cast on Otto's heart.

And yet, there was no mistaking that he would have to face that fear again. He had chosen of his own volition a place to call home where he would surely have to face the Cult again.

He could not just leave Emilia, Subaru, Beatrice, Garfiel, Ram, Frederica, and Petra alone—Otto cared about all of them.

He had never intended to stay in any one place, and yet somewhere along the line it had just become too comfortable. Even knowing he would encounter the enemy that terrified him the most, he could not abandon his home. If it would protect that place he called home, if they needed him to stand beside them, then he would stifle his fear and support them in all the ways they could not support themselves.

Because of that—

"No matter what it takes, I have to take care of my job myself."

His words were to reinforce his fearful heart and also a warning for the enemy to hear.

When Otto stopped moving, there was a small figure standing in front of him.

There was a stone bridge over a canal just ahead, and on the other side was a plaza, where the small figure was standing. There were actually several figures in the plaza, but in the moment, Otto's attention was focused on a single one standing in the midst of them.

The world grew quiet. Painfully so. He could not hear anything at all. The voices of living creatures fell silent as they desperately tried to hide their presences and blend into the background.

Otto Suwen knew that feeling. And because he recognized it, his heart was surprisingly, truly, astonishingly calm, even as the figure before him slowly lowered its arms and its long mess of brown hair and turned around.

"—Hello, mister."

The figure's lips cracked sinisterly as it flashed a terrifying grin.

"—I am Lye Batenkaitos, the Witch Cult Archbishop of Gluttony. Welcome to my feeding ground!"

His red tongue danced inside his toothy mouth as the Archbishop who should not have been there cackled.

—Another unexpected life-and-death battle begins for a noncombatant as well.

<END>

Afterword

—I hope everyone can appreciate just how revolting Regulus is!

Hey everyone, it's Tappei Nagatsuki, the mouse-colored cat! And it seems like this font is actually the default size now!

And with that déjà vu greeting out of the way, thank you very much for following along with this volume of the main story! How was Volume 18?

I suspect all you *Re:ZERO* readers who have followed along through eighteen volumes have realized it by now, but I really love sudden, dramatic reversals! The moment when characters actually manage to turn things around after having been put through the grinder in desperately hopeless situations is just the *best*!

Re:ZERO volumes are often spoken of as being filled to the brim with absolutely depressing developments, but for the author, the happiness afterward is really the main draw! But there is a certain catharsis to it that's proportionate to how intense, deep, and overwhelming the adversity is.

Because of that, an author has to hold back tears while making the characters endure even more suffering. No matter the story, there is always some sort of conflict between the beginning and the end. That is the romance of it all—and fate.

So even while the main characters are enduring horrific circumstances in every volume, the comeback is always lurking just around the corner. Every battle has its ups and downs, and I hope you'll enjoy watching how our favorite cast takes on enemies with their fair share of peculiarities!

And now for the standard thanks in the middle of a packed page!

To my editor, thank you for all the work with the intense fighting without any break at all between this and the last volume! I said that there was conflict between the beginning and the end, but it was practically fights all the way through!

To the illustrator, Otsuka, I'm sorry for all the notes and directions involved this time, particularly with Emilia's outfit change. But Emilia in her wedding dress and Regulus in his white tuxedo and his eminently punchable face were just perfect! Thank you so much!

To the designer, Kusano, I was amazed that you pulled something entirely new out for the eighteenth volume. I can't wait to see what else you have in store, but it was a fantastic job as always this time!

Matsuse's manga version of *Re:ZERO* is entering the climax of the third arc in *Monthly Comic Alive*, and both it and Tsubata Nozaki's *The Ballad of the Sword Devil* are still being serialized to great reviews! Every month is fun to see!

To everyone else at MF Bunko J's editorial division, all the proofreaders, and all the bookstores, thank you very much for all your work!

I have so many other things that I need to share that I can't list them all. *Re:ZERO* could only exist with the support of so many people, so thank you, and I hope you'll keep supporting it in the future!

And finally, to the readers who are always supporting this series, I hope to see you again in 2019!

December 2018
<<While rubbing a stomach that has grown due to busyness>>

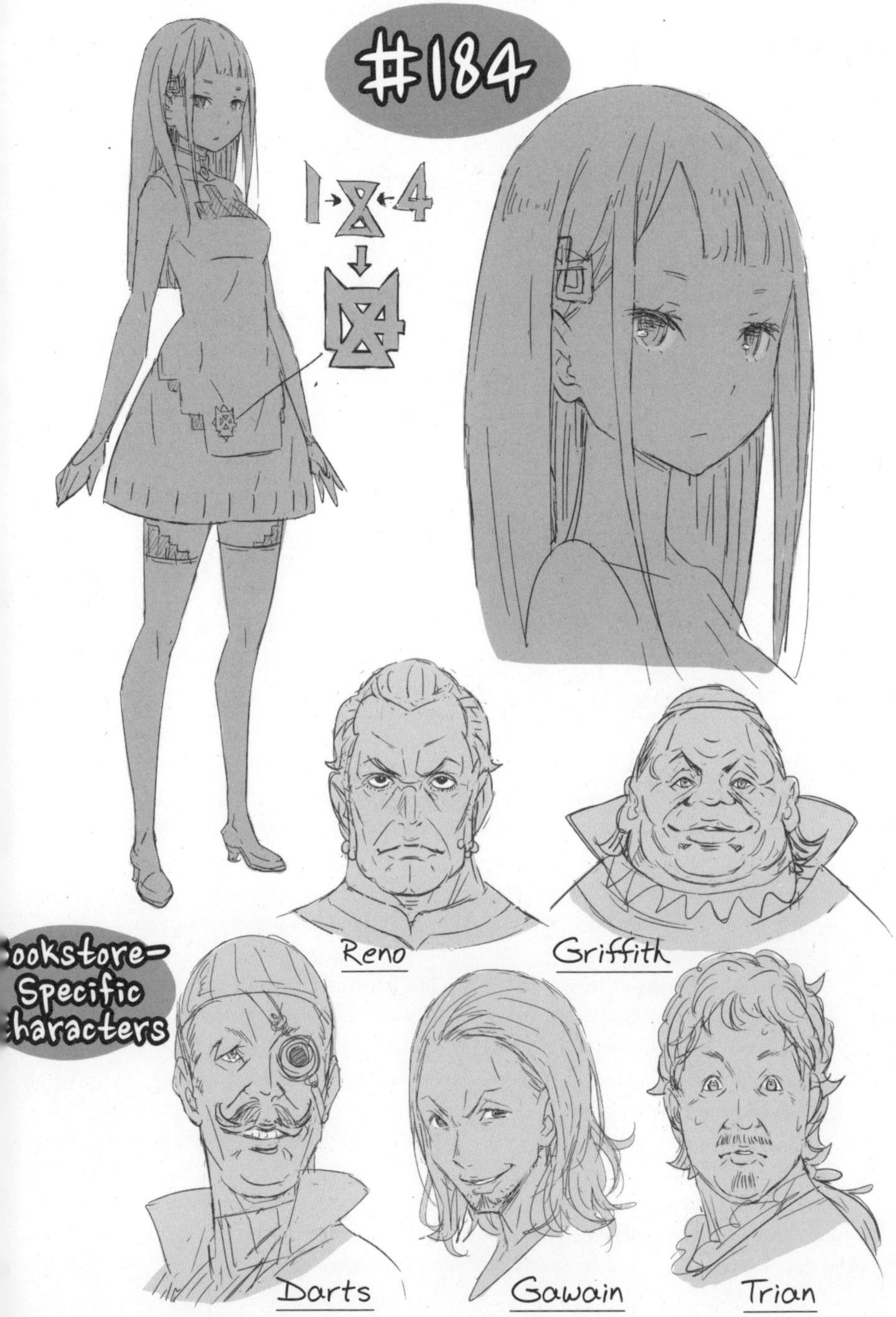
#184
1
4
Reno
Griffith
ookstore-
Specific
haracters
Darts
Gawain
Trian

"You know, I don't know what this preview-for-the-next-volume-or-whatever thing is, but I don't recall ever saying anything about accepting this job or agreeing to handle it, so what exactly were you thinking, pushing it onto me? It's not that I particularly hate it. It's just that there's a certain level of consideration that must be paid. That's the bare minimum of respect in order to not upset the person you are asking for a favor, no? Not even bothering with that is saying that you don't think that person is worth even that bare-minimum level of respect. Wouldn't you say that's practically a form of violence?"

"Yes, that's absolutely right, sir."

"What would you even have me say anyway? That the theater screening of the second OVA, *The Frozen Bond*, has been officially announced? It is some story of my bride #79 and some gray cat meeting, but if you actually think about it for a moment, there are far more important events that could be depicted, right? You should have a bit more consideration when asking me to do this."

"Yes, that's absolutely right, sir."

"And also, you are too slow as it is. When is the next volume? Volume 19! When's Volume 19?! Next year? March 2019? Going on sale at the same time as Volume 4 of the short story series? Do you think that somehow makes up for the amount of time you're making me wait? You know, time is a limited commodity. Everyone only gets a certain amount of it. You certainly can't expect someone to be content with you just stealing away their time like that out of some selfish, egotistical desire. It's sick, I tell you, sick."

"Yes, that's absolutely right, sir."

"Also, what is this? Taking part in the seventieth annual Sapporo Snow Festival? What is that, even? How is that related to anything? You can find more details by going to see the first OVA that's being screened in theaters? What is this?! Who do you think I am?! Don't expect to get away with playing me for a fool!"

"Yes, that's absolutely right, sir."

"There's still more? According to the flyer for the 2019 Sapporo Snow Festival, there is a *Re:ZERO* display in the HBC Finland plaza? Do you expect me to apologize for the oversight? You think tearing a cover in a fit is enough to earn you forgiveness? Where is the sincerity? Where, I ask you!"

"Yes, that's absolutely right, sir."

"And last is something that is a staple by this point—a birthday celebration at Shibuya Marui for the Oni sisters… What even is that?! Exclusive goods are available there, apparently! Some fantastic display or whatever! I'm surrounded by people who don't understand a thing!"

"Yes, that's absolutely right, sir."

"I can't be bothered with this anymore. You know, I'm tired after everything that's been going on, so I'll be retiring for a break. Such a dullard has no qualification to be my wife."

"—Yes, that's absolutely right, sir."

"Ha-ha, that's a good response. Anyway, I'll be leaving here since I'm so busy."

"..............................Just die already."